Love and Other Seasons

Modern Austen Inspired Short Stories

Rebecca M. Fleming

Fairy Jane
PRESS

For the readers who ask for more;
For the writers who dare to take the chance.

Table of Contents

A Tale of Three Christmases

A *Sense and Sensibility* Story

REBECCA M. FLEMING

{Prologue}

Maggie fluffed the pillows in the corner, arranging the biggest ones just so, before burrowing into the pile and wrapping a quilt around herself. At seventeen, she knew she was too old for running to the treehouse, but sometimes a girl just had to hide. Even from here, she could hear Marianne's high-pitched wailing. *She can't even cry without drama,* Maggie thought, wishing she'd grabbed her iPod when she escaped. *It's not like she's the only one who got her heart broken.* Pulling the quilt tighter around her shoulders, Maggie leaned her head against the wall and stared out the treehouse door, tracing the familiar lines of home with her eyes. *I'm going to miss this place as much as I'm going to miss Daddy,* she thought, feeling the familiar burn of tears.

Norland Park was a sprawling, old-fashioned country house, hugged by deep porches with windows glinting gold in the setting sun. It was a house that looked old, and was - members of the Dashwood family had lived on the grounds for generations, ever since some great-great-great relative sailed across the pond from England and settled in the rolling hills of northwest Georgia. The house had no distinct style, as various generations made additions and renovations, at one point demolishing and rebuilding the whole thing. It was a house that demanded attention, but also welcomed company. Maggie knew every nook and cranny of the stately home, and very nearly every inch of the extensive grounds. Norland was the only home she'd ever known, and now in a cruel twist of fate, Maggie, her two sisters, and their mother, would be forced to find a new place to call home.

Even though she was the youngest, and the others tried to keep the details from her, over the last few weeks Maggie had overheard enough whispered conversations to know her father's death meant everything was about to change - in a big way. Because of an obscure family tradition, with roots back in England, the Norland estate only passed to male heirs. Even in twenty-first century America there was no way around the clause - it had been worked into the deed itself. As a result, Norland Park and all its splendor would soon fall into the hands of Maggie's half-brother John, and his wife Francesca.

John assured his stepmother that she and the girls were welcome to stay at Norland as long as they needed; he would not turn them out. Maggie almost idolized John when she was little, and believed he meant what he said, but doubted Franny would be so generous. *If she has her way,* she thought now, *we'd be gone before the moon rises tonight.* There was no love lost between the Dashwood girls and their "big sister" - Francesca had swept into their lives with the unwelcome force and bluster of a nor'easter. The only daughter of a stock market millionaire, Francesca Ferrars craved the respectability an Old Family Name gives to wealth, and when John Dashwood stumbled into her path - she pounced. Maggie still had nightmares about the wedding, some ten years before, the day her mysterious big brother disappeared from family circles.

And now, it's all hers. Every stick and stone of Norland is Franny's. I have no Daddy and no home.

{Christmas Chaotic}

"How are we supposed to have Christmas without Daddy?" Marianne wailed, dropping dramatically onto the leather sofa. "Not just Christmas, but a party! Heartless Francesca and her Yankee family."

Maggie stiffened, biting back a snarky response, as Ellie, the oldest of the three Dashwood girls, drew a deep breath.

"We've been over this, Marianne," she said in the soothing voice so often used with their high-strung sister. "Christmas will happen whether people die or not, and with the holiday comes certain expectations. Traditions that must be upheld. Whether we like them or not, these things do happen."

"But Francesca acts as if nothing horrible has happened, as if someone made her Queen of the World and we're all her servants. Christmas minions or some such ilk. I won't have it. I will not be cheerful. I will not be 'sparkling and vivacious.' And I will. Not. Sing." Hurling herself off the sofa, Marianne punctuated the last words with forceful stamps of her high heel-clad foot. "And you can't make me, Elinor," she cried before leaving the room as abruptly as she'd entered.

"It's going to be a long few weeks isn't it, Ellie?" Maggie asked, moving to perch on the arm of her sister's chair. "If she's this wound up before the 'Yankee family' even arrives, what will she do when Franny's brothers get here?"

Ellie closed her eyes and sighed. "I can only imagine. And it is not a happy imagining. What about you, Magpie? How are you holding up against Francesca's holiday onslaught?"

Maggie wrinkled her nose at the childish nickname, making Ellie chuckle. "Okay I guess. It does seem weird to be getting ready for a party, when we just had a funeral. But at the same time," she hesitated, glancing sideways at Ellie.

"It's okay, Maggie," Ellie assured her, slipping an arm around her shoulders.

"I think I'm sorta glad. I mean," she took a deep breath, "Christmas was Daddy's favorite holiday, and he always loved hosting a big bash, you know? So even though Franny is making it this posh, Yankee thing, it's almost like Daddy's still here and just having a little fun."

Ellie smiled. "I know exactly what you mean. I think Daddy would be rather amused at Francesca's plans, and he'd definitely be teasing her into a frenzy. Not," she warned with a raised eyebrow, "that I am suggesting you should."

Maggie grinned, "Who me?"

"Yes you, Magpie, love of my life. You are more than capable of teasing a saint to distraction, and Francesca is no saint. Mind your manners - you're a lady, so act like one."

"Yes, ma'am," Maggie sighed. "Sometimes, Ellie, you sound like *such* a librarian!" With a shriek and giggle, she jumped off the chair arm and darted out the door, as Ellie tossed a pillow at her retreating back.

A slow rain fell, rendering escape to the treehouse impossible. Maggie found herself wandering the house aimlessly, trying to find a quiet spot to curl up and lose herself in a book, but everywhere she tried to settle, the solitude was penetrated by the animated, shrill voice of Marianne or Franny, sometimes both. In a moment of desperation, she ducked through a door leading to the old servants' stairs, and began to climb. *Nobody will come to the attic*, she thought, *especially not Franny - she might get spiderwebs on her precious shoes.*

The attic was expansive, shadowy, and mostly forgotten. Dormer windows offered little light on a day like this, but Maggie didn't mind. The attic, like the treehouse, was her private domain, and countless hours had been spent prowling and poking in dusty corners. Over the years she created a few special hideaways for herself, depending on mood or atmosphere, and today she migrated toward the broad chimney. With fires burning below, the chimney radiated an inviting circle of warmth. Maggie pulled a blanket from her stash in a nearby trunk, and curled up in the old wingback chair tucked right next to the chimney with a sigh. *This is better,* she mused, opening her book and prepared to spend the whole afternoon in that very spot.

It was too gloomy to read, situated so far from the windows, but Maggie's stash had more than just blankets. Wrapping the blanket around her shoulders, Maggie got up to kneel by the trunk. Moving aside another blanket and tossing a pillow into the chair behind her, Maggie rocked back on her heels and paused. *That's funny,* she mused, *the flashlight and camping lantern should be right – hello, what's this?* As another pillow shifted, something shiny caught Maggie's eye.

Moving the pillow out of her way, Maggie's eyes widened at what she uncovered. The glimmer of shininess that caught her attention turned out to be mirrored glass and silver inlay on the cover of a dark wooden box. Lifting the box out, she was surprised at its weight. Roughly the size of one of her father's law books, the box felt twice as heavy. *Do glass and silver weigh* that *much?* she wondered, running her fingers over the design. The pieces were cool and smooth to the touch, mesmerizing. Unable to decipher the image, she turned the box slowly, hoping each new angle would make a picture fall in place.

"Oh," she gasped suddenly. "It's Norland." Her own voice, though barely a whisper, startled her. Glancing quickly around the attic, noticing the camp lantern further back in the corner, revealed now with the box in her lap, Maggie felt a tingle of excitement. Setting the lantern on the chair behind, letting the light shine down on her, she allowed herself a brief study of the embellished cover, its fragmented portrait of her beloved home. *It really is beautiful,* she observed before curiosity took over, prompting her to run her fingers along the edges, seeking for a way to open the cover and reveal the contents. Finally, she brushed against a small embedded latch and with the softest of clicks the lid opened a fraction of an inch. Raising the lid slowly, carefully, Maggie smiled at what she found inside.

In keeping with the understated elegance of its exterior, the interior of the box was simply lined with deep, rich blue velvet. Resting inside, nearly filling the space, was a thick, leatherbound volume tied with a satiny blue ribbon. Tucked under the bow were an old-fashioned fountain pen and an envelope reading "Margaret Dashwood" in a familiar script. Carefully drawing the envelope from the ribbon, she smiled as she ran her fingers along the letters. *Of course Daddy knew about my hideaway, knew I would need to retreat, but when did he have a chance to stash this little surprise?* she wondered. Lifting the flap, she drew out a Christmas card. Seeing her father's post-production addition of conversation balloons above the family of snowmen on vacation made Maggie giggle. Opening the card, she was surprised to see it filled with his neat, blocky print. As she began reading, tears stung her eyes and she unconsciously drew the box closer to her chest.

My Magpie,

Merry Christmas. My guess is that Christmas is a few weeks away, and you have resorted to hiding from Marianne - not to mention Francesca. I am sorry I had to leave you to fend for yourself. We were always a team. (By the way, I give you leave to tease Franny - just don't let Ellie catch you. She never understood our delight in tormenting her).

You may be wondering about this box, and its contents. I found the box years ago, when you were just a wee girl, among some junk in the barn. After cleaning it up, I kept it a secret, even from your mother, waiting until ... Well, I figured the time would come. And it did, my Magpie.

Of all my children, you have roots sunk deepest in the fertile Norland soil. You've roamed these grounds, inside and out, since you could waddle, and leaving will hit you the hardest. I'm sorry for that too; I wish my ancestors had known that sometimes daughters love the land even more than sons. This box is yours, a small piece of Norland to keep with you, and - I hope - help ease the pain of starting over.

As for the journal inside - Margaret, you have a gift. A way of seeing the world, and teasing out the little details that make up life's ultimate stories. I want you to keep writing, write down everything you hear and see. But for this journal, I have specific instructions:

You may only write in this book during the weeks leading up to Christmas and extending to New Year's Eve. What you write during that time is up to you, it can be caricatures of your extended family (ahem), a record of what has changed, or whatever whimsical idea tickles your fancy at the moment. But only during the Christmas holidays.

Additionally, you may only use this journal for three Christmases. This year, next year, and the year after that. I refrain from explaining my reasons, but trust me. I have them.

Lastly, call me sentimental, but I hope you choose to use the fountain pen when you write. Obviously you can use whatever you like or have handy, but the pen is included in the gift. It was mine, a graduation present, I intended to give to you when you graduate. You know what they say about the best laid plans, so I tuck it in here. The important thing is, you have it.

Look after your mother, Magpie. Ellie will undoubtedly take over the practical concerns of this next chapter, but she will need your support. Keep Momma smiling. Help her settle into the new adventure by maintaining your sense of humor. As for Marianne ... Oh, Marianne. Perhaps the best help is just to be. Avoid getting caught up in the storms, and there will be plenty, but do not shut her out. She can't help herself, poor girl. My hope is that one day, she'll find herself and learn that love bears all things.

Take care of yourself too. You are strong and fierce, my little one, but it is okay to lean on others. I love you, so very much, and wish I could be spending this and every Christmas with you.

With infinite love, Daddy

Maggie could barely read the words through her tears; when she got to the end, she buried her face in her arms and cried. She had refused to indulge in a good cry since the funeral. Marianne was holding her own in that department well enough for the whole family. Now, reading her father's words, Maggie gave in to the sweet release of grieving, really grieving. She mourned the upcoming loss of Norland as much as she did his death, and he had known she would. At last she could cry no more, and her heart felt lighter somehow, as if a small flicker of excitement or anticipation were kindling to life. Wiping her eyes and nose on her shirttail, *Franny will love that*, Maggie untied the ribbon and thumbed through the journal pages.

The leather was soft and pliable, smooth as velvet in her hands and the color of a rich caramel latte. Though the deckle edged pages were crisp and white, there was a hint of the comforting 'old book' smell Maggie found so enticing. A bright purple ribbon marked the first page, where her father had written a reminder: **For Christmases only, Magpie.** She smiled, knowing it would be very hard to resist writing in the book every day. *But I must make it last three years - three Christmases.* As perplexing as she found his limitations, her father's instructions presented an intriguing challenge.

Today is for looking only, she thought, gently placing the journal, pen and card back in the box. *And this is staying safely hidden in my trunk. I can't have Franny, or anyone, finding it.* She tugged a pillow over the box and fluffed a blanket to disguise any suspicious lumps, laughing at herself. *It's not like anyone comes up here but me.* Happy with the look of things, Maggie shut the trunk and moved the camp lantern to sit on top, crawling into the chair and rewrapping the blanket around herself. Unable to concentrate on her book, she soaked up the quiet sounds of Norland until it was time to join the family for dinner. With a secret project of sorts, surviving

Franny's Christmas plans suddenly seemed more doable.

From her hideaway in the treehouse, Maggie could see everything - even hear some of it - without being seen. Franny's brothers were due to arrive any moment, and Maggie wanted to see the kerfuffle without getting involved herself. She had, technically, met the Ferrars boys at Franny and John's wedding, but since her seven year old self spent most of that weekend hiding from all the strangers, her memories were hazy at best. Franny had been particularly agitated at breakfast that morning, fretting about their imminent arrival and hoping they would be suitably impressed with her new domain.

The sudden slamming of a door startled Maggie, and she glanced up to see Ellie storming toward one of the outbuildings near the treehouse. *That's funny,* she thought. *Ellie never slams doors. I wonder whether Franny or Marianne provoked that?* Just as she decided to climb down and see what upset her sister, a tall, lanky man came around the corner, running directly into a very distracted Ellie. As the two attempted - and failed - to regain balance, landing in a tangled pile of arms, legs and a very smooshed hat, Maggie decided her overhead view was best after all.

"I am so sorry!" Ellie's voice was much higher pitched than usual. "I had no idea anyone was out here, and I had to get away - wait, what are you doing out here? Who are you? I'm sorry. That was rude. I don't know what's wrong with me today. I promise I'm not this rude," she stopped to take a deep breath. Maggie was able to see the guy's grin from her treehouse perch, and his deep laughter had a friendly warmth. *Can laughs be warm? His is warm - it makes me feel warm fuzzies inside*, she wondered absently.

"You must allow me to apologize, m'lady. The fault was entirely mine," his voice tinged with laughter.

"I should not have been skulking around corners, avoiding my inevitable destiny. Will you permit me to assist you up, or shall we stay here until someone comes looking for us?" As he spoke, he disentangled himself and moved to sit across from Ellie with a comically innocent expression.

"I, ah, should probably, um," Ellie floundered. "Do I know you?" she suddenly asked, cocking her head to one side. "Oh my word, you're –"

"Edward Ferrars, at your service," he interrupted with a surprisingly formal bow for one sitting in the dirt. "Please don't hold it against me," he added flashing another grin.

Ellie groaned, burying her face in hands, muffling her voice. "Of all people to run into and make a fool of myself, it would be Francesca's brother. I think I am going to die in approximately three-point-seven seconds."

"I wish you wouldn't," he replied in a voice equal parts soothing and teasing. "I think you must be one of the Dashwood girls, and I know my Christmas holiday just got a lot more interesting."

Maggie giggled in spite of herself, quickly holding a pillow to her face to muffle the sound, as Ellie raised her head to meet Edward's frank, open look. "Mmm," she murmured. "I can't decide if that makes me feel better or worse, thank you very much. Yes, I am 'one of the Dashwood girls.' I'm Elinor - Ellie. I must express sincere apologies for my appalling lack of grace and manners." She paused, and Maggie wished she could see her sister's face. "And I should warn you," she continued, her voice eerily steady, "if you tell anyone what you have witnessed here, I will make your life miserable. I am a Librarian, with unending information at my disposal, and I am not afraid to use it."

The expression on Edward's face shifted from teasing to concern to surprise to delight in quick succession, and Maggie laughed out loud in spite of herself.

"Margaret," Ellie sighed, "get down here. Immediately."

As Edward looked around for the mysteriously invisible laughing Margaret, she sighed and climbed down. Jumping the last few ladder rungs, she landed with a soft plop and arched one eyebrow quizzically. "Yes, Ellie?"

"Oh! Another one!" Edward cut in, before Ellie had a chance to scold her. "And a tree-dwelling Dashwood at that," he added, standing and offering a hand to assist Ellie. "I would introduce myself, but I gather you have been snooping the whole time, eh?"

Maggie grinned. "Well, I was technically here first and y'all crashed my party. Why did you come slinking around the corner like that anyway? Weren't you supposed to be arriving in the normal way - by car, at the front door?" She gave him a searching glance, taking in the dusty boots and untucked shirt tail peeking from beneath his heavy sweater.

"Ah, yes, I," he stammered slightly. Suddenly realizing he still held Ellie's hand, he dropped it and took a step backwards - tripping on his forgotten hat. Losing his balance, again, he flailed wildly and caught hold of Ellie as he fell, bringing her down on top of him with an "oomph."

"Oh crud," he muttered, "I am definitely not making a good impression, am I?"

"Well, that would depend on what kind of impression you wanted to make," Maggie answered with a laugh, moving to help them up. She stopped mid-reach when a sudden giggle took her by surprise. "Ellie?" she asked, a note of concern in her voice.

Edward tilted his head, trying to see Ellie's face. "Ell? Are you okay?" His eyes widened when Ellie's only response was to laugh harder, and bury her face in his shoulder. Instinctively he wrapped his arms tighter around her, as an answering laugh escaped him.

Maggie watched the two in stunned silence, before breathing a soft "Wow."

Finally, Ellie's giggles stopped and she breathed a deep sigh, visibly relaxing in Edward's arms. Maggie only had time to raise her eyebrows in reply to Edward's quick wink before Ellie realized where she was and abruptly rolled off his chest onto the grass, headbutting Edward's chin in the process.

"Oof," Edward grunted softly, as he sat up and rubbed his chin.

"Oh crap," Ellie groaned. "Maggie, help me up," she added, waving one hand in Maggie's general direction and covering her face with the other. "What is wrong with me today?"

Edward shook his head at Maggie before gently turning Ellie's face toward him, moving her hand to look her in the eyes. "Hey," he said, his voice low and soft, so Maggie could barely hear the words, running his thumb across her cheek, brushing away a surprising tear. "Correct me if I'm wrong, but your daddy just died, my sister has taken over your home, and strangers will be spending Christmas with you. If that's not a *carte blanche* for having a bad day now and again, I don't know what is. And Ellie," he paused, "I'll give you twenty bucks if you tell Franny to go eat tinsel when she comments on our dishevelment."

Ellie smiled, raising her hand to brush away a stray leaf before resting lightly on his shoulder. "Thank you," her voice soft. "But if you think I'm going to tell Francesca that for a mere twenty dollars, you're insane," she winked as she tweaked his ear. Edward made a grab for her, but she sprang up and away, pushing Maggie between them as a shield.

"Oh good grief," Maggie sighed. "I can't decide if y'all are adorable or ridiculous. This whole family is more than a little ridiculous, in my personal opinion, so maybe you are adorably ridiculous. Are you sure you've only just met?"

"Hmm, well, there was that weekend of Wedding Infamy," Edward tapped his chin thoughtfully. "But I don't remember any ear-tweaking librarians, just a couple skinny, gawky teenagers more interested in their dog than entertaining the debonair Ferrars brothers."

"Funny," Ellie remarked, with one eyebrow arched, "I remember a pair of weasel-y brothers, too caught up in being brooding, mysterious college boys to bother being polite to their sister's new family."

"We were obnoxious, weren't we?" Edward pulled a face. "I hope I have outgrown that phase, and we can be friends this time? Though I should warn you that Rob is still very much a weasel."

Maggie snickered, and Ellie tried to hide her smile. "Mmm," she murmured. "We shall see. What do you say we start by tidying up a bit before –"

"Edward!" Francesca's shriek cut through the yard.

"Too late," Edward muttered, bending to pick up his now very flattened hat.

"Edward Alexander Ferrars! What in thunder are you doing back there? How did you get here? Robert hasn't arrived yet. Come inside this instant and explain yourself!" Francesca stood with her hands on her hips at the top of the porch steps.

Exchanging guiltily amused smiles, Edward, Ellie and Maggie moved toward the house. Maggie fought back a laugh as Franny grew more agitated the closer they got. With a sideways glance so full of mischief even Ellie choked on a laugh, Edward stopped at the foot of the steps. Leaning on the post, he crossed his legs nonchalantly.

"Franny," he drawled, "I do believe your feathers have ruffled. Whatever is the matter, ma'am?"

Franny sputtered, looking between her brother and the Dashwoods with something akin to horror. "Look at you! You're a mess! What have you been doing?" She raised a hand. "No, don't answer that. I don't think I want to know. Edward, you are a Ferrars. And you are a guest at Norland. Behave. With. The. Proper. Dignity." After spitting out the last word, she turned sharply on her heel and stalked into the house, leaving the others in a stunned silence.

"That went over nicely," Edward remarked drily, before offering Maggie and Ellie each an elbow. "Shall we go beard the dragon in her den, ladies?"

The next two weeks flew by. Robert Ferrars was every bit as weasely as Edward promised, arriving three days after he was supposed to, and quickly providing further evidence for Maggie's theory that Edward must have been adopted. *There is no way he shares the same gene pool as Franny and Robert,* she thought regularly. Regardless of where he came from, Maggie was simply glad he came. Edward's friendship was genuine and his company pleasant, even if his delivery was bluntly awkward at times. *Even Marianne likes him,* Maggie noted one day, as her notoriously fastidious sister laughed over Edward's bungling attempts to join family singalongs. *He's completely tone deaf, and she likes him.*

Whenever she could, Maggie would escape to her attic hideaway. The journal beckoned her, and she loved the idea of still being connected to her father in some way. *I know he can't actually read it, doesn't know what's going on,* she thought a few days before Christmas, running her fingers over the soft leather cover, *but he knew I would need to tell the stories, to talk things over the way we used to on coffee dates to Mansfield Perk.* It was hard sometimes to remember to leave pages blank, for next year. The empty pages begged her to fill them with everything from conversations to sketches of the personalities gathered under Norland's roof.

That first day when Edward ran into Ellie and tripped on his own hat? We should have seen it coming: he's all arms and legs, bumping into people – or furniture, sometimes the door – and getting tangled up. He is rather coltish, or maybe like an exuberant puppy, trying to grow into himself. He's so good humored about it. He knows he's a totally spastic klutz, and you can't help but laugh with him. Well, Franny doesn't laugh, but at least she stopped shrieking every time he knocked something over. Now she just grits her teeth and mutters things.

The one she should be muttering about is Robert. He's such a creeper, and gets worse and worse the longer he's here. I caught him slinking about the hallway where our rooms are the other day, looking extra sketch. He didn't even have the decency to look guilty when I came around the corner and saw him. He looked annoyed. I must remember to tell Ellie we should probably all use the keyed locks with him around. Too bad John can't kick him out for being a weirdo.

I can't decide if I like John or not. Horrible, I know. I have all these memories of him from when I was little, in the Pre-Franny Era, and even though he didn't come to Norland often, he was wonderful. Rather like Edward, actually, but not so klutzy. Ellie looked at me like I was delusional when I mentioned it, so possibly my subconscious has a selective filter. However he was then, he is very different now; more withdrawn, maybe a little lost. Sometimes I think he really wants to be a big brother to us, but he either doesn't know how or he isn't allowed. I'm fairly certain Franny wears the pants in their relationship. And we all know how she feels about the Dashwoods lingering in the home. (Does she forget she is a Dashwood too, I wonder?)

Edward has a crush on Ellie, I've decided. They really do make a cute couple: the professor and the librarian. Nerds. They're adorable. He makes her laugh, and brings out a mischievous streak we'd all forgotten. In turn, her friendship and support, her ability to listen and understand his weird academic passions, have made him more sure of himself. I hope they're able to explore the potential, but Franny saw them talking the other day and got a queer look on her face. They are always talking, about everything and anything. One day, I found them in the treehouse; Ellie was telling him how we used to keep bees and that beeswax candles are her favorite smell in the world, because they remind her of summers. Whenever Ellie talks, Edward focuses intently on what she's saying - you can tell he's really listening. He listens to all of us, of course, but with Ellie it's something deeper.

John was able to gently persuade Franny that perhaps a Christmas dinner for family and a few close friends would be in better taste than a party, considering the recent death of our father. She relented, and the evening was surprisingly not horrible. Christmas itself was quiet, and restful actually. Edward gave Ellie a necklace with an enameled beehive charm (he said he ordered it from With Love; I looked them up online, and it's the sweetest florist and gift shop in Oregon. Makes me want to visit just to meet the owner and poke around the place), which made Franny's eyebrows skyrocket. I think she finally figured out her brother might have a serious interest in the eldest Miss Dashwood. Since then, we've all been kept busy with errands and sorting through belongings. It wasn't until tonight, New Year's Eve, that things came to a head.

Marianne made a comment about Edward and Ellie, and Franny lost all pretense of composure. It quickly turned into a screaming match, Franny vehemently declaring her brother would never connect himself to the Dashwoods, that their father had plans for him to marry a wealthy heiress and create a dynasty. Marianne felt the need to point out that marrying a Dashwood had been quite good enough for her, and why not let Edward make up his own mind. It was shocking. Edward and Ellie both were bright red, and John looked as if he wished to run away. Momma ended everything with a quiet announcement: "We're leaving," and left the room.

I guess our time at Norland is really over now. But where do we go? Where will I be next Christmas?

{Christmas Cursed}

Somehow, another holiday season had arrived, with Christmas just around the corner. Maggie hoped they could stay home and celebrate in their snug little house, but Franny had been planning a grand "Southern Christmas Soiree" since the first week of football season. Apparently, she had designs to out-dazzle last year's fete, which was "necessarily subdued coming so soon after the death of the family patriarch," with hopes to firmly entrench herself in Society. Maggie had her doubts, but if she had to suffer through another of Franny's parties, at least it would be at Norland. *And Edward is sure to be there.*

The promise of seeing Edward and Ellie together again made her smile. In spite of good intentions, Edward was not able to visit them in Barton as often as hoped, and his last visit had been particularly awkward. Outgoing, teasing and comfortable among the 'Dashwood Belles' as he dubbed them, Edward had been oddly tense and withdrawn, often starting to speak before abruptly stopping himself and leaving the room. *But with Marianne being so emotional and dramatic about Wills leaving, I think* life *was awkward.* Maggie sighed. The last few months had been as emotionally tense as the months after Daddy died - worse if you asked Marianne. Maggie tried to avoid her sister as much as possible since Wills skipped town; instead of getting over his sudden departure, Marianne was spiraling deeper and deeper into emotional denial. *If that's what having a boyfriend does to you,* Maggie mused during an afternoon ramble through the winter woods, *I'd rather not have one. Ever. There's plenty of things to do without a boy.*

Giving in to the temptation to climb a lovely gnarled old apple tree, Maggie began to mentally compose her first Christmas entry. *Only being able to write at Christmas is quite cumbersome,* she thought. *A whole year has gone by, and so much has happened! I should catch a ride into town with Ellie tomorrow, spend some quality time with the comforts of Mansfield*

Perk. It's going to take a rather large drink to get the Marianne-Wills saga explained in a way that makes sense and still captures the intensity.

The next morning, Ellie dropped Maggie at Mansfield Perk on her way to work, with promises to collect her at lunch. After getting a chocolate chip muffin and the largest hot chocolate they served, Maggie found a table by the window, soaking up the sun, with a view of the whole shop. *There is the best people watching here,* she thought, noting several college students frantically cramming for approaching exams. Settling in, she pulled the journal from her oversized purse. Sipping her cocoa, she browsed through last year's entries, chuckling to remember some of Franny's meltdowns and surprised at how many pages she used for the first Christmas.

She sighed a little, reading the last entry - written on New Year's Eve, per Daddy's instructions. *Poor Franny tries so hard. I wonder if she'll ever figure out that things go smoother when you don't force them. Just let it happen - regardless of how it will happen.* Almost a year later, and Maggie could still hear Franny and Marianne shrieking at each other, and Mother's quiet "We're leaving" silencing the room. *It all seems so silly now,* she thought. *I hope things go better this Christmas, though with Marianne sulking about Wills I probably shouldn't hold my breath.* Turning the page, Maggie blinked in surprise. Where her ribbon marked a clean page, the start of the second Christmas's story, a green envelope rested. Certain she would have noticed it last December, Maggie wondered who had been poking among her things. Drawing the card out of the envelope, she gasped.

Merry Christmas, Magpie!
You're starting to write your second Christmas, and I hope this year is better than last. I have a hunch Francesca is having an elaborate bash, and you're all spending Christmas at Norland. Enjoy the homecoming, my girl, and don't let Franny's overzealousness for Proper Society ruin Christmas. Try not to

let Marianne steal your cheer either - that girl loves an excuse for melodrama, and a morbid anniversary is prime drama potential. Especially if Franny tries to make her sing in public. I rather wish I could see that showdown.

Your special task this Christmas is to make Ellie relax and laugh, I feel certain she has taken on great responsibility this year. She is capable of great love, though I think it scares her sometimes. Also, hug your mother often. It will be hard for her to be a guest at Norland, during Christmas.

Don't hide in the treehouse too often, mind your very best manners - you are, after all, an adult now. 18. A true lady. So grown up, my little one, and still so very young. Revel in your youth, and cherish this Christmas.

With infinite love, Daddy

Maggie read the card twice, but there was no denying her father's hand. *How on earth did that happen?* she wondered, flipping through the journal. Nothing else lurked in the pages, and she opened to the blank page once more. *Impossible, and yet... I have the card in my hand.* Propping the mysterious card open against the window, she took up her pen to write.

The strangest things happen in this family. This year has been no less strange, and I hardly know where to begin. When Momma made her announcement New Year's Eve, the resolve, the very quietness of her tone, shocked us all. Imagine our greater surprise a few days later when she relented and gave us the rest of the news! Her aunt, hearing about Daddy's death through the wonder of the Southern Grapevine, phoned with the news that we could move into her little house in Barton. Apparently Aunt Jenn is a widow herself, and when her husband - a Middleton, of the Barton Middletons you know - died, he left her a small fortune. Including a rather substantial estate outside of Barton with not one, but two houses. Turns out Aunt Jenn lives in the big house, and said we could have "the cottage." (Spoiler alert: It's nowhere near as big as Norland, but it is definitely not a cottage.)

We made the move to Barton mid-January, and settled nicely. The house is cozy and neat, with delightful nooks and the best window seats. Barton and the outlying country is beautiful. Expansive and green, and the trees! It feels a lot like Norland, only wilder. Freer. Less gentrified. Marianne calls it barbaric. But she liked it well enough when she and Wills were an item - she met Wills because of the wildwood surrounding our new home, and she's not forgiven the trees yet. It's not the trees' fault that Marianne got lost, in the middle of a tantrum-induced walk, right as a March storm broke. If Wills hadn't been having his own Byronic fit, she might have wandered all afternoon and into the evening, but he found her and was able to escort her home. From that point on? They were disgustingly inseparable.

Marianne, I believe, truly fell in love. Or what she thinks is love. She has so many dramatic, overwrought ideas, sometimes I wonder whether she even knows the rest of the world operates differently from the tricked out version in her head. To say she fell head-over-heels for Wills would be an understatement. I think we all had a crush on him at first, even Momma - and definitely Aunt Jenn. Who wouldn't? Willoughby Allenham has movie-star looks. Dark, broodingly dark, eyes; wavy, just too long hair that curls against his collar and falls across those eyes; a devilish grin and the deepest dimple you've ever seen. The only flaw marring his perfect looks? A scar, faintly visible, tracing the line of his jaw on one side. His dark perfection was a stunning pairing with Marianne's golden beauty - the way a church steeple stands stark against a steel grey sky before a storm. They were too perfect for each other.

Things got intense, Marianne fell harder and harder, and we started to get a little creeped out by Wills's broodiness. (By we, I mean Ellie and myself. Momma listened to our concerns, but didn't want to make Marianne unhappy). One temperamental artist in a relationship is more than enough, and lo and behold! We soon learned Wills is a cellist with the Atlanta Symphony, showing much promise and with an illustrious future ahead of him. He said he was taking a leave of absence from symphonic duties before embarking on a tour - mysteriously vague about details, this only added to Marianne's enchantment. And when he learned she sings like an angel? You could literally hear the wheels spinning. I believe he honestly thought they could take their show on the road and find fame and fortune.

And then, he left. With barely a goodbye, and no explanation, after nearly eight months of an intense and tempestuous relationship, he vanished. To say Marianne did not take it well is vast understatement. Her emotional distress, and general agitation, has been even worse than when Daddy died. She lost herself so entirely in Wills and the idea of their coupling, she's floundering. The only thing to spark her interest, even a little, was Aunt Jenn's gift of new dresses for Franny's Christmas shindig.

Though you wouldn't guess to look at her, Aunt Jenn really is a fairy godmother. When she first told us we were having custom dresses made, Marianne went wild. All her emotions funneled into sketches and designs for one stunning dress after another. After chatting with the designer and mastermind behind Cate's Creations, we were instructed to send only our measurements, our color of choice, and specific hemline and neckline details. I was dubious at first, we all were, but when the dresses came, we were dazzled. Cate must be a magician. We sent her the barest of guidelines, as requested:

Marianne: Red; Halter; Asymmetrical layers with beads

Ellie: Navy; Ballet neck; 3/4 sleeves; Tea length fit-and-flare

Me: Dark Emerald; Knee-length; Surprise me

Somehow, from those few descriptions, she created dresses that perfectly reflect our personalities and preferences. It's amazing. From now on, anytime I need a special dress, I am only wearing one of Cate's Creations. Even Marianne was pleased, and the rich red Cate picked brings roses back to her cheeks. I hope the dress is the start of a Christmas miracle and she can shake free of the whole Wills debacle.

Pausing in the arched doorway to survey the scene, Maggie had to admit Francesca had outdone herself. When the Dashwood women arrived a few days before, they were sternly informed no one was to go into either the formal dining room or the adjacent 'drawing room' until the night of the party. Maggie attempted to peek several times, but was never able to catch more than a whiff of fresh paint. Apparently Franny set screens in front of all the doors, and covered the windows, to preserve her surprise. *She certainly had something worth hiding,* Maggie marveled now, eyes wide. *This is a winter wonderland if there ever was one!*

From her place in the doorway, Maggie could count half a dozen Christmas trees glittering and shining in the light of who knew how many candles. The bulbs in the antique chandelier, a family heirloom acquired on some long ago trip to Europe, had been replaced with the flickering kind. Looking closer, Maggie realized not all of the candles were really candles; wall sconces and standing candelabra lamps were also fitted out with the flame-like bulbs. Every metal surface was polished to a high sheen, and glass was everywhere - colored, mirrored, crystal - reflecting and refracting the light. *There are real candles in there somewhere,* she thought, wrinkling her nose at the scent of vanilla hanging heavily in the air. *You can't even smell the trees. I bet they're fakes.* Regardless of their origin, the trees were spectacular, decorated in what Maggie could only define as "classic Franny."

The whole wonderland had a very "classic Franny" feel, but a bit more tastefully executed than some of her previous demonstrations, Maggie noted with some relief. *There's no denying this is beautiful. I wonder if she hired a decorator.* The color palette was overwhelmingly creamy, antique whites with deep green and gold accents. There was a surprising lack of red, and Maggie idly wondered how Franny would react when she saw Marianne's dress. Greenery twined with thin gold ribbons was everywhere, in many places sprinkled with tiny gold Christmas balls, and massive pots of white poinsettias were artfully tucked in corners. The abundance of twinkling light and glass elements gave the space a sense of sparkling, as if the air were somehow alive and dressed for the party too. *It might not be our Christmas, but it is definitely a Norland-worthy Christmas*, Maggie decided, stepping into the room.

The furniture had been rearranged to accommodate decorations and soon-to-arrive guests. The double set of French doors between the dining and drawing rooms were propped open, tiny fairy lights woven in the greenery flanking the door frames. Moving further into the dining room, Maggie realized not only had the table been shifted closer to the wall, but nearly all of the furniture from the drawing room had been removed. The space felt almost vast, in spite of the mini Christmas forest, and the rugs had been pulled up too - revealing a highly polished wooden floor, perfect for a spontaneous dance. A sudden flurry of notes made her jump, and she turned to see several members of a strings group warming up in the corner by the bank of windows. *Oh boy*, Maggie thought, *this could get interesting. Very interesting indeed.* Since Wills's disappearance, Marianne adamantly refused to listen to classical, instrumental, or any other string-heavy music that reminded her of Wills. *And everything reminds her of Wills.*

"As you can see, the architecture and design of Norland lend so naturally to entertaining, we barely had to do anything to prepare for tonight's gala." Franny's voice entered the room ahead of her, and Maggie rolled her eyes at the "Southern diva" tone she was using. *Edward sure labeled that right*, she thought, turning to see who she was talking to. Stifling a giggle, Maggie was happy to be mostly hidden from view by one of the larger trees. Slipping a little further into its shadow, she watched as Franny continued to pontificate to the Steele sisters.

Anne and Lucie arrived the day before, and Maggie had yet to deduce their connection to the Dashwoods or Norland, even a Ferrars connection was suspect. Though Lucie had taken a queer interest in Ellie, spending most of the previous evening trying to lure her into confidential girltalk over Franny's spiked eggnog, the Steeles seemed to want little to do with anyone. *Except Franny,* Maggie noted with a quirked mouth. *I wonder what they're up to, because nobody is that fascinated by Franny's prattling.* Fortunately, Franny's lecture on the importance of tasteful decor was interrupted when Robert and Edward walked in, arguing about something or other, in their usual style. The effect their entrance had on Lucie was instant and intriguing, and Maggie wondered if she had stumbled upon her answer.

"Edward, Robert," Franny snapped. "Manners. We have company present, and a larger party expected soon. Schoolboy antics are strictly forbidden tonight, do you understand?"

"Perhaps the Christmas spirit has made them restive," Lucie purred. "I, for one, am all aflutter with anticipation for tonight's revelry. I have never been to a true Southern Christmas soiree, you know." As she spoke, Lucie cast coy glances at the Ferrars men. Maggie rolled her eyes again and decided the time was right to make an appearance.

"Maggie!" Edward smiled, opening his arms to hug her. "You look beautiful tonight. Very festive as well," he added, giving the tinsel garland in her hair a light tweak.

Maggie returned the hug, then stepped back and gave a quick spin. "We discovered a fairy godmother in Barton," she laughed. "When did you get here? I was beginning to think you weren't going to make it in time."

Edward blushed. "I was delayed by a University matter," he mumbled. "Unpleasant business, definitely not acceptable party conversation."

"The important thing is you made it," Maggie replied, squeezing his arm. "Have you seen the others, do they know you're here?"

Before he could reply, Marianne swept into the room. "Edward! I'm so glad you're here, we were worried you were going to miss Christmas! Wait until you see Ellie; you won't believe how pretty she is tonight." As she spoke, Marianne seemed to float to Edward, air-kissing him on both cheeks, and smiling broadly. Maggie knew she was overcompensating for post-Wills doldrums, but wagered the others would not. A sharp hiss cut through the air, and Maggie glanced at Lucie in surprise. The younger Steele sister quickly schooled her features back to simpering, as Franny found her voice.

"Marianne, that dress is -"

"Red, Franny. My dress is red," Marianne interrupted, spreading her arms. "That is, I believe, a color commonly found in Christmas decorations."

"I was going to say highly inappropriate," Franny replied evenly, one eyebrow arched. "This is a Christmas dinner soiree, a very dignified and respectable affair. And I don't think I need to remind you the stateliness of the home demands a certain refinement of character, carriage and dress. I would suggest you go upstairs and find something more suitable."

Marianne's eyes glinted dangerously, and Maggie started backing slowly to the door, wondering if she could find Ellie in time to prevent a screaming match. Before she made her escape, Edward stepped forward, placing one hand on either woman's shoulder. "Ladies, ladies, ladies," he began, a small smile on his face and diplomacy in his tone. "It's Christmas Eve Eve, Santa is watching, and red is an acceptable color for Christmas, Franny. If the design is a bit, ah, flamboyant, we must remember that

Marianne is a musician, and has a creative, expressive spirit. Now, can we all be family and host a good party?"

"Oh, Edward," Franny sighed, pulling a face before reluctantly nodding her head. "Okay, fine. I still question the appropriateness of that dress, but you make a little sense. And thankfully you didn't come in black, Marianne. I'm glad you seem to have put your mourning behind you."

"Mourning? Did you wear actual mourning for your father?" asked Lucie, cocking her head and blinking.

"Oh no, dear," Franny said, in an almost-whisper. "She has been mourning a lover, it was a nasty breakup."

"You poor thing," Lucie cooed, "I hate to think about suffering a breakup, and so close to Christmas! I feel so sorry for girls who find themselves in that place."

Ellie, walking in with Mrs. Dashwood at that moment, startled as if she'd been struck. Maggie cast a quizzical glance her way, but Ellie merely smiled and commented on the decorations. Lucie chimed in with more gushing, and Maggie worried Franny might begin pontificating again, but John wandered in, mentioning the first guest had pulled in the drive. Franny gave frantic instructions on where to stand, or not stand, for greeting the guests as they arrived, with an especially piercing glance at the Dashwood sisters when she added "And interact, pleasantly!"

The evening went smoothly, much to Maggie's delight, though she frequently caught strange glances being exchanged between Lucie and Ellie, Lucie and Robert, and Ellie and Edward. There was a strained quality to their interactions, but Maggie was able to detect nothing truly amiss despite her close attention. *Franny may have succeeded in pulling off a successful party*, she thought after dinner, as everyone moved back into the drawing room space. *No catastrophes, and everyone appears to be having a genuinely good time. Even John is relaxed and more like the big brother I remember from ages ago.* Sipping a flute of sparkling cider, Maggie turned to find an out of the way spot to people watch, and found herself face-to-face with Wills.

"Oh," she gasped, as his face drained of color. Before she could fully process this development, Marianne's voice sliced across the party noise.

"Wills! Oh, Wills!" The desperateness in Marianne's voice tore at Maggie's heart, but it triggered a steely resolve in Wills. He clenched his jaw as Marianne joined them. "Wills, you're here! Oh, I didn't think you'd come, why didn't you tell me you could make it? Surprises are wonderful, but I'd rather have known. And where have you been during dinner?" Finally taking a breath, she beamed at him, a hopeful expectancy flushing her cheeks.

"I have been here the whole time, ma'am," Wills replied stiffly. Formally. "I am here in the employ of your hostess and sister-in-law, as a musician."

Marianne staggered back, and Maggie quickly wrapped her arm around her sister's waist. "I don't understand," she began.

"There is nothing to understand. I am here to play mood music, and Mrs. Dashwood is paying for my services. That is all."

"But, Wills - Willoughby," Marianne's hopeful smile was fading fast. "I don't understand," she whispered.

"Marianne," John stood at her elbow, surprisingly protective. "Are you okay? What's going on?"

"That's Wills," Maggie spoke softly. "The one who broke Marianne's heart when he disappeared without a trace last month."

"John, make him answer me," Marianne's voice wavered, her eyes filling with tears.

"I think we should take this somewhere private," he said instead, giving Wills a look that brooked no argument. "The three of us, and your mother, are going to my office. Now." Beckoning Momma, John ushered them out of the room, leaving Maggie to field questions and smooth over their absence. She quickly told Ellie and Edward what happened, and the sisters exchanged worried glances.

"Poor Marianne," Lucie murmured, causing both to jump. "And in the middle of such a merry party too. I call that very bad luck. Don't you?" She turned and gave Edward a piercing look. As he blushed and shuffled his feet, Lucie continued. "Fortunately, there are still men who keep their promises." Maggie squinted at Lucie, wondering about the strange tone in her voice, as if she were trying to relay a message - or threat.

"Maggie," Ellie said softly, "let's go, Marianne will need our support, whatever is happening."

Long after the party ended, and everyone went home, Maggie stole away to her attic hideaway, journal in hand. Finding everything as she left it, almost a year ago, she sighed in relief and sank into the old chair.

That was a Christmas party like no other. Franny wanted to make an impression on society? She succeeded, though perhaps not quite the way she intended. There were weird undercurrents all night, before the party even started. It was only a matter of time before everything exploded, but I don't think anyone foresaw how that would happen.

Marianne and Wills are definitely, irrevocably over. Ellie and I slipped into John's office just as Wills was starting his "defense," if you can call it that. Apparently, his leave of absence from the symphony was a forced leave, while he was investigated for a number of nasty side jobs. Fraud, embezzlement and extortion, nice friendly charges. It would seem the very charming Wills conducted affairs with a number of women in positions of power, using them to curry favors and access funds. One of them discovered his unsavory scheme and outed him, thus the investigation. His departure from Barton was a result of being informed he was facing charges and needed a lawyer. All his assets frozen, he was forced to resort to playing small gigs, like Franny's. Thankfully, Francesca and John truly did not know Wills was the devil who broke Marianne's heart, but it was still a dicey situation. Marianne is more distraught than ever, and swears she will never be involved with men or music again. Oy.

Just as John kicked Wills out, there was a bone-chilling screech from the dining room, quickly followed by the sound of shattering glass and garbled shouting. In the minute it took to get from John's office back to the party, Franny managed to topple a Christmas tree, throw a candlestick through the French door (she has very bad aim, fortunately), and generally scandalize her guests. John quickly swept Franny into his office, and Ellie and I did our best to send everyone home with reassurances and Christmas wishes. Robert conveniently disappeared, Anne Steele looked traumatized, Lucie looked like the cat who ate the canary, and Edward looked even more miserable than Franny. It took some time, and not a little whisky, before we were able to get answers out of anyone. The answers were shocking indeed, and I understood why Franny reacted so. I should like to throw something myself - and my aim is much more accurate.

Lucie took advantage of the Dashwoods being preoccupied neatly out of the way to propose a toast to "the first of many Ferrars Christmases, and a lifetime as Mrs. Edward Ferrars." Chaos and calamity ensued. Nobody saw it coming, nobody had an inkling. Nobody wanted to believe it. When pressed for answers, Lucie merely smirked and said they had been engaged for several months (that would explain the awkwardness when he visited last month, if true), and involved far longer. Edward said nothing, only looked more and more miserable, meeting Ellie's confused glance with so much raw pain in his eyes it made me want to cry.

Lucie's weird overtures toward Ellie make sense now, the veiled threat in her sugary words. She must have known Edward has special feelings for Ellie, must have known this Christmas could have been something special for them. I'd suspect Franny as mastermind behind the plan, except for her total shock and distress. There is some queerness afoot, something isn't ringing true. I just can't prove it. And I shan't have a chance to investigate further, because Momma decided we're returning to Barton. Tomorrow. It looks like I'll get to celebrate Christmas at home, after all.

My consolation is the Steele sisters have been kicked out. John, wonderful John, has come into his own tonight and informed Lucie that while he cannot control what Edward does or does not do with his life, he would not tolerate such rude, ungracious behavior from guests. "Norland is a resting place, and you have disturbed the peace enough." I love that. I think Norland is working magic on John, restoring him to his former goodness. Maybe John can find the answers; I hope.

   This Christmas is officially cursed. It has to be. Leaving Norland and spending Christmas at home seemed like a good idea. And this morning, gathered around the tree, handing out gifts, everything did feel right. Almost. Marianne's eyes were swollen from crying, and Ellie has been more quiet than usual since Lucie's bombshell. But still. It was good. Until Ellie opened a beautifully wrapped box that appeared under the tree. Her name was printed on the label, but no one else's. As she carefully lifted the lid, a sweet, familiar scent wafted on the air. Beeswax candles. Inside, a small card with the elegant logo of With Love rested on a ribbon-tied bundle of long tapers. Ellie blinked away tears, and handed me the card. It was from Edward, and only said "I'm sorry. I hope to have answers soon, for everything. I hope these can brighten your days, and remind you of happier ones. I'm sorry, Ellie, so sorry."

   Once Ellie started crying, Marianne teared up again. Then the phone rang. Aunt Jenn called to let us know before we saw it on the news: Wills eloped with the socialite daughter of a wealthy and prominent senator. Apparently his new family could help clear his name, and reinstate his income. Christmas was officially a lost cause.

There are so many mysteries, so many questions unanswered - and unasked, and so many hearts broken. Christmas should be happy, not sad. The new year looks bleak. I don't think I shall write again until next December. There will only be disturbing things to record in the days to come, and next year ... Next year, we are due a good Christmas!

{Christmas Charmed}

Christmas music played softly in the background, and Maggie hummed along to Michael Buble's crooning as she wiped down tables and pushed in chairs. After spending so much time there as a patron, Ellie convinced her to apply when Mansfield Perk advertised an open position, and Maggie had been an official barista-of-all-trades since June. She found she enjoyed the work, and being paid to learn the ins and outs of drinks while getting to know the other people who appreciated the shop's cozy atmosphere felt incredibly lucky. As much as she loved establishing relationships with the regulars however, her favorite customers were the travelers, the passers-through.

Maggie, now a Creative Writing student at the local college, let her imagination run wild creating stories about the people here one day and gone the next, sipping their drinks and living mysterious lives. She often scribbled first impressions or hurried thoughts on napkins, stuffed in her apron pocket, to be smoothed out and explored in her writing journal later. One day she hoped to compile her character sketches into a series of short stories to serve as entrance portfolio for an MFA program – a dream she kept tucked close to her heart, out of the public spotlight. Today though, her thoughts kept drifting to another journal.

Only one section left, she mused, straightening the creamer station. *I wonder why only three Christmases were allowed? Why not every Christmas? And how do I even begin to end this?* Her father's last gift had been a lifesaver, there when she needed it most, and a way to work through the ups and downs of Dashwood family drama. Even as she dreaded having to set down her pen and close the journal, saying another 'goodbye,' Maggie found herself anticipating the release of sharing a year's worth of family news. *But not tonight*, she remembered. *We're going to Ellie and Edward's to decorate the tree!* The promise of an evening spent in her sister's home, with family, tinsel and festive treats galore, made Maggie smile. *And their story is the happiest Dashwood news of the whole year, I'm going to enjoy revisiting that in the writing.*

"Why are you smiling like the cat that ate the canary, Miss Magpie," asked a familiar voice.

"Brandon!" Maggie looked up in surprise, her smile broadening. "When did you get back? We didn't expect you until Christmas Eve!"

Brandon grabbed her hand and twirled her in for a hug. "I finished the job early, and couldn't stay away from the Dashwood girls a minute longer. My life was getting boring, I needed entertaining, and y'all are always good for a laugh." He winked.

"Right," she laughed. "You can't fool me, you missed Marianne. Have you seen her yet? Does she know you're here? Are you coming to Ellie and Edward's tonight? Please say yes!"

With a laugh of his own, Brandon set his hands on her shoulders. "Easy, Magpie. Take a breath, girl. You got me: I was pining for Marianne. Aching and wasting away to nothing. No, she doesn't know I'm here yet - and yes, I'm coming tonight. And don't tell her, it's a surprise."

"Eee!" Maggie squealed, before clapping her hand over her mouth. "Brandon, are you going to -"

"Maggie," he interrupted with a raised eyebrow. "Hush. I need to pick up a dozen of those amazing muffins y'all sell; I promised Ellie I'd bring something and we all know I can't cook to save my life."

As she boxed up the muffins, Maggie tried to coax more information from Brandon, but he just smiled and told her to wait and see. "Okay, be that way," she sighed dramatically, handing over the box and taking his money.

"Oh, I will," he said with another wink, turning to go. "See you tonight, Magpie. And don't be late! I'd hate for you to miss anything exciting."

Maggie couldn't help laughing as she watched him leave. *He is the best thing to ever happen to Marianne*, she thought.

Later that evening, after everyone had eaten way too many savory treats, and the finishing touches were being placed on the tree, Maggie curled up in a corner of the sofa with a mug of cocoa, surveying the scene. The old farmhouse was drafty and neglected when Edward bought it in the spring. He and Brandon did all the renovations themselves, working through the hot Georgia summer to get the house ready for Ellie. While the men focused on structural and practical aspects like patching holes, stripping floors and busting out walls to expand rooms and add closets, Ellie made the house a home. *It's beautiful,* Maggie thought now, *not as elegant as Norland perhaps, but it's homey and cozy. It's so Ellie.*

The large room downstairs where they gathered now was as warm and welcoming as her sister and brother-in-law. Edward made sure Ellie always had beeswax candles from With Love, and tonight their soft honeyed fragrance brought to mind childhood memories. Watching the two of them now, heads bent together as they tried to untangle ornament hooks, Maggie knew this Christmas would be the best yet. Her gaze wandered to their mother, and she smiled at the look of utter contentment on her face. *I know just how she feels,* Maggie mused. *This is what peace feels like.* The smile deepened as her eyes found Marianne and Brandon. *He must be teasing her about something, look how she blushes!*

Even though he was a relative newcomer to both the area and the family circle, Brandon Delaford slipped into place as if he'd been born a Dashwood. His unassuming manner and genuine desire to be of help in any way quickly won their friendship. A skilled builder, it was some months into their acquaintance before the Dashwoods learned their new friend was in fact a much sought after architect. The discovery only cemented their regard, and as they grew closer it became apparent Brandon had a special appreciation for one of the Miss Dashwoods.

After the fiasco with Wills, Maggie thought her sister might actually follow through on her declaration to never even look at another guy. To the relief of everyone, Marianne 'found her way out of the black depths of brokenness,' with a little gentle prodding from Brandon and his guitar. It had been a slow process, and the healing tempered Marianne's spirit even as she learned to laugh - and love - again. The over-the-top dramatics once so annoying to Maggie had given way to a simple embracing of life, the good and the bad, a change that brought all three sisters closer together. Now, watching her sister laugh at Brandon's teasing, Maggie knew everything was turning out just as it should. *Maybe that last entry won't be so hard to write after all,* she thought. When Brandon pulled out his guitar and began to strum as Marianne softly sang Christmas carols, Maggie hoped for many more nights like this - cozy and familiar, surrounded by the people she loved and the love they shared. And she knew that life for the Dashwoods was finally headed toward a happily ever after.

Much later that night, Maggie stole away to the attic, thankful once more their house in Barton had an actual attic with dormer windows. Maggie convinced her mother to let her commandeer one of those dormers in the spring, creating a cozy nook where she could work on homework, read or just soak in the silence. She sat for a moment, her favorite quilt wrapped around her shoulders, looking at the leather book in her hands. It was even softer now, after two Christmas seasons, and its comforting weight in her hands settled her restive mind. "Okay, Daddy," she whispered. "The last Christmas awaits."

Tugging on the ribbon marker, and opening the journal, Maggie smiled when a blue envelope fell into her lap. *I don't know how it happens, but I love that it does,* she thought. *Some things, you just don't ask questions about.* Drawing out the card, she wondered what message awaited her this year.

Merry Christmas again, Magpie.

Your third and final Christmas for scribbling in this journal has arrived and, if I know you, there are only a few pages left. I can picture you so clearly, hunched over the journal, scribbling furiously, with the slightest of furrows to your brow. You get so lost in your writing, the whole world could fall away and you would never notice. I love that dedication and intensity in you, my Magpie. But don't let it take over.

By now, I feel certain you have all settled into a new routine, a happy new way of living. I hope Ellie has found love with someone who looks out for her, and that Marianne has learned to walk in grace and not just gracefully. And you ... You are now 19. A wonderful age, on the very brink of a new decade.

I have one final instruction for you, Margaret: Live. Embrace the adventures given to you. Write the words that must be written, but do not forget to live in the world. Take care of you now, Maggie. Your sisters, your mother, they're going to be okay. It's your turn to fly, and I pray you soar.

I love you to infinity, and beyond, my little Magpie.

Daddy

Blinking back tears, Maggie slipped the card between the pages of the book and closed it gently. *Oh, Daddy.* Turning off the little lamp, she leaned her head back against the wall and looked out the window into the night. *December stars are always brightest*, she mused, searching out her beloved winter constellations. *And Daddy knew me well. It is so easy to hide behind the writing, to lose myself in the story.*

Some time later, Maggie turned the lamp back on and opened to her final pages.

Every year, there's a new story to tell. This year at last it is a happy story, a happy ending.

Our happiness began early, surprisingly, when John worked with Edward to unravel Lucie's claims and procure his freedom without making a scene in the public eye. She had been a student of his one semester, and was attempting to coerce him into marriage or else face charges of harassment and discrimination. I don't know what evidence she had, or thought she had, but her scheme was destined to fail. (I think she knew that, somehow, and that's why she kept making digs at Ellie, even after Christmas. Misery wanted company, perhaps?) Turns out she ultimately wanted an additional monthly allowance, conspiring with Robert, the mastermind behind the plan and now her husband, in her attempts to blackmail Edward. Yup. Weasely Robert Ferrars. Talk about brotherly love. Franny was furious, banning Robert and Lucie from Norland indefinitely. She even decided that Ellie was a good match for her brainy brother, and helped smooth their transition from cute friends to an adorable couple. In a moment of true grace, she and John offered the grounds of Norland for the wedding in September. It was beautiful, and Ellie is blissfully happy. At last.

I have a hunch Marianne will follow her down the aisle soon, Brandon is head over heels in love and I feel certain he is going to propose before New Year's. To see her happy and in love - really in love, and not a dramatic pretense of love - has been our delight. She returned to music as well (also thanks to Brandon), and I expect her new sound will take her far. Certainly farther than Wills will ever make it - hard to be a renowned cellist from a federal penitentiary.

I will always miss Norland, especially at Christmas, but life in Barton is everything I could hope for. I am surrounded by family and friends; the world is full of promise and hope. I've taken time to hide and heal, and now I emerge ready to conquer anything. Daddy knew exactly what he was doing, and I trust him in this as ever.

Here's to loving, laughing, and most importantly: living.

This is [definitely not] the end.

Acknowledgements

I count myself incredibly privileged to be part of this awesome group; Jessica, Melissa, Kimberly, Cecilia and Jennifer have been wonderful to work (and laugh) with – and tell amazing stories. Thanks for letting me join the fun, ladies!

Thanks also to Steven, my beta reading guinea pig, even though this is not your genre of choice. Your commentary made me laugh out loud sometimes, and was tremendously helpful.

And, of course, the biggest "Thank you!" of all goes to Jane, for writing it first and letting me fall in love with these characters over and over again.

Emma's Inbox

An *Emma* Story

*For the Emmas who don't see their hero in
front of them;
and the Knightleys who love them regardless.*

To: IsabellaWKnightley@yourmail.com
From: EmmaWritesHartfield@yourmail.com
Date: 15 Feb 20**
Subject: <u>Wedding Bells!</u>

Grab a drink, Izzy, and make sure the kiddies are distracted: this is going to be one long email. There is much to say.

It's official: Anne Taylor has married Jack Weston. Finally. I take full credit for their trip to the altar, no matter what Knightley says. We have watched them engage in a lackadaisical, romantic pursuit of sorts (sorry, I can't help but shiver - even if she is my dearest confidant and mentor. I simply cannot think of people Father's age flirting without getting a horrid mental image) for twenty years. Twenty. Years. They probably would have kept it up for another twenty, if I had not given them a slight nudge in the right direction.

Knightley, of course, says Anne and Jack's marriage – their whole romance – has nothing whatsoever to do with me. He says my little New Year's Eve soiree last year had nothing to do with their Valentine's engagement. Silly man. I think he's still sore I knew you were going to marry John years before it happened, while he swore it never would. I love him dearly, of course, but sometimes I wonder if he has any idea how relationships work. Leaving things to Fate is all well and good in books, but in real life people never see things as clearly. They need a nudge, a gentle push toward each other.

The wedding was beautiful, Izz. Sweet and simple, in spite of the best attempts of the Bateses (although I will say Missy has some astonishing ideas for new ways to use tulle). The only thing lacking, to my eyes, was the appearance of Frank Churchill. You'd think he could make time in his schedule to see his father get married - there were text messages exchanged - but nope. No Frank. And so the myth and mystery surrounding Hartfield's idol continues to grow.

I digress. The wedding. Anne was a dream bride, and the weather perfection. It was surprisingly warm (I desperately hope spring comes early this year!), and the sun set the wintery decorations to sparkling. Father was, of course, preoccupied with drafts, certain Anne would catch her death in such a frivolous gown (it had no sleeves!). Of equal concern was the very real chance the snowflakes or tinsel would catch fire from the candles on the altar. He did approve of the way our new minister, Elton Phillips, handled the ceremony and related events - and his proper deference to "the women of the congregation" and their traditional role concerning all things social.

Poor Elton. I almost feel sorry for the guy - fresh out of school, and a big city internship (do ministers intern? student preach? hmm, I should probably know that), having no idea what awaits him as the new minister in a small Southern town. Almost. He's cool as a cucumber most of the time, but when the ladies of Hartfield start fussing and clucking over him like mother hens, he smirks like a fox in the henhouse. Of course, they haven't started playing matchmaker with him yet - that will change everything.

Here's a secret, Izz. I decided, during the wedding, that third time's the charm. I am going to find our dashing young Elton a bride before the ladies of Hartfield swoop in for the kill. Not only will it serve as a nice diversion, with Anne married and beginning her new life with Jack, but Elton is new. He knows nobody in Hartfield. So when I find his perfect match, and they begin a life of happiness and romance, Knightley can't deny that I played a role.

Speaking of new people in the community - it appears we are to have a new church secretary to go with our new minister. I thought Anne would be taking an extended leave, by way of a glamorously long honeymoon, and Missy Bates was going to "fill-in." Anne has decided not to return to the Church Office however, and instead turn all her energies to life as Mrs. Weston (Jack has so many plans for them, his enthusiasm is cute). When Elton found out, he decided to just hire a brand new secretary. An ad has been placed, and Mrs. Goddard and myself have been tasked with finding the perfect replacement.

Things are indeed changing here in little ol' Hartfield. A fact I find thrilling, and Father finds unsettling. Poor dear. I keep reminding him I am going nowhere, and that nothing too terrible can happen with Knightley at the helm.

It still makes me laugh, his being mayor. I'm not sure why - it's the perfect position: he can boss everyone around, instead of being stuck only bossing me. Ha. Really though, Izz, when did we get so old? How is it possible that you have been married for seven years, have two children under the age of 5, and another on the way? (How are you feeling by the way? Just a few months, and I will have a lovely baby niece to spoil! I'm already making plans - Aunt Emma, already cool to the dashing Knightley Nephews, will rise to new heights of glory as Aunt-to-a-Princess! You think I'm kidding; I assure you I speak truth. Consider yourself forewarned, dearest big sister).

What was I saying? Oh yes. How old we have all become. While you have been busy growing another baby for me to snuggle, I have settled into my role writing for the Hartfield Herald. It may only be a biweekly rag, but there's no denying the immense responsibility: we at the paper take all things community-related very seriously. Anne and Jack's wedding is going to be on the front page of the next edition, with pictures. I'm also working on a piece about the new - and familiar - faces popping up around town. Jane is coming back, did you know? I'm sure Knightley must've told John, but in case my darling brother-in-law did not pass along such a tasty tidbit of Hartfield news, I will.

You know how Missy Bates goes on and on and on about Jane and her friend Tricia Campbell's PR company? From all accounts, it would seem they had a rather lucrative little set-up, with actual A-list clients. While you would think this a good thing, and it was - for Tricia - it ended up backfiring. You see, Tricia fell hopelessly in love with Dixon Greene, who is not only one of the hottest players in the history of baseball, but also a client. Apparently marrying the people who hire you is frowned upon, and since Tricia no longer *needs* to work (I'm not sure she ever did, actually, I think her little enterprise was more entertainment than anything), she signed over their clientele to another firm and left Jane without a job. She did get a very nice payout however, which she used to buy the sweetest little loft in the new building downtown. Until she figures out what direction her career is going to take, Knightley has brought her on board to coordinate PR and planning for the town. And so, Jane Fairfax, the wonderfully talented and going-somewhere-special epitome of awesomeness that has haunted *my entire life* is back in Hartfield. This should be fun.

I know, I know. I can hear you clear as day: "Be nice," "Jane can't help it." I know that, but you have to admit - everyone has praised her so much, on scholarship at swank private schools in glamorous cities around the world, then starting a PR firm in New York. It grates on my nerves. I'm only human, after all. (See? I can admit my own humanity!) Knightley says the affair with Tricia and Dixon rattled Jane more than she lets on, and she overworked herself dreadfully in NYC, handling all the real work herself, a combination that has made her even more reserved than normal. I suppose we'll find out for ourselves soon - I hear she is to arrive in the next week or so, after handling some of Tricia's wedding details. (Seriously, can this girl do nothing for herself without Jane being involved?)

I must go finish my column ... Kiss the boys for me! And send Knightley home, Hartfield is strangely quiet without him.

To: EmmaWritesHartfield@yourmail.com
From: IsabellaWKnightley@yourmail.com
Date: 15 Feb 20**
Subject: RE: Wedding Bells!

I'll have to reread later, to digest everything. Can't wait to see pics, and you're right about Jane: Be nice!

Must you persist in calling Noah "Knightley"?

To: IsabellaWKnightley@yourmail.com
From: EmmaWritesHartfield@yourmail.com
Date: 15 Feb 20**
Subject: RE: Wedding Bells!

That's his name, that's who he is. I can't think of him as Noah - and I have tried, believe me - it feels weird. Real weird. Too weird. Knightley he is, and Knightley he's called.

Knightley: Did you cry at the wedding?
Emma: No comment. Father did.
Emma: I still can't believe you missed the wedding.
Knightley: A mayor's work is never done, Emma.
Knightley: Don't feel sad. Anne will be back after her honeymoon before you know, and you can help redecorate poor Weston's entire house. That level of meddling should make you happy :)
Emma: OMG. Did you just use an emoticon!?
Emma: Ha. ha. ha. I don't meddle.
Emma: But that will be fun.
Knightley: I have been known to emote. When the moment is right.
Knightley: ;)
Emma: I just fainted from shock.

Love, Hartfield: New Faces in the Crowd
By Emma Woodhouse, Staff Writer

Change is in the air, Hartfield! After the dismal weather we've experienced since November, I for one am welcoming the unseasonally sunny warmth with open arms and no questions asked. If the swelling buds in the Highbury Hills orchards are any indication, spring is coming early this year. Along with the changes in nature, we are experiencing some social changes as well - what an exciting time it is to be in Hartfield!

Anne Taylor and Jack Weston were married over Valentine's weekend, and there is a beautiful story on the front page (and more pictures on pages 6 and 7) for your viewing pleasure. It was a glorious wedding, and I am sure you all agree their marriage will be a story of hope and encouragement for others in the community. The ceremony also served as the formal introduction for our new minister, Reverend Elton Phillips, to the hospitality and communal spirit of Hartfield.

If you haven't heard, Rev. Phillips joins us following a stint in Oxford (England, not Mississippi), but hails from Atlanta. This will be Rev. Phillips's first small-town experience, but I am sure Hartfield will roll out a true Southern welcome. It's a season of all-around change in the church office - a new office manager has been hired to fill the place vacated by Anne Weston. Harriet Smith, a recent graduate of Barton College, will begin work next week. I had the pleasure of meeting Ms. Smith during the interview process, and believe her cheerful, welcoming personality will be an asset to the church office and Hartfield society.

Among the new additions, a familiar face will be returning to the streets and gatherings of Hartfield in days to come. Our own Jane Fairfax is coming home, and will be settling into City Hall as Public Relations and Planning Coordinator. In this role, Ms. Fairfax will work closely with citizens and local government, bringing her years of experience in the big city to make dear Hartfield sparkle all the brighter.

Here's to the arrival of new friends, and an early spring!

To: IsabellaWKnightley@yourmail.com
From: EmmaWritesHartfield@yourmail.com
Date: 24 Feb 20**
Subject: Matchmaker, matchmaker ...
I have found Elton's match, Izzy. The genius of it is he opened the door for me. Remember I mentioned Mrs. G and I were going to handle the interviews for a new secretary? Wait, excuse me: office manager. Apparently the term "secretary" is not comprehensive enough for the position. Elton delivered quite a spiel about the differences (not to mention the outdatedness of the terminology to begin with). ANYWAY. Interviews. We only conducted three - the first two were doozies, let me tell you. (I'm actually surprised Missy Bates didn't apply, but maybe with Jane moving home she's going to be too occupied for occupation). Third time was the charm however, and Mrs. G and myself were in immediate agreement on the matter. Not only is she the perfect candidate for the church office, but she will suit beautifully as candidate for "minister's wife."
Name: Harriet Smith
Age: 21 (almost 22)

Education: Barton College, BA in Performance Art, minor in Bookkeeping

Okay, so Performance Art is perhaps not the ideal background for an office manager, but you have to admit it will come in handy planning and staging church socials! Plus she worked in the ticket office her entire college career, in addition to the minor in Bookkeeping (I didn't know that was a thing?). Mainly, she's got this great, bubbly personality that will set people at ease. And she's adorable. Ah-dor-ah-ble. Seriously. You know the girls who are so dang cute you kinda want to hate them, but they're so sweet and genuinely nice that you love 'em instead? That's Harriet Smith.

I've only chatted with her briefly, outside the actual interview, over dinner at Mrs. G's, but my instincts tell me she is the perfect match for our charismatic young minister. Elton is quite the charmer, Izz, and he has The Ladies eating out of the palm of his hand. The Bateses adore him, and he can even make Mrs. G giggle! Giggle! It's amusing to watch him flirt and cater to them - smart move on his part. Nothing happens in the church, shoot, in the town, without The Ladies' stamp of approval. I can only hope he will employ the same level of charm in his interactions with Miss Harriet Smith. A little careful nudging may be in order, some interactions on neutral ground, shall we say. I will keep you posted.

Away I fly ... Knightley wants to see me - in his Mayoral Chambers - about something or other. Kiss the kiddies for me!

To: EmmaWritesHartfield@yourmail.com
From: IsabellaWKnightley@yourmail.com
Date: 24 Feb 20**
Subject: RE: Matchmaker, matchmaker ...

The minister and the church secretary (sorry, I am not going to use "office manager") ... Not the most creative pairing, Em, but I guess you can't help it if the occupations are such a cliché match. Haha. Do keep me posted, sounds like it could turn out very interesting.

Anne: Office manager??? What on earth is an office manager?
Emma: You saw the column?
Emma: Why are you online during your honeymoon? Aren't those supposed to be sacred? ;)
Anne: Yup. Wanted to see what pics from the wedding they used, then I had to read your column, of course.
Emma: Elton has some interesting ideas. Thus the job title change.
Anne: Apparently. What's she like? Have you already worked out a match for her?
Emma: Anne! Whatever gave you such an idea?
Anne: I know you. Come on, 'fess up. :)
Emma: Yes. I have. But you have to wait until you get home.
Anne: Deal. See you soon, Emma-love!
Emma: I can't wait! Enjoy the rest of your honeymoon.

To: EmmaWritesHartfield@yourmail.com
From: NoahKnightley1978@yourmail.com
Date: 25 Feb 20*
Subject: Odds and Ends

    Emma, I wanted to reiterate the particulars from our conversation yesterday. You seemed a bit distracted, and I'd like your full concentration and cooperation in this matter. You have considerable intelligence, and the ability to see things from a more creative vantage point than I possess. In addition, whether you admit it or not, you have a position of some standing in the community - people respect your opinion(s), and will follow your lead.

    As you know, Jane Fairfax is returning to Hartfield in the midst of a chaotic and rocky season. While she has not mentioned anything specific, my gut instinct is there is more behind her return than the dissolvement of their firm and Tricia's upcoming wedding. I mentioned before, Jane seems much more reserved and withdrawn than previously - I can't help but think something has happened on a personal level. To that end, I strongly encourage you to extend and offer your friendship. I know you two have spent your whole lives being compared, a forced rivalry of sorts, but even with the differences in your temperament and experiences, I find you to be very similar. I think it could be beneficial for you to have a peer of such equal standing, and I know your friendship would be a very good thing for Jane. As your friend, and as your Mayor, I charge you - Emma Woodhouse, unofficial Queen of Hartfield - with personally ensuring Jane Fairfax feels welcomed and accepted back into the community.

Official business completed, I also wanted to let you know I'll be able to join your dinner party on the 28th after all. I do have to make that trip to Atlanta on the 27th, but I anticipate my business concluding quickly enough to return to Hartfield well before dinner.

I do hope you aren't up to any more matchmaking mischief - you were rather too coy in the inviting. You've been rather secretive in general since the wedding, and I am half-afraid you're taking yourself too seriously. You were lucky in your guess about Isabella and John - perhaps the close relationship you share with Isabella let you see things before the rest of us did - but you are in no way responsible for the Westons. I've said it before, and I'll say it once more: Jack was preparing to take things further before your little party. (And really Emma, do you think men so simple minded that one candlelight dinner - even in as lovely a setting as the Highbury Hills formal dining room - would persuade someone to turn a casual fling into a lifetime commitment?)

I'm sure I'll see you before heading to the big city, but do try to behave while I'm gone.

To: NoahKnightley1978@yourmail.com
From: EmmaWritesHartfield@yourmail.com
Date: 25 Feb 20*
Subject: <u>RE: Odds and Ends</u>

Has anyone ever told you you sound like an old man? ;)

Don't worry, everything is under control. It's true, I was a little distracted during our meeting - I ran into Harriet Smith on my way into your office and half my mind was still on our conversation. I did pick up the general vibe of your lecture however, and the extensive details provided above definitely cover all the bases. Yes, I will be welcoming and friendly toward Jane when she arrives. I may even host a party to celebrate her return! But I desperately hope you're wrong about her reserved nature, or this "friendship" will not progress well ... Even I can carry a conversation only so far without assistance.

As for your other point of business ... If I am up to any 'matchmaking mischief' as you put it, you can rest assured it shan't affect you in any way. Lord knows it would take a great deal more than a candlelight dinner to turn your thoughts to romance - after all, you're the charter member of Hartfield's Forever Single club. ;) It's one of the things I love about you: I'm always guaranteed a wonderful escort to parties and events. We're perennial loners, you and I. So don't you worry your mayoral head about matchmaking and whether it is happening or not, leave it to the experts.

Knightley: You are impossible sometimes, Emma Woodhouse
Emma: I know :) But you love me for it
Emma: Are we still on for lunch?
Knightley: Of course. On both counts.

Unknown Number: Hiiiii! U wanna grab coffee 2day?
Emma: I'm sorry, who is this?

Unknown Number: Omg, my bad. Its Harriet :) Got ur # from Elton

Emma: Oh, hi! Sure. When do you finish for the day?

Harriet: Get 2 leave @ 4. Good 4 u?

Emma: Perfect! I'll meet you at Mansfield Perk at 4:15

Harriet: :D C u then!

Emma: Izz ... Am I getting old?

Izzy: Well. Yes. If you're still alive, you're getting old. Duh

Izzy: :)

Emma: Ha. Ha. I just got several texts from Harriet, and felt the strangest urge to correct her grammar

Emma: Who knew the generation gap started at 8 years? It's like she was speaking another language!

Izzy: Hahaha ... Now you know how Noah feels when you needle him

Emma: Unfair! That's totally different.

Emma: Knightley and I have an understanding.

Emma: And the difference in our age doesn't impact our communicating.

Emma: And we are only 6 years and 5 months apart in age.

Izzy: Methinks she doth protest too much

Izzy: Are you second-guessing your matchmaking now?

Emma: No, I still think Harriet + Elton = ♥

Emma: But I hope her texting isn't an omen of things to come

Izzy: Keep me posted. This is better than tv!

Knightley: How was your coffee date with the adorable Harriet Smith?

Emma: It was lovely. She's darling! So perky and bubbly... I think she'll fit in nicely here in Hartfield

Emma: And thankfully she doesn't talk the way she texts. ;)

Knightley: Mmm. That is good.

Knightley: Would I be correct in guessing she is the victim of your current matchmaking plot?

Emma: I told you not to worry about that.

Knightley: Like that will make me not worry...

Knightley: Just be careful Emma. You really don't know much about her, she hasn't been part of your life forever, like Isabella and Anne.

Emma: That's what makes it so fun and exciting! Don't worry. I know what I'm doing.

Knightley: That's what I'm afraid of.

Izzy: Isn't tonight the big Harriet + Elton = ♥ dinner?

Emma: Yes! Everything is going according to plan, and I've got a good feeling about this.

Emma: So long as Knightley behaves.

Izzy: Ha. Doesn't he always?

Emma: He's been razzing me about matchmaking Harriet, not to cause trouble, blah blah blah…

Izzy: hahahahahaha

Emma: Not funny

Izzy: Oh, it kinda is. And by kinda, I mean very.

Izzy: What time is show time?

Emma: People should arrive at 6:30, dinner will be served at 7

Izzy: Eating late, like the rich and famous, are we? ;)

Emma: More like making sure Knightley has time to get home and cleaned up, ha. He's been in Atlanta on mysterious mayor business.

Emma: He refuses to tell me anything about that mysterious mayor business.

Izzy: Maybe he has a secret life … a secret romance he doesn't want you to know about …

Emma: Oh do be serious, Isabella. That is absolutely preposterous.

Izzy: Not necessarily ;)

Emma: Do you want to know how the party goes tonight?

Izzy: Okay, okay. You know I'm just teasing.

Izzy: You really are touchy about Noah these days, btw

Emma: I'm not even gonna give that a response.

To: IsabellaWKnightley@yourmail.com
From: EmmaWritesHartfield@yourmail.com
Date: 1 March 20**
Subject: Operation: Dinner Party

Consider yourself forewarned, Izz: This is another long email.

Operation: Dinner Party was mostly successful, though it may take a little more encouragement (*cough*finagling*cough*) for Harriet + Elton = ♥ to happen. (And don't you dare tell Knightley! He'd consider that admitting failure, and never let me live it down). It all began well, everyone showing up on schedule - Harriet, Elton and Knightley of course, and also Missy Bates and Mrs. Goddard, so it wouldn't be too small or awkward. (Plus Mrs. G volunteered to bring a batch of her famous chocolate truffle brownies - and we all know those are my kryptonite). It was definitely a diverse mix of personalities, but everyone is generally agreeable and, with Elton and Harriet still so new, conversation was wide-ranging and amusing. Even Knightley contributed to the exchange, though I'm not sure the others picked up on what he was leaving unsaid. He makes it so hard for me to maintain composure sometimes! I was cracking up, not just at what he was saying but that everyone else was completely missing it, and could not laugh. Worst part was he knew what he was doing, and kept giving me this devilishly innocent smirk. It was such a relief to move into the dining room.

I was excessively careful in the seating arrangements, positioning Elton and Harriet to my left and right, so they were across from each other. Close without being obvious, perfect for a magical candlelit conversation. I placed Missy and Mrs. G on Father's end of the table, and Knightley next to Harriet. It did bother me to have that empty chair, but alas ... I've promised Knightley to include Jane, so when she arrives (today? Tomorrow? I forget; soon!), she can fill the gap. Although Anne and Jack come home today - we'll still be short a person. Unless Frank comes to visit; then I'd still have an empty chair... Sorry, rabbit-trail ... Where was I? Oh. Yeah. Dinner. The easy conversation from before did not transfer to the table. I'm not sure what happened, but something shifted. Harriet kept chatting away merry as can be - she has simply fallen in love with Hartfield, you see, and wants to get to know simply everyone and discover all the best local hangouts - but Elton seemed distracted. Almost edgy, actually. Knightley wasn't too charming or chatty himself - you would almost think something happened between them, looking back, but I'm not sure what could have possibly happened. Or when. Who knows.

The important thing is that Elton and Harriet were able to interact outside of their work roles, in a more natural and 'friendly' environment, and I still believe they have potential to be a wonderful couple. She is perhaps a little young, a little excitable, but I think once she settles into her role in Hartfield things will level out. The ball has started rolling, and I hope when we meet for lunch on Wednesday, I'll get a peek into whether things have shifted in the dynamics of their interactions.

Harriet: OMG, thnx so much for inviting me last night!
Emma: You are most welcome! I hope you had a good time. Hartfield is a quiet town, but we do enjoy each other's company - and good food.
Harriet: Totes! Those brownies were 2 die 4!
Harriet: Hey, so ? for u ... Why do u call him Knightley?
Emma: Oh, haha. Long story very short, I met him years ago while writing a story for the high school paper. He was a star player on the Barton minor league team at the time.
Emma: I got so used to hearing & referring to him as Knightley in that sports/paper context, that it stuck.
Harriet: Cool. He was a bball star? OMG! No wonder he looks so good!
Emma: For a while, yes. But he realized he wanted to settle here, and gave it up.

Harriet: I think Elton played baseball. How many men play in Hartfield?

Emma: Ah ... Well, we do have quite a number of baseball fanatics. Some Southern towns are football towns - we do baseball.

Harriet: I totes dig that. Baseball boys r so hott, lol

Emma: You're a fan then? :)

Harriet: Of the players & their uniforms? Heck yes! The game is dumb

Harriet: Have u seen that show Phenomena?

Emma: Noooo, I don't think so

Harriet: Its awesome! This Russian sounding chick goes around & like ghost hunts. I watched like a thousand episodes the other night.

Emma: Sounds interesting. What exactly does she do?

Harriet: Oh, idk. I just like the places she goes & when she interviews hott guys

Emma: Ah, gotcha.

Emma: So I'll see you for lunch on Wednesday, right?

Harriet: Totes! Thnx again for dinner! I love ur house!

To: EmmaWritesHartfield@youmail.com,
JaneFairfaxPR@Hartfield.gov
From: NoahKnightleyMayor@Hartfield.gov
Date: 1 March 20**
Subject: Meeting - High Importance!

I need to see the both of you, as soon as possible. Would first thing tomorrow morning work?

Jane, I know you're just getting settled in, and apologize for "rushing" you into things, but something has come up that requires immediate attention. It's a good problem, I think, but I will need your PR expertise and Emma's general knowledge of the pulse of the community to pull this off successfully.

To: NoahKnightleyMayor@Hartfield.gov,
JaneFairfaxPR@Hartfield.gov
From: EmmaWritesHartfield@youmail.com
Date: 1 March 20**
Subject: RE: Meeting
     Well you've definitely piqued my curiosity. Sure, I can make it tomorrow ... What time? And please, please, please promise me there'll be coffee if it's before 9 ;)
     ps: Welcome home, Jane!

To: EmmaWritesHartfield@youmail.com,
NoahKnightleyMayor@Hartfield.gov
From: JaneFairfaxPR@Hartfield.gov
Date: 1 March 20**
Subject: RE: Meeting
     I can make it also, just tell me when and where. And I second Emma's plea for coffee.
     ps: Thanks, Emma. It feels as if I never left - so little has changed. :)

To: JaneFairfaxPR@Hartfield.gov,
EmmaWritesHartfield@youmail.com
From: NoahKnightleyMayor@Hartfield.gov
Date: 1 March 20**
Subject: RE: Meeting
     Perfect. Let's plan on my office, 9am. And to show my appreciation for your flexibility and willingness to accommodate such short notice, I'll swing by Mansfield Perk and get coffee and baked goods.

To: NoahKnightleyMayor@Hartfield.gov,
JaneFairfaxPR@Hartfield.gov
From: EmmaWritesHartfield@youmail.com
Date: 1 March 20**
Subject: RE: Meeting
     You're so my favorite, Knightley! See y'all at 9!

To: EmmaWritesHartfield@youmail.com,
NoahKnightleyMayor@Hartfield.gov
From: JaneFairfaxPR@Hartfield.gov
Date: 1 March 20**
Subject: RE: Meeting
    Sounds good, Noah. See you guys in the morning! (And thanks in advance for making the MP run!)

Emma: What's all this mysterious urgent meeting stuff???
Knightley: You'll find out in the morning.
Emma: You know I can't wait that long! What is going on?!
Knightley: It's less than 24 hours, Emma. Patience, my padawan. Patience.
Emma: Does it have anything to do with your trip to Atlanta?
Emma: What if I bat my eyelashes and say 'pretty please'?
Knightley: You want a chocolate croissant in the morning?
Emma: Yes please! :)
Knightley: Then stop wheedling.
Knightley: And that never works on me anyway, remember?
Emma: I'm glaring at you in my mind.
Knightley: :)

To: EmmaWritesHartfield@yourmail.com
From: IsabellaWKnightley@yourmail.com
Date: 1 March 20**
Subject: RE: Operation: Dinner Party
    Maybe Noah figured out you're trying to matchmake Harriet and Elton, or thought you were trying to matchmake him with Harriet while claiming Elton for yourself.
    It does sound as if something has started, though I can't make out what exactly. Do keep me posted ... Maybe lunch with Harriet will offer more insight. But perhaps you should be careful Emma, if she really is so young and excitable - things may end up backfiring if you proceed too quickly.

To: IsabellaWKnightley@yourmail.com
From: EmmaWritesHartfield@yourmail.com
Date: 1 March 20**
Subject: RE: Operation Dinner Party

Claim Elton for myself?! Really, Izzy, that's taking preggo brain to the extreme.

First of all, why on earth would I want Elton? Why would I want anyone? I am thoroughly pleased with the life I lead now, and when I need an escort for functions, I have Knightley.

Second, Elton is so not my type. If I were looking to get involved with someone, he'd be more like … like … like Frank Churchill! Definitely not Elton Phillips.

Third, Knightley knows I have absolutely no interest or design in matchmaking him with anyone. If he did work out that I'm trying to matchmake Harriet and Elton, and found some fault or complaint with that - I don't even know what that could be. But he'll be sure to tell me, if it exists.

Fourth … I don't even remember. "Love Me Tomorrow" just came on the radio, and now I'm wondering what it'd be like to slow dance to it with Frank. ;)

To: EmmaWritesHartfield@yourmail.com
From: IsabellaWKnightley@yourmail.com
Date: 2 March 20**
Subject: RE: Operation: Dinner Party

Slow dancing with Frank Churchill! And you say I have preggo brain ;) Haha! (Actually, Jack Weston would probably adore having you as a daughter-in-law … He'd try and convince you to let him experiment in the Highbury Hills orchards, but hey, you'd have Anne as a mother-in-law! I'm teasing. Sorta.)

Elton may like you however, and it's possible that Noah picked up on that interest. He is surprisingly perceptive when it comes to reading the minds of men. Blame it on being so close to the arrival of your niece, but I'm definitely advocating more caution as this progresses. You know I love ya, baby sister, and I'd hate to see you in a pickle.

To: IsabellaWKnightley@yourmail.com
From: EmmaWritesHartfield@yourmail.com
Date: 2 March 20**
<u>Subject: RE: Operation Dinner Party</u>
      Love you too, big sister.
      And why would Knightley care if Elton were interested? Which he's not. He'd be stupid to be interested in me, when Harriet is right there in front of him.

To: EmmaWritesHartfield@yourmail.com,
NoahKnightleyMayor@Hartfield.gov
From: JaneFairfaxPR@Hartfield.gov
Date: 2 March 20**
<u>Subject: Rough Draft Plans</u>
      Okay, several hours and much caffeine later, I've managed to compile the notes from our meeting this morning and draw up a rough plan of attack. Talk about hitting the ground running! And here I thought working for Hartfield would involve community picnics, Eagle Scout honors and the odd tourist. :) Below is a recap of our conversation, and an exceptionally rough draft of the plan(s) - I welcome your input and suggestions for tweaking things. Especially from you, Emma, since you seem to have an uncanny handle on the ins and outs of Hartfield. The actual logistics will be simple enough, but the local connection and determining the best course of action for Hartfield ... That will require more thought.
      Summary:
      Augusta Hawkins, agent to the stars of Nashville, has reached out to Noah and Hartfield for assistance arranging a sabbatical of sorts for a client - without making it seem like a necessary sabbatical. Ms. Hawkins is leaving the 'spin' to us, on the condition that she sign off on whatever we decide

before it is publicly released. It would appear that Ms. Hawkins's client, country music sensation (and hometown hero) Frank Churchill, is teetering on the edge of a breakdown and in need of rest and seclusion. Entertainment business being what it is however, he cannot be seen as *needing* a break - it'd be bad for his 'Golden Boy' image. Our task is to present his forced vacation in a positive manner.

In the interest of full-disclosure, I have worked with Frank Churchill before - in New York - though he was not signed with Ms. Hawkins at the time. Assuming he has not had a major personality change, Frank is surprisingly laid back and easy to work with (perhaps a result of his Hartfield roots - although, correct me if I'm wrong, he has not lived in Hartfield since preschool, yes?). Perhaps his fame has become too heavy, and he needs some quiet time, or who knows what - unfortunately in my line of work you see the sad truth behind the glitz and glamour. Regardless, our mission: Bring Frank home, without raising suspicion.

The Plan(s):

Frank is the son of Jack Weston, so he has a legitimate tie to Hartfield. Doesn't Hartfield Church have a special musical program around Easter every year? I remember Aunt Missy telling me about her adventures with set and costume design. Granted, we have a new minister this year so things may be different, but, what do you say to this proposal ... Frank comes to Hartfield to celebrate his father's recent marriage, and work in some connection also to the annual spring musical. We'll have to clear everything with Ms. Hawkins, of course, but I think this should work. Maybe we can even arrange to have him sing with the choir (town ensemble? Who does the music for this, exactly?), as a super special touch.

If this sounds like something logical and feasible to y'all, we can send it to Ms. Hawkins, and then Emma can write it up in a column - get a little local energy stirred up, and keep it from being an absolute surprise when Frank and his entourage roll into town.

To: JaneFairfaxPR@Hartfield.gov,
NoahKnightleyMayor@Hartfield.gov
From: EmmaWritesHartfield@yourmail.com
Date: 2 March 20**
Subject: RE: Rough Draft Plans
    Jane, you're a freakin' genius! :) I love it! We'll need to get Elton involved, see what's going on with the Easter program this year, (I haven't heard anything yet, and it's only a month out), but if this Hawkins woman is okay with it, I think we've got a plan. I'll start drafting something now, and then once we have details I can plug them in and have a column ready for print.

To: JaneFairfaxPR@Hartfield.gov,
EmmaWritesHartfield@yourmail.com
From: NoahKnightleyMayor@Hartfield.gov
Date: 2 March 20**
Subject: RE: Rough Draft Plans
    Excellent work, Jane. I agree, it sounds like we have the solution to our problem - provided we get the clearance from Ms. Hawkins. Send me your draft Emma, and I'll include it when I send our proposal. Additionally, I will go ahead and check with Elton about the program plans, I have to meet with him about some things later today, so that's perfect timing. Good work, team!

Love, Hartfield: Exciting Things Afoot!
By Emma Woodhouse, Staff Writer
    It isn't often the Love, Hartfield column makes front page, but readers, there are exciting things afoot!
    As you are all aware, country music heartthrob Frank Churchill is the son of our own Jack Weston. We have chronicled his rise

to fame and fortune in these very pages, from the very first audition for American Talent to celebrating his latest single "Love Me Tomorrow" holding the #1 spot for a month. Hartfield loves music and hometown talent, and we have long loved and adored Frank Churchill from afar. Now, after more than twenty years away, Frank is coming home!

Next week, Frank and members of his band will be rolling into our quiet town, prepared to stay through Easter. Taking advantage of a break in his touring schedule, Frank decided to come visit his father and new stepmother, and reconnect with his Hartfield roots. While here, arrangements have even been made for Frank to take part in the annual Hartfield Church Easter program! Final details are pending, but you know this is going to be a special night.

Harriet: OMG!!! FRANK CHURCHILL IS COMING THIS WEEK!!!
Emma: Yes!
Harriet: I LOVE HIS BAND!
Emma: We all do, haha … I can't wait to see how the final details for the program shape up
Harriet: Me & Elton r working on that for the mtg 2morrow!
Emma: Great! Looking forward to it!

Emma: Hi Jane, it's Emma. I'm not sure if you had my number or not. After the meeting tomorrow, wanna grab dinner?
Jane: Hey Emma, that sounds fun, but I'll have to take a raincheck - got a lot of stuff to sort out, and work on the Churchill project

Emma: Oh. Okay. Well, we have to at least get coffee soon! I want to hear about New York!
Jane: Maybe so.
Jane: New York wasn't really that great. Hartfield is so much nicer.
Emma: Really? I mean, I love Hartfield, but New York is so ... glamorous?
Jane: Touche. NYC definitely wins the glam battle. But the people are better here.
Emma: :)

Anne: Emma! Frank will be here in a few days!
Emma: I KNOW! I'm so excited! I will finally get to meet the man behind the voice that haunts my dreams ... ;)
Anne: Hahaha, oh my. Let's not get too carried away, dear
Emma: No worries. Knightley has already lectured me on handling things professionally, since I am officially on the planning committee for this event and blah blah blah
Emma: But a girl can still appreciate things ;)
Anne: True. And you are a close friend of the family
Emma: Amen!

Emma: Hey Izzy? Guess who just walked into Knightley's office
Izzy: You?
Emma: Nope! Frank Churchill himself! He came a day early, totally surprised us in the middle of our planning meeting
Izzy: !!!!
Izzy: Is he as gorgeous in person?
Emma: Oh yeah. Totally. He's rendered we females breathless, speechless and who knows what else ;)
Emma: Elton seems less than enthused
Izzy: Hahahaha
Izzy: Is Harriet there too? Maybe Elton is seeing Frank as competition
Emma: My thoughts exactly.

Knightley: Get off your phone. Texting during meetings is rude.

Knightley: As is drooling over the arrival of a guest ;)
Emma: I'm not drooling! And you're on your phone too :P
Knightley: Emma …
Emma: Knightley …
Knightley: Can we please just finish this meeting? I'm going to need your help here, Jane seems very flustered by the unexpected appearance of Frank.
Emma: On it, Chief!

To: EmmaWritesHartfield@yourmail.com,
JaneFairfaxPR@Hartfield.gov,
NoahKnightleyMayor@Hartfield.gov,
GuitarHero@FrankChurchill.com
From: RevElton@HartfieldChurch.org
Date: 20 March 20**
Subject: Final Plans
        Greetings,
        I hope everyone is as satisfied with the results of today's meeting as I am. My office manager, Harriet Smith, and I have just finished adjusting the copy for the programs and sent the file to the printers. I have high expectations for this event, and feel certain it will be a resounding success, in spite of the short preparation. Thankfully, it would appear the members of Hartfield Church are excellently trained in the art of production, and Ms. Smith has been of great assistance with her background in performing arts. You, of course, are the guest of honor Frank, and as a true professional will have no problem stepping into the part we created for you. As we only have a few weeks to rehearse together, I will count on each of you and your varied talents, to help shoulder this burden.

To: RevElton@HartfieldChurch.org,
EmmaWritesHartfield@yourmail.com,
JaneFairfaxPR@Hartfield.gov,
NoahKnightleyMayor@Hartfield.gov
From: GuitarHero@FrankChurchill.com
Date: 20 March 20**
Subject: RE: Final Plans

    Y'all are awesome to work with, and I'm totally excited about this. It's been so long since I've seen a good ol' Hartfield Church production, and now I get to be in one! Groovy! :)

Emma: Okay, I think I see where you were coming from earlier...
Knightley: How's that?
Emma: Elton. Is. Weird. As. Crap.
Knightley: Emma... That is not what I said.
Emma: Maybe not, but you were thinking it. You know I'm right
Knightley: No comment.
Emma: Ha!
Knightley: I was serious though - if you have been trying to matchmake Elton and Harriet, as I suspect, it will only end badly.
Emma: I don't understand why you are so against the idea of Elton + Harriet
Knightley: Harriet, for all her "adorableness" as you put it, is young and more than a little silly. Elton, while not entirely sensible himself, knows he is considered both attractive and intelligent.
Knightley: He will not settle for a silly wife. He has his eyes set rather higher I'm afraid
Emma: Yes, she is a little silly. But she is so agreeable, and they seem to work well together! Just look at how they've collaborated on this Easter program!
Emma: And I know for a fact that Harriet has developed a major crush over the last few weeks. She hasn't admitted to

crushing on Elton, but who else would she be spending so much time with?

Knightley: That doesn't mean they have a relationship ahead of them.

Knightley: Just be careful. And perhaps spend more time with Jane than Harriet.

Emma: Now you sound like a fussy old man again ;)

Knightley: You make me feel like a fussy old man sometimes

Knightley: I want you to shine, Emma. You know I've always been your biggest fan.

Emma: Aww :)

Knightley: And I can't help but think this has potential to get messy. I don't want to see you get hurt.

Emma: I won't, I promise.

Unknown Number: Hey Emma, it's Frank. Dad gave me your number. I'm looking forward to getting to know you the next few weeks

Emma: Hi Frank! I'm pretty excited about that myself, it's so weird to "know you" without knowing you. Glad to change that now.

Frank: I feel like I know you too, Anne and Dad have told me so much about you the last few days. :)

Emma: All good things, I hope!

Frank: Of course. Who could say anything bad about you?

Emma: Aww! I'm gonna blush!

Frank: Wanna grab coffee this afternoon?

Emma: Sure! I've got a meeting, but should be free by 4. Meet me at Mansfield Perk then?

Frank: It's a date ;)

Emma: I've got a date with Frank Churchill!

Izzy: Squee! When?!

Emma: 4ish, Mansfield Perk

Izzy: Not the most romantic of first dates, but hey. It's Frank!

Emma: Haha, so true, sista! :)

To: IsabellaWKnightley@yourmail.com
From: EmmaWritesHartfield@yourmail.com
Date: 2 April 20**
Subject: What just happened?

Whew, Izzy, I have no idea what just happened ... I'm hoping it was a horrible April Fools prank, but I have this creeping feeling it's all true. Especially since everything still feels tense and awkward, and April Fools was yesterday. :(

So you know it has been an absolute madhouse around here lately, scrambling to get rehearsals scheduled and costumes for Frank and the band, and we've all been spending a crazy amount of time together. After that first coffee date, Frank and I have hung out some but nothing serious. He's not as dreamy in person as I thought - I think he's been flirting with me out of obligation to the Westons, ha. He's been a good buffer actually, Elton was not interested in Harriet Smith. At all. By any stretch of the imagination. And apparently he even thought my activity in trying to bring them together, or my visits to Harriet at the church office, were ways to spend more time with him. Turns out, ol' preacher boy has been plotting and pining for me. Yesterday he cornered me after rehearsal and started babbling about not being able to keep silent anymore, and how Fate itself orchestrated our meeting and subsequent developing relationship, and while I was trying to figure out WHAT exactly he was saying, he leaned in for a kiss. I ah ... Well, I punched him. Square in the nose. He's gonna have a great shiner for Easter services.

As if that wasn't bad enough, Missy Bates came around the corner and saw the amorous advances - and bounced back apologizing for disturbing us and etc, missing the punch. So the whole choir ends up hearing about it, and I lost all control of my temper and snapped at Missy, while Elton is over there howling like a banshee about my unprovoked attack and how could I deny our affections and It. Was. Horrible. Knightley just stood there watching, stern and disapproving. I felt like I had failed him, especially when Frank came and put his arm around me telling Elton to buzz off and leave me be. There was the strangest look in his eyes, Knightley's I mean, and it made a queer ache start in my chest. So much chaos, Izzy, such a wreck.

I've apologized to Missy and she was perfectly understanding - bless her heart. Jane isn't speaking to me at the moment, and Elton ... well Elton is stalking around in high dudgeon. Harriet finds the whole thing weirdly amusing, and Frank is busy being uber charming to smooth over the tensions. I have a bad feeling about the performance Saturday night ...

To: EmmaWritesHartfield@yourmail.com
From: IsabellaWKnightley@yourmail.com
Date: 3 April 20**
Subject: RE: What just happened?

Oh Emma ... I wish I could give you a big hug and eat five dozen cookies and tea while we hash this over. I had a suspicion Elton was more interested in you, but I can't believe he acted on his feelings in such a way. I'm glad Frank has been a good friend, though I'm not sure his role as 'buffer' is doing much to dissuade the gossip coupling your names together. (Oh yes, even I have heard the buzz.) I'm not sure I have any advice for you - I'm still trying to figure out what possessed Elton to act in such a manner, and trying to picture that shiner. ;) I hope the program is all the better for the trouble beforehand - don't they say a horrible dress rehearsal is a good omen?

To: EmmaWritesHartfield@yourmail.com
From: NoahKnightley1978@yourmail.com
Date: 3 April 20**
Subject: Wanted to let you know ...

Emma, wanted to let you know I'm leaving town on a business trip and will miss the big Easter 'production.' I know you and Jane have put a lot of time and energy to make this a success, and look forward to reading the write-up in the paper. I hope the night is everything you want it to be.

Because I know you will badger me, as usual, to know all the details - I have been invited to participate in a local government exchange program. The program was brought to my attention in the fall, and after several months of deliberation, I have decided to accept the invitation to attend an information conference in Solvang, California. It's an excellent program giving members of local governments the opportunity to travel and see how issues are handled around the country and the world. Being selected for invitation is something of an honor, and I am very interested in learning what international prospects are available. I fly out tonight, and the conference will last through Wednesday, but I will be staying through the week, possibly longer. Barton Winery, host site of the conference, is rumored to be beautiful in the spring, and I need the time away from the distractions of Hartfield to make decisions regarding my participation in the exchange - and other things.

Emma: What. The. Crap?!
Emma: I just read your email. You couldn't even come tell me that in person?
Knightley: You're busy getting ready for tomorrow night's show, and I need to pack.
Emma: When did you decide to do this thing?
Emma: When were you going to tell me?
Knightley: I told you, I've been thinking about it since the fall
Knightley: I've got to finish packing. I'll see you when I get back.
Knightley: Emma … Remember who you are. Be the best you. Don't change you.
Emma: Now I really am going to cry. Be safe, see you sooner than later I hope, and don't agree to anything rash, please.

Emma: Did you know about this exchange something or other international program Knightley is joining?
Izzy: What are you talking about?
Emma: He just sent me this crazy email saying he's skipping town tonight and doesn't know when he's coming back, but he's considering an overseas exchange program???
Izzy: Oh, that. Yeah, he and John were talking about it the other day
Emma: Isabella!
Izzy: Relax, Emma. It's just an informational conference. In Cali. Not the moon.
Izzy: And even if he does one of the international exchanges, he'll come home. His whole world is in Hartfield
Emma: But he's going to miss the program, and Easter, and he never told me anything about this!
Emma: He tells me everything!
Izzy: Maybe he knew you'd overreact
Izzy: I love you dearly, but Noah does have a life of his own, Emma.
Emma: Hmph

Love, Hartfield: The Easter Program of the Century!
By Emma Woodhouse, Staff Writer

Oh, Hartfield. What an Easter program we had this year. We knew we were in for something special, when Frank Churchill and his band rolled into town and joined the show, but we never expected it to be quite so memorable!

The ladies of Hartfield Church did a magnificent job, as usual, decorating the sanctuary, overcoming the unique challenges of accommodating band equipment with enviable ease. The choir rose to the occasion and sounded better than I have ever heard them - and Hartfield, I have heard many Hartfield Church choir performances. Frank Churchill's smooth voice added new depth to familiar anthems, and I am sure many in town will agree when I say that I hope Frank's next album will feature that amazing rendition of "Amazing Grace." The glamour of the Nashville music scene mingled seamlessly with the comforting sounds of home, and I have high hopes for future church programs.

You see, the musical was not the only item of noteworthy interest this Easter weekend. At the end of the performance, to the warm applause of Hartfield, Frank Churchill took the mic and poured out his heart to our fair Jane Fairfax. I will never be able to listen to "Love Me Tomorrow" without thinking of the look in his eyes as he spoke the chorus directly to Jane before dropping to a knee and begging her hand in marriage. Every lady in the house had a tear in her eye, myself included. It was a beautiful moment, and when Jane agreed to marry him? Hartfield, these are the moments we dream of, in our sleepy Southern town. Two of our brightest stars, wandering afar for years, finding their way home - and to each other.

Love is in the air, and I'd go so far as to say we have a full-fledged case of spring fever on our hands, Hartfield.

Knightley: Emma, I've just arrived back in town, earlier than anticipated.

Emma: Oh yay! I've missed you! What made you change your plans?

Knightley: I heard the Frank + Jane news.

Emma: I'm not surprised. It's the talk of town!

Knightley: Are you ... How are you handling it?

Emma: Handling it? I hope to get dibs on writing it!

Knightley: You seem rather unruffled... not as upset as I'd have expected

Emma: Why would I be upset?

Knightley: Everyone thought it would be Frank + Emma

Emma: Oh. That. No, we were only ever going to be friends. He's a darling, but not for me.

Emma: Actually, this makes so many things make sense.

Knightley: Oh. I see.

Knightley: So ... You really weren't interested in Frank Churchill?

Emma: No, I wasn't.

Emma: The man for me is so far removed from Frank, it's amusing to think I could have entertained a celebrity crush on him for so long

Knightley: Oh. You do have an interest?

Emma: Knightley, I can see you sitting in your car ...

Knightley: Where are you?

Emma: Mansfield Perk. I'll meet you outside.

Emma: I think we have things to talk about ... One particular thing to talk about.

Knightley: Should I be worried?

Emma: No. But I am. A little.

Knightley: Why?

Emma: Because I'm not sure if you'll agree with me or not.

Knightley: I think you need to come on outside, this is getting silly, texting from the sidewalk, seeing you through the window.

Knightley: And if your smile, and the look in your eyes, is any indication, I very much agree :)

Emma: Hey Izzy, I've got some news, and knowing Hartfield it's gonna spread like wildfire. You should hear it from me first.

Izzy: OMG, what's wrong? Is it Daddy? Are you sick? What's happened?

Emma: Oh, no, it's good news. Sorry, didn't mean to scare you :)

Izzy: Don't do that to me! I'm nine months preggo, crazy woman!

Emma: Sorry!!! I think you'll like this though

Emma: I think you'll like it a lot ...

Izzy: Suspense is also not good for pregnant women

Emma: Emma + Noah = ♥

Izzy: !!!!

Izzy: WHAT?!

Emma: :) It's true.

Izzy: WHAT?!

Izzy: How?? When??

Izzy: TELL ME EVERYTHING!

Izzy: And you're using his NAME!

Emma: Hahahaha, I knew you would pick up on that ;)

Emma: Get John and put it on speaker, we'll call and tell y'all everything.

Knightley: I should probably apologize for earlier ...

Emma: Whatever on earth for?

Emma: Oh! I need to update your contact... Noah :)

Noah: I can't help but feel like I could have handled things better.

Noah: Or at least picked somewhere other than the absolute middle of town

Emma: Oh, haha ... I didn't mind. Honest.

Noah: That's what I love about you :)

Emma: Oh really?

Noah: You know me for who and what I am, and you accept that.

Emma: That goes both ways, buddy. You know all my deep dark secret flaws, and you still believe in me.

Noah: You're a remarkable woman, Emma Woodhouse

Emma: Backatcha, cutie ;)

Emma: Er, minus the woman part. You're a remarkable man.

Noah: HAHA! Oh Emma :)

Emma: You're emoting a lot these days, btw
Noah: You do something to me. If I loved you less, I might be able to talk about it more.
Noah: As it is, you'll have to make do with kisses on the sidewalk and emoticon-riddled text messages :)
Emma: I think I can handle that. :)

To: EmmaWritesHartfield@youmail.com
From: MusicLoverJane@youmail.com
Date: 15 April 20**
Subject: Love is in the air!

Emma!!! First let me say again how very, very sorry I am for the way things played out with Frank and us and everything ... I didn't handle the pressure very well, and in hindsight if I had just been more open to your offered friendship, this whole weird interval would have been better. Much better. I am sorry, and hope we can move forward and become real friends. :)

I feel I owe you the whole story - I'm sure Anne and Jack have told you most of it, and Aunt Missy is doing her best to share the news with all of Hartfield. I met Frank last year, when he came to Tricia and I for assistance with a charity concert. Tricia handled most of the legwork, but I had enough contact with Frank for a friendship to develop. Or casual acquaintance, perhaps - Tricia was already dating Dixon, secretly, and I was edgy about getting too involved with a client. I could tell Frank was interested in being friends, at the very least, and I could see the appeal (who am I kidding? I had a mad crush on him! Ha), but couldn't reconcile the risk. New York isn't like Hartfield - the world is not like Hartfield - if you mess up, that's it. And if you mess up with someone in the spotlight, there's definitely not a second chance. I tried explaining some of that to Frank, but it just got awkward and I finally told him even the casual stuff needed to stop.

When Tricia decided to dissolve the firm, Frank called and asked me out - said my reasons were invalid now, and to give him a fighting chance. We hung out, my crush gained momentum, and just when I thought things were going to get more serious, he signed with Augusta and everything imploded. Augusta, as I'm sure you noticed, is the ultimate micro-managing agent, and she made no secret of her dislike for me. She packed Frank's schedule with events - oh, all good things, as I'm sure you know - essentially making it impossible for him to see me. I will give her this: she's good at what she does. While Frank was gaining good publicity and public adoration, he had no idea what was taking place on a more personal level. Augusta was direct in her dealings with me; she knew I worked with Frank previously, and promised to take action, professionally, if I did not end the relationship.

I bolted, Emma. It was cowardly, taking the easy way out, but I couldn't see anything beyond losing everything I worked so hard for. You know my story, you know how steep the climb has been. Augusta Hawkins had it in her power to destroy everything, and I panicked. In hindsight, I should have fought her, recognized the hollow threat for what it was - but who thinks clearly in that situation? That's why I ended up back home in Hartfield, bruised and broken and far too prickly for my own good. You tried to be a friend, and I was probably a bit rude - especially once Frank came to town. Again, I'm sorry.

When I made my escape, it nearly broke Frank. I changed my number, I wouldn't answer his emails, I literally disappeared. That's how he ended up in Hartfield too - there's something about this place that calls you Home when you need to recover, need to discover that goodness - that love - still exists. I'm not sure how he convinced Augusta to let him come, but I know he had no idea I was here licking my own wounds. During all the hoopla surrounding the musical, and whatever the heck happened between his drummer and the church secretary (you're her friend, what was that? Spill, sister! ;) Kidding, sorta), we managed to find moments alone and talking happened.

You know the rest: we're engaged - sudden, I know, but after fighting it so long, there's something so sweet about surrendering to destiny. (Okay, okay, that's incredibly cheesy, but you know what I mean). Frank is going to continue touring musically, but focus more on charity work - he genuinely enjoys that, something Augusta did not anticipate - and move his "home base" from Nashville to Hartfield. I will of course stay here in Hartfield, continuing to work with Noah for the town as well as handling Frank's more relaxed publicity needs. Eventually there will be a wedding, but we both want to enjoy the engagement for a while. And that's my long, sad, crazy story ... You'll have to help me spin into something better for releasing to the wider public - they're crazy about a celebrity love story. ;)

Now, tell me something, Miss Matchmaking Knows-All-The-Things Chronicler of Hartfield ... What's this I hear about you and Noah kissing in the streets??? Don't get me wrong, I knew that was gonna happen from our very first planning meeting. But still. Tell the story!

To: MusicLoverJane@youmail.com
From: EmmaWritesHartfield@youmail.com
Date: 15 April 20**
Subject: RE: Love is in the air!

Hahahahahahahaha, that's quite a title you have bequeathed upon me, Miss Forbidden Romance ;) (Though I think I finally see what Noah meant: I wasn't making any matches, I was just able to see their development before others, because of the close relationships).

The story ... I don't even know where it began. We've always been friends, the best of friends, and I never in my wildest imaginings anticipated we would end up here - and now? Now it feels so very right. There could never be anyone for me but Noah. Nobody else could complement and 'handle' my crazy with as much understanding. He's been part of my life for so long, his friendship and respect treasured for years, and now ... Now I have his love - and he has my heart.

I suppose, on some level, I have you and Harriet to thank for everything. Anne was the first to pick up on your 'star-crossed romance' vibes, convinced you were madly in love with Noah (or he with you), and the whole supervisor/workplace dynamics were keeping you apart. Her insistence made me realize, perhaps for the first time, that Noah could be seen as "a catch." I found I wasn't particularly fond of that idea. Then Harriet, bless her heart, started crushing on him, and I was so set on her marrying Elton that I didn't realize the guy she kept referring to, that she was so fixated on, was Noah until he went to that conference in Solvang. After the program, she came up to me, a bundle of nervous energy, and told me that she expected to be relocating overseas in the immediate future. As I listened to her hopes and plans, I had a sudden, painful, realization that if Noah really was going overseas, and taking someone with him, it should be ME. In that moment, I saw my heart so clearly - every bit of it entwined with his - and felt the world shatter around me. I was seeing the truth too late, I had lost him. Happily, I completely misunderstood her - no doubt subconsciously influenced by my own unease about the unexpected trip to Cali - and she was actually talking about Robby Martin. Crisis averted! ;) (And I still haven't figured out what happened there! Haha)

The bit about kissing downtown is true, hahaha ... He came home thinking I was heartbroken about you and Frank, I thought he was heartbroken about Harriet and Robby, and in one big crazy confusing and overlapping conversation we realized how absolutely ridiculous the whole thing was. Then he kissed me - on the sidewalk, not in the street - and my heart found Home.

As for you and Frank - of course I'll help you write it up and give it a spin. It really is a lovely story, something straight out of a novel. I'm sorry if my flirting with Frank upset you, and of course you are forgiven a thousand times over for your distance. I assumed you were missing Tricia, and having a hard time settling back into the slower pace of Hartfield after so long away, I never dreamed there was so much more afoot! Here's to love, and everything finally being as it should!

Emma: Hey Noah?
Noah: Yes?
Emma: Emma + Noah = ♥
Noah: :)
Noah: Emma + Noah = ♥ x Infinity

Acknowledgements

This has been another wonderful experience working with the ladies of Holidays with Jane - Jessica, Jennifer, Melissa, Kimberly and Cecilia: y'all are awesome, hilarious, and the best group of writing buddies I could ask to work with on such a project. I love our 'brainstorming' rambles, and the crazy conversations that happen.

I also owe huge thanks to the friends and family who have been so supportive of this adventure, listening as I ramble my way through the writing process and teasing me about "all that Austen stuff."

And again, the biggest thanks of all to Jane - her stories and characters are timeless and I fall more and more in love with them. Especially Mr. Knightley, who has recently edged Darcy out as my all-time favorite.

Once Upon a Story

A *Northanger Abbey* Story

To everyone who believes the story is worth telling – and the cast of characters who keep life interesting.

Sunday, 1 November 2015

Catie cradled her steaming mug of tea and stared at the paper in front of her. *Maybe if I look at it long enough, the headline will go away,* she thought. "Battlefield Legend A Fraud! Unmasked by Professor Daughter and Local Student During Annual Fall-o-Ween Festival." No matter how long she stared at them, the words never changed. *I wanted an adventure,* she sighed, *and there it is, in full color, on the front page of the paper. The* whole *front page.*

"Dear, are you okay? You look as if you've seen a ghost." The softly accented words were accompanied by a touch on her shoulder that made Catie jump out of her skin.

"Oh!" she squeaked, nearly spilling her tea.

"I am sorry, I did not mean to startle you." As she spoke, a woman moved to stand beside Catie. "You do look rather –" she paused, visibly searching for a word. "Perturbed. You look rather perturbed."

Catie glanced at the woman, taking in her dark hair and friendly eyes. She was a complete stranger, and yet something about her seemed familiar. *Maybe I've seen her around campus,* she mused, *she reminds me of Eleanor.* The woman touched her on the shoulder again, "dear, are you okay?"

"Oh," Catie blushed. "I'm sorry. I was trying to figure out if I knew you from somewhere, and forgot – yes, I'm okay. It's just been a very long and very strange weekend," she paused. "I have no idea what I think about anything anymore."

The woman gestured to the chair across from Catie, "may I join you?"

"Of course," Catie smiled. "I'm sorry; I'm really not this spastic normally. My name's Catie, by the way."

"I'm Cassie," the woman offered, taking the seat. "My sister Jane was planning to meet me here, you don't mind if she joins us do you? I have a feeling your story – and I can tell you have one, so don't try to pretend otherwise – will interest her greatly."

Catie shrugged, "No, that's fine. I'm sorry, but I have to ask. *Do* I know you from somewhere?"

The woman, Cassie, laughed. "No, I don't believe so. I have never been to Northanger before, and I'm fairly certain I'd remember if you came to Chawton. The perk of living in a small town, you understand."

"Are you in town for the festival then? Do you like reenactments, or were you here for the football game? You wouldn't be the first English lady to foster a secret love of American football," Catie smiled.

"Oh no, though I have been enjoying the festivities. Your football is a strange game; I cannot begin to understand its popularity. Jane had to come to the States for an English conference of some sort in Atlanta; when she offered me the chance to tag along I couldn't refuse. She always gets to have adventures, and I wanted a chance of my own."

"Now that is something I can totally relate to," Catie said emphatically. "Atlanta is a decent drive from here though, how did you find Northanger?"

"Oh, we've been touring the state of Georgia, making a real holiday of it. We've spent time in Barton and Hartfield, but so far Northanger is my favorite. Something about it reminds me of home. Oh good, here's Jane now." As she spoke, Cassie waved to the woman just walking in.

"Welcome to Mansfield Perk," the barista – *he's new*, Catie noted absently – called to the woman. She smiled at him as she walked over to join Catie and Cassie.

"Jane, you simply must meet my new friend Catie," Cassie said. "And Catie, this is my sister Jane, the Queen of Stories. Now that she's here, you must tell us yours."

Jane gave her sister an indulgent smile, "I'm not sure I'd call myself the 'Queen of Stories,' but I do love to hear a good one. Catie –" she paused. "You wouldn't by chance be Catie Morland, from the story in the paper?"

Catie blushed. "That's me," she sighed. "I keep hoping this is all a nightmare, but if you've read the article, it must be real."

"Unless we are part of the nightmare too, dreams are tricky things," Jane winked. "Come now, it can't be all that bad. I have read the article, yes, and my instincts tell me there is much more to this story. Let me just pop to the counter and snag some tea – and maybe a muffin, I have become addicted to Mansfield Perk muffins this trip – and then tell us all, dear. Every single delicious detail."

"Okay, I can do that," Catie agreed. "Maybe telling it to someone who doesn't know everything will help it all make sense."

"I think I need a muffin too," Cassie added, "but I need something stronger than tea. I may go wild and get an espresso!"

As the two sisters went to the counter to order, Catie sat back and watched them. *I'm having coffee with complete strangers, about to tell them the most humiliating event of my entire life. There is probably something very wrong with this scenario, but I don't care. At least we're in a public place – it's not like they can kidnap me without witnesses. And I like them, there's something very familiar about them somehow.* She smiled as Jane said something that made the barista blush and her sister burst out laughing.

"Isn't he a doll?" Jane asked, coming back to the table. "I just love to make redheads blush, is that horrible of me?"

Catie laughed, "I don't know that I've ever thought about it before."

"Don't encourage her," Cassie added. "She really and truly can't help herself; for reasons unexplored she has a major weakness for redheads. Between you and me, I think it's because her first boyfriend was Irish, and poor Tom ruined her for other men. Now, enough about redheads – let's get to the really juicy stuff. Tell us the story!"

"Yes, we're both familiar with the article – I read it out loud to Cassie over first breakfast this morning – but tell us how it all began."

"Well," Catie drew the word out, thinking. "Everything happened so fast, I hardly know where to begin. Maybe –" she paused, "okay, we'll start with the phone call from Bella, the day she met my brother..."

Early September 2015

"It was a dark and stormy night. Waves tossed on the shore; a fierce wind tugging Amelia's skirt as if trying to strip it from her slender frame. The pounding rain made it impossible to see beyond the reach of her own hand, but even as she cursed the vision-obscuring downpour, she was grateful it hid her tears. If anyone observed her unkempt and sodden appearance, they would assume the storm had wreaked the damage – and not a broken heart. Aye, her heart was truly and completely broken as she watched Lorenzo stride away into the storm."

Catie looked up from the page and sighed. She knew her time would be much better spent reading her English assignment, but *Captive of the Storm* was just getting to the good part, and she had to find out what would happen with Amelia and Lorenzo. "Just one more chapter," she murmured, taking a sip of now-lukewarm tea and settling deeper into her pillow nest on the bed. Before she could lose herself in the perilous romance, her phone chirped. Glancing at the screen she smiled before answering, "Hey, Bella."

"Ohmigosh, Catie you will never believe what just happened!" Catie rolled her eyes and smiled at her friend's high-pitched enthusiasm. Bella Thorpe always sounded like she had just won the lottery; everything was A Big Deal. "You'll never guess, so don't even try," Bella continued. "I'm going to have to tell you, because you will never in your wildest imagination figure this out!"

With a laugh, Catie finally got a word in. "Unless you finally got Prince Harry's phone number, I cannot possibly guess what has you so excited at 4:30 on a Monday afternoon."

"Girl, don't I wish. I'm still working on that one!" Bella laughed. "Okay, so here's the thing. I had to meet with my advisor today, right? That was such a drag – apparently I have to officially declare a major like, next week, or I won't be able to graduate on time. I mean seriously? Whatever. I'll deal with it later. Anyway, after that meeting I simply had to have caffeine, so I popped into Mansfield Perk and you will never *believe* who I ran into!"

"Well it wasn't Prince Harry, so ..."

"Your brother!"

Catie blinked. "My brother?"

"Yes, silly. Your brother Jamie. You never told me he was such a hunk!"

"My brother Jamie was in Mansfield Perk? Here in Northanger?"

"Yes! I told you you'd never in a million years guess," Bella crowed.

"Why was Jamie in our Mansfield Perk?" Catie wondered. "He never comes to Northanger if he can help it."

"Oh, he said something about being in town with his coach to meet with your father," Bella replied. "I think there's a football scout involved too, or was it a trainer? I don't remember the details. I was listening; I just kept losing the words for staring into his eyes. Dang girl, why have you never mentioned that your brother has eyes that green?"

"Uh, I guess it never –"

"And, you'll never guess what else!" Bella interrupted. "Don't even try to guess, because you're never going to in a million years. Your brother Jamie and my brother Jack are in the same fraternity at Sotherton! Jack knows I've been wanting to meet his fraternity brothers, but he never invites me to any of their events – says I shouldn't travel so far for a party, blah blah blah. Anyway, when Jamie mentioned he had just pledged, I let it drop that my brother just happens to be chapter president, and wasn't that a small world? Just think, here we are at Abbey College – hopefully to soon be sorority sisters in addition to BFFs, and yes, I am going to keep pushing you to rush so you might as well give in – and all the way across the state, our brothers are brothers! How funny is that? I just love it. Fate, you know."

"Mmm," Catie murmured, settling in to listen, knowing that Bella would carry the rest of the conversation herself.

"So Jamie and I are talking and talking, it's like I've known him my whole life – I think because he is so much like you, Catie. You're both so quaint and old-fashioned, though he doesn't seem to live in a dreamworld the way you do. No, I'm not teasing, you know I love your imaginative take on life. It's refreshing, especially when you come from as jaded a background as I have. Swear not to tell a soul, Catie? But I think I've developed a very fast and very serious crush on your big brother. He's not just the hunky football player, he's *so sweet.* I think I've been waiting my whole life to meet someone like him. And to think, if I skipped meeting with my advisor, I never would have needed a coffee pick-me-up, and then I'd never have met him!"

"I suppose that helps justify not picking a major, huh?" Catie couldn't resist teasing her friend.

"Totally! I can't wait to tell my advisor that after our meeting I met my soul mate! Don't laugh, Catie, you'll understand what I mean when you see us together."

"Oh? And when will that be?" Catie knew her brother was unlikely to stay in Northanger any longer than he had to – though the two were close, Jamie had always fought the constraints of the small town. Catie on the other hand adored living in a place where everyone knew everyone else.

"This weekend! It's a bye week or Thursday game or some-such, and Jamie is free. When he asked me out, I said I absolutely could not begin to think of saying yes, unless he agreed to make it a double date."

"I thought you fancied yourself madly in love-at-first-sight with him?" Catie asked in confusion.

Bella laughed again. "Of *course* I am, silly. But as soon as I found out he knows Jack, I realized that you would be perfect together. Sooooo, I convinced your doll of a brother that the four of us should double! It's so perfect! And you and I can spend all day getting ready – we can get our hair and nails done, and plunder our closets for the best outfits. It's going to be so much fun!"

"When did you say this was happening?" Catie asked.

"Saturday!" Bella chirped gleefully. "The boys are picking us up around 7, but we can spend all day getting ready."

"Bella," Catie groaned. "I can't do that. You know I work with Eleanor on Saturdays."

Bella made a sound that strongly resembled a snort. "I'm sure she can do without your assistance for one day, Catie. After all, these people have been dead for thousands of years. It's not like they're going anywhere."

"Not quite that long, Bella." Catie sighed. No matter how many times she explained it to her friend, Bella never quite remembered things correctly. "She counts on me to help her with the transcribing, and I enjoy it! I could maybe leave early enough to be able to change before the guys got here at 7, but I cannot – I will not – take a whole day off."

With a huff, Bella muttered something that sounded like "doesn't know a good thing when it bites her in the butt," before ending the call with a more audible "we'll talk about this later, but now I've got to call Jack and find out everything he knows about Jamie! Cheers, darling!"

As her phone flashed "Call Ended," Catie blinked at the screen. *That was a little weird*, she finally decided. With a sigh, she marked her place in

Captive of the Storm. "Being shanghaied into a date means I have to finish this assignment now," she told the colorful novel, setting it on the shelf behind her. "Eleanor may let me leave early, but she won't let me slide on reading for class. At least I like it." Catie rolled her eyes as she realized she was talking to her books. "Maybe I need a night out on the town after all," she laughed, settling her notebook on one knee and her Anthology of Southern Literature on the other.

Sunday, November 1, 2015

Catie paused, taking a sip of her much-cooler tea and glancing at the sisters across from her. Jane and Cassie had listened carefully – Catie never had such an obliging audience from anyone other than Eleanor and Henry. *Don't think about Henry,* she told herself.

"Well then, this is an interesting beginning," Jane murmured.

"Okay, so I have two questions. Who is Bella, and how'd you meet her? And why wouldn't you want to go out with her brother if she's your BFF?" asked Cassie, leaning forward. "Don't deny it, I could tell from the way you told the story you had no interest in meeting this brother."

Jane cocked her head and squinted slightly. "I'd wager there was another boy on her mind. Am I right?"

"I, ah–" Catie stammered. "Sort of? I would have prefered to be planning a date with someone else–"

"A particular someone else?" Cassie interrupted.

Catie nodded. "Yes. A particular someone else. But that seemed a very remote possibility at the time, considering I hadn't heard from him since the semester started. It's not like I was waiting on him, that'd have been pretty pointless, ya know? There was just something about the way Bella talked about her brother at times – I'm not really into the whole Greek scene, and the Thorpe family very much is. They're kinda fraternity royalty, or so they would have you believe."

Jane nodded thoughtfully. "Yes, yes I could see that being the case," she murmured to herself. Cassie shot her a quick glance, and Jane merely smiled.

"So, Bella?" Cassie asked again.

"Oh, sorry. Bella – Isabelle Thorpe, of the Texas oil money Thorpes – is the quintessential sorority girl. There is no better way to describe her," Catie laughed a little.

"I can think of a few choice words," Jane muttered under her breath, earning a sharp glance and an elbow to the ribs from Cassie.

"We met by accident during Orientation Week. In the library, of all places."

"Orientation Week? You aren't a freshman though, are you?" Cassie blinked in confusion.

"Oh no, I'm a hybrid," Catie laughed. "I have the hours to be a junior, but I'm only a second year student. But I spend a lot of time in Fullerton Library, and Mrs. Allen, one of the librarians, asked me to help out at the last minute. Apparently several of the students scheduled to work Orientation decided to take one last beach trip, which they conveniently forgot to mention. Since I know the place inside out and backward, and had no plans, I was happy to pitch in and help."

"Fullerton Library – I believe they have an extensive collection of first edition novels," Jane mused.

"That's right," Catie nodded. "I love to do homework in the Special Collections room. Being surrounded by all the amazing stories, with their fading gilt and that warm musty smell of old paper and leather somehow makes math more bearable. And my math needs all the help it can get," she laughed. "They're primarily works by Southern authors, though there are some others in the mix as well, including quite a few of your British writers," she added with a cheeky grin.

"Jane, that sounds like your kind of Heaven," Cassie looked between her sister and Catie. "You two are seeming more and more alike."

"She does seem to be a kindred spirit," Jane agreed. "But then, I suspected as much from the article this morning. I planned to contact Eleanor Tilney and leave a message for the both of you – I suspect she is also one of our tribe – but this is rather more fun."

Catie cringed, "Oh that article. That blasted, cursed article. Meeting you was providential, since I'm not sure the Tilneys will be wanting much to do with me for a while."

"My girl, it's surely not as bad as all that," Cassie murmured. "Tell us more of the story, and we'll see what's to be done with things. You mentioned that you met this Thorpe girl at the Library, but not the rest of it."

"Oh," Catie replied. "It was one of those meetings that sets things in motion, you just don't know how or where. Bella is a force to be reckoned with."

Early August 2015

Catie straightened the stacked folders and bookmarks again before glancing at the clock. Orientation sessions were held in the auditorium across the quad every two hours, on the hour, and the first group would be arriving at for Library Orientation any minute now.

"Ready for battle?"

"I was born ready," Catie smiled at Mrs. Allen as she came to join her behind the desk. The librarian was a favorite among students, equally available to be a listening ear as to help find materials. The older woman had taken particular interest in Catie as she navigated her first year at Abbey College, gently guiding her toward the events and activities best suited for the quiet English major. It was Mrs. Allen who first suggested using the Special Collections room as her private study area, after Catie mentioned how noisy her dorm tended to be, and now she couldn't imagine studying anywhere else.

"I'm sure you remember what it was like to go through Library Orientation from last year," Mrs. Allen said. "And of course you've read over the materials, so this should be a fairly easy assignment. If the last couple years are any indication, our crowd will likely be small. And those who do come probably won't ask questions – most students would rather bypass Orientation altogether."

"Until their first exam or paper is due," Catie laughed. "Then you'll be swamped with questions!"

"Very true," Mrs. Allen nodded. "If they paid a little more attention to the Orientation information and a little less attention to what their fellow students are wearing, there'd be a lot less panic. Ah well," she sighed, "to be young and fancy free, falling in and out of love at every coy grin or dashing wink."

Catie smiled. Mrs. Allen loved to tease the students about their flighty romances, but Catie had spent enough time in the Library to guess the truth: Mrs. Allen was a hardcore matchmaker. *I wonder if she starts making her plans during these Orientation Week sessions*, she wondered now, watching as the librarian turned to greet the first group of students straggling through the Library doors. *And so it begins*, she thought, standing at attention and ready to begin distributing folders at the end of Mrs. Allen's welcoming spiel. Catie's job was primarily crowd control and making sure there were enough informational materials available; Mrs. Allen was handling the welcome lecture and directing students to the other areas of the Library to explore as they wished, giving Catie ample opportunity to observe her new fellow students.

Glancing over the crowd of students in this first group, Catie noticed a tall, striking blonde in the back. *She's not exactly pretty*, she thought, *but she's definitely a looker. I bet the guys fall at her feet by the dozen.* The thought made her smile, *I read way too many romance novels*, and to her surprise the girl caught her eye and smiled back. *She's got movie star teeth*, Catie noted, and gave a slight nod. The girl started moseying her way along the outside edge of the students, until she was close to the desk where Catie stood, a triumphant gleam in her eyes.

While Mrs. Allen concluded her welcoming spiel and fielded questions from a few overeager students, the girl grabbed a bookmark and scribbled something on the back. Sliding it across the desk to Catie with a dazzling grin, she walked out of the Library. *Huh, I wonder what that was about*, Catie thought, flipping the bookmark over to read what the message. "I'm Bella Thorpe, and I've decided you're my new BFF. I'm never wrong about these things. Meet me at Mansfield Perk at 4pm, and we can get to know each other. Mwah! XOXO!" Her curiosity piqued, Catie reread the message. *I'm going to do it*, she decided. *It may be crazy*, she *may be crazy, but if nothing else it's a simple afternoon coffee break that may be an interesting story later.*

Sunday, November 1, 2015

"And that's how I met Bella," Catie leaned back in her seat. "We were inseparable before I even realized it – one of those fast friendships that typify the college experience. My father will likely point to the lack of discernment in establishing such a close friendship so soon after making her acquaintance. Looking back, I guess I was sort of starved for friendship, for someone I could connect to outside of class. I certainly could have aligned myself with someone that produced far worse results. Not that Bella was particularly *good* in hindsight, but you know what I mean."

"Interesting," Jane murmured.

Catie toyed with her empty mug. "We did have some good times, before things got weird. I've never had many girlfriends – Eleanor was actually my first close girlfriend, she's more like an older sister really, we're friends but she's also my professor which makes it tricky – so it was lovely to have someone to do girl stuff with. We had sleepovers, watching sappy rom-coms and giggling over boys. She introduced me to new bands – I am completely in love with Willow Bee now – and I got her hooked on BBC period dramas. It was fun," she sighed. "But I wonder now if any of it was real, or if she had an ulterior motive all along. When you stop and think about it – I really haven't known her very long."

"There, there, love," Cassie said, reaching over and squeezing Catie's hand. "If I can sound like the big sister I am for a moment, even with parts of the story still to be told, I think her offers of friendship were genuine in the moment. You're cute as a button, the kind of girl people *have* to be friends with. If she later decided to capitalize on that friendship, it shows a weakness in her character and reflects no fault of your own."

"She has a point, dear," Jane added. "From what you've told us so far, it sounds as if this Bella Thorpe found you to be a refreshing addition to her customary circles. Is she a psychic that she could see into the future and know you'd lead her to your brother – or whatever other circumstance occurred to make you question the friendship?"

Catie shifted in her seat, hugging one knee to her chest. "Hmm," she murmured. "I never thought about it that way before," she said slowly. "Maybe Bella really did want to be my friend, but she sure has a funny way of showing friendship."

"It's possible she doesn't know how to be a friend," Jane said thoughtfully. "If she is from a Texas oil family, as you say, and has always been assured of having a place in society – both from her family's economic standing and the Greek tradition – it's possible she's never had to *make* a friend in her life." She paused, taking in the way Catie and Cassie were staring at her. "What?"

"Where in thunder did that come from?" Cassie asked. "You have always been the Queen of Snark when it comes to the Bella Thorpes of the world," she added, sounding as if she were trying very hard not to laugh.

Jane did laugh. "Believe me, I could unleash the snark. However this is a very interesting little phenomenon for me, as I sit here thinking about it – I'm wondering how much of Bella's problem is her nature and how much is a result of her nurture."

Cassie groaned. "Oh brother, you've been reading Henry's psych journals again haven't you? I need to remind him what happens when you start reading science."

"I have no idea what you're talking about," Jane brushed aside her sister's comment before turning to Catie. "Are you alright, dear? You just turned very white and very red in quick succession."

"Oh, I'm, um," Catie stammered. "I'm fine, I just–" she paused. "I think I need some more tea, before I finish telling the story. If you still want to hear the rest?"

"Of course! Every juicy detail!" Cassie smiled.

Jane looked at Catie for a moment before nodding, "yes, we do want to hear the rest of your tale. If I may," she added, "I would suggest getting one of those large hot chocolates with an extra caramel drizzle. The sugary goodness will make the telling easier, and I have a hunch that barista can do wonders with chocolate."

Catie laughed, "I'm definitely a fan of the cocoa here, so I'll probably take that advice. What makes you think he can do wonders?"

"Just a hunch, and a lady never explains her hunches," Jane winked.

"I'll come with you, Catie," Cassie stood as she spoke. "I feel like trying one of the hot chocolates myself. Actually, let's just have hot chocolates all around, I'll pick one up for you too, Jane. No, no," she waved a hand at her sister as she began to rise. "You save our table, and we'll spare the poor boy another round of blushes."

Once Catie and Cassie were settled in their seats once more, with steaming mugs of cocoa and a plate of scones to share, Jane leaned forward with an eager smile. "While I am dying to know how the double-double date of Morlands and Thorpes went, I think we should first find out who Eleanor is – how she plays into things."

Catie smiled, something wistful in her eyes. "Eleanor Tilney is amazing," she began. "I already mentioned she's my first real girlfriend – although it's so much more than that. She's the big sister I always wanted, but she's also this brilliant scholar. I think she's about ten years older than me, and working on her PhD, teaching at Abbey College while completing her research. Her class is my favorite, hands down and absolutely. We met last semester, in the spring I mean, at an English department function – she was giving a lecture on her research, actually – and before you could blink, our friendship was cemented and I began spending every Saturday working with her at the Vic. It's funny how naturally everything fell into place ..."

Late February 2015

Catie walked into the lecture hall and sighed. It was a grey day, and she'd rather be curled up reading a novel, but Mrs. Allen insisted that Catie attend the new English professor's presentation. "Trust me, it will be worth your time," the librarian had promised. *I hope she's right*, Catie thought, glancing around the room and waving at a few classmates before slipping into a seat, just as the Chair stepped forward to introduce Eleanor Tilney. *At least I can find out if she'll be teaching anything interesting.*

In the final stages of her doctoral studies, Prof. Tilney was deeply involved in a project tracing the similarities and differences that arise when reading personal writings through the lens of literary analysis, with a particular focus on Southern manuscripts from the late 18th and early 19th centuries. Catie was fascinated – after steamy romances and dark, twisted gothic novels set in the South, Catie loved reading Antebellum diaries above all things. She listened with intense focus, and before Prof. Tilney's presentation ended, she was a card-bearing fangirl of the quiet young woman.

During the meet-and-greet afterwards, Catie lingered at the edge of the crowd until the other students wandered off to other social engagements. As the room cleared, she approached Prof. Tilney, all but trembling with enthusiasm. Prof. Tilney was soft-spoken and reserved, until conversation turned to her current research – in Catie she found an equally animated audience. Following several coffee dates at the Mansfield Perk near campus, Eleanor offered Catie the opportunity to join her project – earning valuable experience, as well as indulging their shared love of the past.

A few weeks into her assistantship, Catie could not imagine spending her Saturdays anywhere other than the quiet rooms of the Northanger Historical Society. The NHS shared space with the Northanger Visitor Information Center in an old house near the center of town. Catie loved wandering down Bath Drive, looking at the hodgepodge of houses with their picket fences and heirloom plants. You could trace the history of Northanger walking along Bath, and she loved to give her imagination free reign, wondering what stories the houses would tell if she could unlock the spell. The rambling Victorian that housed the NHS was fondly referred to around town as "The Vic" – a nod to both its design and the Visitor Information Center. Catie had yet to discover why a town as small as Northanger needed an information center – it had very limited operating hours and even fewer visitors – but supposed it had something to do with being a college town. Eleanor theorized the nearby battlefields also played a contributing role, as they certainly aided funding and interest in the Historical Society.

The NHS made use of the entire second floor, each of the various rooms having a different theme or focus. The members of the Society, primarily older ladies whose mortality Catie sometimes questioned, took great care keeping the rotating exhibits neat and orderly. Overflowing boxes, trunks, and bags regularly appeared, filled with things to sort through and either file away for posterity or be prepared for display. Catie loved when new boxes arrived, and the Society Ladies often let her try on clothing and jewelry from the collection. Eleanor liked to tease her about being the Society pet, but even she could be persuaded to join the fun when a particularly interesting donation arrived. Eleanor's personal office space was tucked in a corner of the third floor attic. Though the space was barely contained chaos, home of all things unused, Eleanor had cleared an area large enough for a desk and several work tables. She and Catie even unearthed a pair of mismatched wingback chairs and drug them in front of the dormer windows. It was a strange office space, but homey and relaxing. The two spent countless hours poring over documents, typing up every passage remotely applicable to Eleanor's project.

It was only natural, after such an immediate recognition of "kindred spirit at first sight," that working in such proximity allowed a close friendship to develop. For Catie – the second eldest and only girl of her parents' six children – spending time with Eleanor was a welcome haven away from the world of football, wrestling, and hunting that defined her family. In Eleanor, Catie found the big sister she always wanted: someone she could talk to in her native tongue of literature and fancy, someone she could turn to for advice on navigating the tricky waters of being a co-ed. The relationship seemed to meet a need in Eleanor's life too, and when Catie's parents were offered a chance to go to Canada for the summer, Eleanor extended an invitation for Catie to stay with her in Northanger. Rev. Morland agreed on the condition that Catie enroll in two summer courses and continue her research assistantship at the NHS – neither condition being disagreeable, everything was quickly settled.

Sunday, November 1, 2015

"Jane, we must visit the Historical Society before we leave," Cassie said when Catie once more paused in her telling.

"Indeed," Jane nodded. "And I rather fancy a glimpse of the third floor attic too. Do you think, if we asked politely, we could be given clearance?" she asked, with a surprisingly impish smile.

Catie smiled as she nodded, "I think that can be arranged with very little effort. And you'll love it, the attic is my favorite part – and that's saying something, because I never knew how much I could love a Historical Society!"

"Quick question," Cassie raised a finger. "Where are you from, Catie? Are you a daughter of Northanger, or here as a student?"

"Oh, I'm from here. Ish. My family lives outside of town, sort of in a no-man's land between here and Barton actually, but we claim Northanger. I've always known Northanger as home, and Abbey College has a great English program," she paused. "My father wanted me to go to Barton, tuition reduction, you see, but I worked hard in school and managed to earn enough scholarships to stay in Northanger and attend Abbey for almost nothing." Catie blushed. "I probably shouldn't talk about money and needing scholarships – but I *earned* those!" Her eyes flashed with quick emotion.

Jane tilted her head slightly and studied Catie. "A girl has to do what a girl has to do, especially when her education is on the line. Brava to you, my dear," she said quietly.

"Tuition reduction at Barton?" Cassie blinked in confusion.

"Yes," Catie said, crinkling her nose. "My father is the college chaplain there, and as such his children can have reduced tuition. Jamie was able to go to Sotherton because of football, but I'm not an athlete by any stretch – and since I was so determined to major in the frivolous field of English, Dad said he'd only pay for my studies at Barton." She sighed. "I've wanted to attend Abbey College my whole life, so I fought for it. I found scholarships all over the place, and a couple found me," she laughed. "It took work, but I've managed to take care of it all. When I showed Dad, he grumbled but couldn't find a reason to say no. And here I am." With a slight shrug she sipped her cocoa.

"What does he think of your work with Eleanor Tilney?" Jane asked.

Catie paused, thinking. "He is pleased with the project. History is a useful field of study – even though Eleanor is looking at these primary documents as literature, Dad views it as unadulterated history. He even made some inquiries among the family circles and found a few diaries for us to peruse. So he is definitely in favor of the project – it's why he let me stay here, instead of going with everyone to Canada. Of course," she pulled a face and gestured to the paper on the table, "he is unlikely to look kindly at this story."

Jane picked up the paper and glanced at the article. "But wasn't this 'unmasking' a result of your work with Eleanor?"

Catie blushed. "Ah, yes and no. It began innocently enough, and then things got out of control and took on a life of their own. There is so much more to this story."

"And you have put the family name on the front page of the paper in a deliciously engrossing way, quite out of keeping with a minister father's preference," Cassie said quietly. "That's something we are well familiar with eh, Jane?"

Jane snorted. "Oh, our poor father. It must be so trying to balance being a minister in good standing and the father of many children."

Catie smiled a little. "I imagine it might be, and at least my affair is only a trifle compared to when Jamie makes news. The trials of being a football god in the South," she sighed dramatically.

"Okay, now we've got things settled on that count, what about spending the summer in Northanger with Eleanor?" Cassie leaned forward. "I have a hunch things are about to get interesting."

"The summer was simply amazing," Catie smiled.

Early June - Mid-August 2015

After weeks of planning and countless phone calls, emails, and three rescheduled meetings at Mansfield Perk, Catie was finally able to wave an affectionate "Bon Voyage!" to her family as they ventured north of the border. *I hope Canada is ready for the Fearsome Foursome*, she thought, watching as her four younger brothers tussled over seat assignments and comics books.

"Do you wish you were going?" Eleanor asked with a smile, joining Catie and offering a wave of her own.

"Nope," Catie said emphatically. "I'm sure Canada is lovely – one day I want to visit P.E.I., but I do not want to have such an important literary experience overshadowed by one of the boys finding a lobster or claiming to see Sasquatch."

Eleanor laughed, "I believe Sasquatch is more commonly found in western Canada. But I understand." She paused, arching one eyebrow slightly. "I'm surprised you admit to reading *Anne of Green Gables*, my friend. Isn't Montgomery a little tamer than your normal taste?"

Catie grinned. "Hey, you have to start somewhere! Anne and company have been my bosom buddies for life. 'Sides," she added with a wink, "Anne's got a crazy imagination!"

"This is true. Wonder who that reminds me of?" Eleanor mused.

"I haven't the foggiest idea," Catie laughed. "Shall we begin our summer adventure, now the travelers are off?"

"Sounds good to me. What do you say we swing by Mansfield Perk on the way into the Society offices?"

Catie nodded, "seems the only logical way to start. Especially since we have a box of new treasures to sift through."

Several hours later, Catie looked at Eleanor over the stack of dusty books on the floor. "Remind me again why we're going through this box? I haven't seen *anything* that relates to your research – they're not even primary documents."

"Because one of the reenactors in my father's unit decided to donate his entire collection, and my father seems to think there is valuable information in the mix," Eleanor sighed and promptly sneezed. "He won't come out and say so directly, but I think he hopes we will find something they can use in their reenactments. Apparently there's a big anniversary coming up, which means a bigger hoopla around all the regular battle events than normal. I think they're even talking about playing a bigger role in the Fall-o-Ween festivities this year."

"Whoa," Catie said. "They take this stuff seriously, huh?"

"You have no idea," Eleanor rolled her eyes and smiled. "Dad's the General, so we can blame his obsession on his position, but the others? Who knows. But since I'm the resident expert on all things historical – don't even try to explain that historical analysis of literature is not the same as being a historian – I inherited these treasures."

"Which means I did too," Catie laughed. "If we have to sift through this stuff, maybe we really can find something interesting for them to use. Or," she paused, an impish twinkle in her eye, "we could always make something up."

Eleanor laughed, "we shouldn't, that'd be very poor conduct on all levels – professional and familial."

"I'm not saying that we absolutely have to, but we *could*," Catie winked.

"On that note, I think we can call it a day – let's get you moved in to the apartment, and then we can do something fun before dinner at The Homeplace." Eleanor arched an eyebrow, "you'll get to meet the General, and can decide whether it's worth the risk of making up a historical discovery."

A few hours later, standing in the foyer of a rather grand old house on the outskirts of town, Catie began to see Eleanor's point. General Tilney cut an imposing figure; Catie could easily imagine him leading men into battle – reenactment or otherwise – instantly realizing why everyone referred to him simply as 'the General.'

"Have you ever been to one of our reenactments?" he asked now, voice gruff.

"Ah," Catie stammered. "No, I haven't."

"Catie's brother is a football star at Sotherton, Dad," Eleanor interjected. "And with four younger brothers, I feel certain the whole family spent every weekend at various football games."

"Well then," the General nodded. "I don't suppose I can argue with family devotion. An admirable quality sadly lacking in modern youth."

"Aww, Dad, you know that's not true."

Catie startled, turning to see a guy a little older than her walking in the door.

"Henry!" Eleanor exclaimed, a smile spreading across her face. "I didn't know you were coming tonight." As she spoke, the guy crossed the foyer and wrapped an arm around her shoulder.

"I was able to wrap things up sooner than expected, and decided to surprise everyone," he smiled. "Hello, we have a newcomer," he said, turning to Catie.

"Catie, this is my younger brother Henry," Eleanor introduced them. "Henry, this is my student and intern, Catie. She and I will be doing hardcore research this summer."

"I hope you won't let Eleanor steal your whole summer – all work and no play makes for a very boring summer," Henry winked as he shook her hand. "I plan to do nothing more than frolic and read novels," he continued. "What say you to that, sir?" he asked his father, with an impish grin.

"I think it is time for dinner," the General grumbled. "And for you to grow out of your teasing ways," he continued, one corner of his mouth twitching suspiciously.

"Eleanor mentioned the amount of research you put into preparing for reenactments, do you often find new elements or details?" Catie asked over dinner.

"Now you've done it," Henry leaned over to whisper. "Get him started and he'll drone for hours."

"Hush, boy," the General shot Henry an exasperated look. "Catie is working with Eleanor, she obviously likes research. Unlike some people. Yes," he nodded. "I do frequently discover things that need to be changed – typically it's merely a matter of personnel placement or an adjustment in accoutrement. However," he paused to take a drink, "when I first began my reenacting career, I made an astounding discovery – one that changed my life. I met the Northanger Ghost."

Catie's eyes widened. "There's a Northanger Ghost?"

"You don't get out much do you?" Henry teased.

"No, not really," Catie agreed with a laugh.

"The Northanger Ghost is tale best suited for stormy nights or deep, dark woods," Henry continued. "The General puts on a performance at every Fall-o-Ween event, so your ignorance is inexcusable."

"The game was played at Sotherton last year," Catie countered, "and I was there watching my brother dazzle the crowds."

"Touché," Henry nodded.

"Though he teases, Henry makes a valid point," the General interrupted. "The story of the Northanger Ghost is one you should *experience* – I feel certain the right moment will come. Until then, let your imagination dwell on this one detail: the Ghost is the true hero of every battle fought in these parts. Without him, there would be no reenactment. Now Henry, tell me about this new internship."

From there, the conversation flowed aimlessly, and Catie was pleased to discover the General a more amiable host than first impression indicated. It was the first of many meals shared, and as the summer passed Catie found herself ever more drawn to the family. She knew the summer would strengthen her connection with Eleanor, binding the two in a true sisterhood of shared experiences and confidences. Though she did not see him often, the General was gracious and cordial to Catie, often extending ambiguous invitations to join the family for vague future events. He never mentioned the Northanger Ghost again, a fact she found puzzling, until Henry mercifully satisfied her curiosity.

Henry was an unexpected surprise of the best variety. A graduate student, he was taking the summer off before beginning an internship at Barton College in the fall. Protective and supportive of his sister, Henry possessed a smart aleck sense of humor that delighted Catie. The combination of his kindness and snark proved lethal, and Catie found herself living the cliché of falling for her friend's brother. Happily, it seemed to be a mutual experience, and as the end of summer drew close, Catie began to hope for the acknowledgement of everything left unsaid.

After a particularly hot and muggy day near the end of July, Henry and Catie were on the broad covered porch of the Vic, watching an evening storm while Eleanor finished a conference call. "I don't tell the story the way the General does," Henry began, bumping her shoulder, "but if you want to hear a short version of the Northanger Ghost legend, this would be a good setting."

"Yes please," Catie smiled, startling at a particularly loud crack of thunder. "This is perfect story weather."

"Okay, it was a dark and stormy night – quite a bit like this one," he began.

"Henry," Catie rolled her eyes.

"No really, I promise that's how the story goes!" he winked. "Anyway. It was a dark and stormy night, and there were soggy soldiers camped out throughout the woods outside of town. One of them couldn't sleep, between the rain and his nerves about the impending battle, so he started wandering around camp, checking on things, you know? On the far side, closest to enemy territory, he runs into a man. Surprised to find someone else out in the murky weather, he strikes up a conversation. The stranger, who only gives the name 'Clay,' tells the soldier that if he wants to win, the charge should come from the west. Our soldier is skeptical, but the next day he mentions the encounter to his commanding officer, and the officer takes the advice. Changing their course to attack from the west, our soldiers win.

"A month or so later, on the night before another battle, another soldier can't sleep and runs into Clay in the night. Clay tells them to attack from the south, if they want victory. The soldier told his commander, they don't take the advice, and suffer a mighty defeat. That night, Clay appears by the commander's bedroll, but the commander never told anyone what happened. From that night forward, anytime a battle was being fought anywhere near Northanger, including Barton, Hartfield, all the surrounding area, Clay would appear to a soldier and give him a plan of attack. When the commanders listened, they won."

When Henry paused, Catie turned to face him, sitting sideways in the swing. "So the Northanger

Ghost that changed your father's life was, like, a battle guru ghost?"

Henry laughed, "I told you I don't tell it the same as the General. But, in the most basic terms, yes – I suppose he is something of a battle guru."

"Hmm," Catie murmured, looking past him into the rain.

Henry reached over to squeeze her knee. "Whatcha thinking?"

Catie glanced down at his hand on her leg and smiled. "I'm thinking there's more to the story, of course. It's almost too simple."

"You have a crazy imagination, you realize that right?"

"Of course I do. But that's why you told me the story, because you love my crazy imagination," she winked, before leaning in to kiss him lightly on the cheek. "Thank you for telling me, and thank you in advance for agreeing to help me get to the bottom of the real story."

"Always," Henry whispered, his eyes searching hers intently. Raising his hand to cradle her cheek, he was just leaning closer when the screen door slammed making them both jump.

"Whew, I didn't think that call would ever end," Eleanor sighed, walking toward them. "Uh, did I interrupt something?" she asked, glancing between the two as Catie blushed and Henry smiled.

"Henry was telling me the Northanger Ghost story, a very short and factual version, teasing me for thinking there's more to it, and wanting to find out more," Catie said in a rush.

"But not tonight," Henry said, standing and offering a hand to Catie. "Tonight is for enjoying the last bit of summer, and ignoring the bothersome demands of academic life."

"I say amen to that," Eleanor laughed. "Come on, let's find something to eat and see what mischief we can make in the next two weeks!"

"No argument here," Catie smiled, relishing the feel of Henry's fingers intertwined with hers. "It's been a summer to remember, why waste what's left by stopping early?"

Sunday, November 1, 2015

"And Henry is the one you were not-waiting for when Bella tried to set you up with her brother, Jack," Cassie said with a sigh. "No wonder! He sounds wonderful. I wonder if he has an older brother?"

"Actually," Catie laughed, "he does. But from what I can tell, Rick is not even half the man his brother is. I haven't really met him, we exchanged a half dozen words in passing, but there's something smarmy about him." She paused, cocking her head slightly. "If this were a romance novel, he'd be the type to try and seduce the heroine away from the hero, perhaps resorting to drastic measures."

Jane laughed, "I know *exactly* what you mean! That's the beauty of novels, isn't it? How well fiction can illustrate and even reflect everyday life. I never open a novel without reading about someone I know – and often meet people I'm already familiar with from the pages of a book."

Catie smiled. "Well, I can't honestly say I've had that experience, but I do find novels very nifty for explaining weird relationships or interpersonal dynamics."

"Now that we have our cast of characters: you, Eleanor, Henry, Bella, Jack and your brother," Cassie counted them off on her fingers as she spoke, "and a little background information to build on, what happens next?"

"Don't forget General Tilney," Jane added. "Considering the headline of today's paper, I think he is going to play a fairly significant role in what comes next."

Catie nodded. "Mmhmm, General Tilney definitely plays a role – although I confess to only knowing a small portion of that role. From things said last night, I think there was a whole other plot afoot that nobody suspected. I certainly never guessed."

"When does Henry come back into the story?" Cassie asked. "When Bella tried setting you up with Jack, you hadn't heard from Henry in several weeks right?"

"That's right. I had told Bella about Henry, of course, and her advice was that I couldn't just sit around waiting for something that would probably never happen. She has so much more experience with boys than me, and assured me I wasn't the first girl to fall into the trap of a summer fling only to find myself forgotten again in the fall." Catie crinkled her nose. "I should have listened to my instincts – I knew that I knew Henry wasn't that guy, but I wanted to trust Bella."

"It can be difficult to know who to trust and when," Jane murmured.

"I did agree to go on the double date," Catie continued. "But I also stood my ground and spent the day working with Eleanor per usual."

"Did she know about the date?" Cassie interjected.

"Yes, I told her about it," Catie nodded. "I also told her I was going primarily as moral support for Bella. In part because I was holding out hope something would happen with Henry, but even if nothing ever did, a fraternity president was definitely not at the top of my list."

Jane snorted. "No, somehow I don't see that pairing happening."

"Poor guy never had a chance," Cassie sighed. "I'd love to tease you about that, but I can't really blame you."

"I felt a little bad about it, especially since Bella was *so excited* about the idea," Catie admitted, "but he wasn't Henry. And when Henry called right before the guys were supposed to pick us up, I regretted agreeing to the date even as moral support."

"Oh! He called you that night?" Cassie leaned forward. "Did Eleanor tell him you had a date?"

Catie laughed, "No, she promised she wouldn't say anything. It just happened that way. He had been ridiculously busy working through some snags concerning his internship at Barton College and his graduate coursework, and time got away from him. Everything was finally sorted out and he was calling to ask me to dinner. He apologized profusely for the last minute invite, and I hated having to tell him I was on my way out, but we made plans for the next weekend."

"I wager that made for an awkward dinner," Jane remarked.

"Did it ever! Bella made a point of telling Jack straight away that he had competition, and the whole night turned into the Jack show, all about his wonderfulness. It was obnoxious." Catie shuddered. "What made it even worse was the way he kept acting as if we were already a couple. I'd never even met him! Apparently that made no difference. It was weird. In hindsight, I think he and Bella must have talked more than she let on."

"Did he ever realize you weren't interested?" Cassie asked.

"It took a while," Catie admitted. "Bella kept encouraging him in his 'pursuit,'" she made air quotes with her fingers, "and even Jamie wanted me to give him a chance. Jack kept calling and trying to set up dates, and the more I resisted dating her brother the more distant Bella became. Although, not exactly distant – different, I guess. Cooler, less affectionate. The nature of our friendship definitely changed, and she began to trick me into trips to the mall or the movies that turned into double dates. A few weeks ago, Jack finally realized I was seriously not interested." Catie smiled mischievously.

"That's a smile with a story behind it, young lady," Jane said with a pointed look. "What made Jack finally realize his pursuit was doomed to fail?"

Catie grinned. "It's possible he walked into the Historical Society one Saturday, attempting to surprise me, and got a surprise of his own."

"Catie Morland, what did you do?" Cassie's eyes were wide with anticipation.

"Let's just say that Henry also came by that day, and Jack walked in just in time to bear witness to a stolen kiss."

While Cassie burst out laughing, Jane quirked an eyebrow. "I have a suspicion it was a kiss freely given, but that is a wonderfully effective means of communicating your preference."

"It wasn't planned that way, but it did work beautifully. He blustered and growled before he left, but he stopped calling me." Catie paused. "Strange, I just realized – I don't think he told Bella what happened – she would definitely have made a big deal about it. Interesting. Anyway, when he left the Historical Society that day, it was the last I heard from him until he showed up last night at the Fall-o-Ween debacle."

"If you're kissing Henry in the Historical Society, I'm guessing your instincts were right and it wasn't just a summer fling, you were able to work things out. Worth the waiting and suspense from the first part of the semester?" Cassie asked, picking up her mug to take a sip and discovering it empty again.

Catie's smile faded. "I'd like to say yes, but I don't know anymore." She looked down, toying with her mug, as Jane and Cassie exchanged a quiet, knowing glance.

"Why do you say that, dear?" Jane asked softly.

"Because after last night, I don't think Henry will want anything to do with me ever again," she whispered. "Everything went backwards somehow. We were just settling into an 'us,' and then that happened, and he's lost to me."

"Did he tell you that himself, or are you letting the drama of the situation cloud your judgement?" Jane continued.

Catie raised her eyes to meet Jane's. "No. Yes. I honestly don't know. He didn't say he never wanted to see me again, but you've read the article. And Jack was so horrid. I don't see how he could want to keep being my friend, let alone anything more."

"I'm going to get us one last round of drinks, and then I think you should tell us what happened last night."

"You just want to torment that poor barista again," Cassie laughed as Jane stood.

"Perhaps," Jane nodded. "And perhaps I think we need a spot of tea for the end of the story – although I have a strong suspicion this isn't really the end. Don't tell her anything good until I get back," she told Catie before heading to the counter.

Catie and Cassie watched as Jane placed the order. "If she doesn't make him blush in the next 30 seconds," Cassie mused, "I will be exceedingly surprised." As if on cue, Jane leaned against the counter and said something that provoked a blush. Catie and Cassie laughed.

"What is it about redheads? You mentioned her first boyfriend?"

"Yes, Tom. He was a great guy," Cassie nodded. "Jane was absolutely crazy about him, but something happened – I have theories, but I've never been able to prove them – and he left. Jane has dated a few guys since then, but she's never fallen for anyone. I think she will always love Tom best. I suspect that's why she focuses her studies on the classic romances." Cassie raised her voice slightly as Jane approached the table, "and I know that's why she torments every helpless redhead she meets."

"Torment?" Jane scoffed. "I did no such thing. I merely mentioned that he looks uncommonly good from behind. It's a compliment!"

Catie burst out laughing, "Ohmigosh, did you really tell him he has a cute butt?!"

"Of course I did," Jane winked. "I may not be a co-ed anymore, but I'm certainly not dead. I'd wager your friend Eleanor would agree with me – life is more fun in your late thirties. People can't make you behave anymore," she laughed.

"People have never been able to make you behave, Jane," Cassie laughed. "Remind me to put a generous tip in the jar before we leave, to make up for your antics."

"Oh hush," Jane smiled. "He liked it, I'm sure. Now, Catie, tell us your version of what happened last night."

Catie took a sip of her tea, savoring the soothing warmth. "It all began over the summer, with the story of a ghost hero. The idea wouldn't let me go, and I started looking for more information on that battle, as well as looking for other accounts of a battlefield ghost. Eleanor helped me when she could, and together we discovered a surprising amount of information – with startling results ..."

Saturday, October 31, 2015

An insistent pounding on her door pulled Catie from a deep sleep. *What on earth*, she wondered, blinking in confusion. *Who in the world is beating my door down at* – "Crap!" she exclaimed aloud, finally able to focus on the clock. "It's after 10 already?!" Wrapping a throw around her shoulders she stumbled to the door.

"Finally," Bella huffed. "Catie! You aren't even dressed! I thought you just couldn't hear me over the shower or blow dryer or something." Her eyes narrowed speculatively. "You were asleep!"

"Um," Catie began.

"Never mind, just start getting ready, girl! We are going to be so late!" As she spoke, Bella swept into the room and made herself at home on the foot of Catie's bed. "You don't have time for a shower now, you'll have to grab one after the game."

"Remind me again why we have to be there so early?" Catie muttered, looking for a pair of jeans. "I've been going to my brothers' games my whole life, what makes this one so special I have to be there a million hours before kickoff."

"Well," Bella said, arching an eyebrow with practiced delicacy. "Someone woke up on the wrong side of the bed. What is with you today, Catie?"

"I was up until almost 5 o'clock this morning, looking for my flash drive. The flash drive that has all of my research about the battlefield –"

"Not those jeans, wear these," Bella interrupted, reaching over and snagging a pair of dark wash skinnies from the closet. "They'll go better with the Fall-o-Ween game shirts we pick up at the stadium, and look super cute with your boots and a scarf until we get there."

Catie turned and stared at her friend. "My boots."

"Duh. Tall boots and skinnies are like, the quintessential look for fall. You know this, silly," Bella looked at her.

"Tall boots at a football game," Catie repeated.

"Yes, Catie," Bella sighed. "We really need to get some caffeine in you."

"Bella, you realize we will be on our feet for a million hours right? And football stadiums have a tendency to be messy – thousands of people trying to eat and drink while cheering for their team spill things."

Bella sighed again, rolling her eyes dramatically. "To be such a dreamer, you are so practical. Don't you see? Big football games like this are to see and be seen! You have to look like you're a college somebody if you want to be a college somebody."

"Maybe I don't want to be a college somebody," Catie muttered under her breath, pulling on the jeans and a dark pink thermal.

"And to look like a college somebody," Bella continued, ignoring Catie's muttering, "you need to look carefully casual. Tall boots and skinnies give you polish, while the game day shirt will give you that 'I've got school spirit'-vibe. Oh," she nodded. "I like the choice of pink. I have it on good authority today's game shirts are black, and that's really going to pop once you layer them."

"Great," Catie chirped with false enthusiasm. "Plus, it's the perfect color to match my Chucks!" She held up a hand to cut off Bella's protests. "I'm not wearing my boots to the game, and nothing you can say will change my mind. Now," she smiled sweetly, wrapping a band around the end of her hastily braided hair, "you mentioned something about caffeine?"

With much muttering, sighing, and eye-rolling, the girls left the room. *This could be a very long day,* Catie thought with a sigh. *And I still don't know where my flash drive is.*

By the time Catie made it back to her room, she found herself desperately wishing for a time machine. Anything to erase the day and start over again. *I can't even appreciate that the sunset looks like a fireball,* she thought with a sigh, *because my feet and head hurt too bad for anything to be interesting. And the day still isn't over.* The thought made her whimper. The first few bars of the *Indiana Jones* theme interrupted the beginning of her pity party.

"Henry," she smiled, answering the phone. "How did you know I desperately needed a friendly voice?"

"I'd love to claim supernatural abilities, but you texted me from the game, remember?"

"Oh, I did," she laughed. "It's been one of those days, and I just want it to end. Or a do-over. Can I have a do-over? Also, you may be the only guy I know who calls instead of texting. Why is that?"

Henry laughed. "Call me old-fashioned, but I like to actually hear my girl's voice when I'm talking to her. Even when she sounds on the verge of a meltdown. What happened to make today so bad?"

With an exaggerated sigh, Catie flopped onto the bed. "Where should I start? Did Eleanor tell you my flash drive is missing? The one with *all of my research* on the battlefield legend."

"You never made a backup copy, did you?"

"Uh, no," Catie admitted. "I was going to, but I wanted to wait until I got everything finished. The slideshow was so close, I just had a few tweaks to make and it'd be ready to go for the conference next month. Now," she sighed. "I think I'm screwed."

"Mmm," Henry murmured. "I disagree."

"Henry, I spent almost four months working on this presentation, with your sister's help, discovering the truth behind the infamous Northanger Ghost, and now –"

"I made a copy," Henry interrupted.

Catie blinked. "You made a copy?"

"Yes, last week – so your most recent changes won't be saved, but the bulk of your research and work is safe."

"You made a backup copy of my research?"

Henry laughed, "is that so hard to believe?"

"Right now? Yes," Catie laughed. "But you are so ridiculously awesome it probably shouldn't be surprising. I don't know how to thank you – saying the words doesn't come close."

"I can make suggestions, but we can talk about that later," she could hear his smile in his voice. "Now we have that resolved, what else happened today?"

Catie groaned. "Why did you remind me? I had almost forgotten. Maybe I'm hyper sensitive because of the whole flash drive thing, but it was just a really weird day. I should have stayed in bed, ha."

"But the Lions beat Sotherton, right?"

"Oh yeah, we totally stomped 'em. The game was great," a little enthusiasm crept into Catie's voice. "It felt weird to cheer against Jamie's team, but a girl's gotta do what a girl's gotta do. He played well," she added. "The game wasn't the problem."

"Bella," Henry stated simply.

"Mmhmm," Catie agreed. "It was strange. You know things have been increasingly awkward since the whole Jack thing, but today it was a whole different level. We were both snappish and snarky – granted, I got maybe five hours of sleep last night, but still. It was tense. Nothing I did was right; every time I tried to answer her 'what is wrong with you, Catie?' questions, she cut me off before I could explain about the missing research. I'm dreading the rest of the Fall-o-Ween events tonight," she sighed. "Do I have to go?"

"Yes, because I spent my day waiting to wander among crazed masses of college students with a beautiful girl at my side," Henry replied. "And you don't want to miss the General's final performance as the Northanger Ghost."

"I hate it when you're right," she laughed. "Okay. Fine. I'll go. But I refuse to act like a 'college somebody,' just so you know ahead of time what you're getting into."

"A who? Actually, don't answer that. Just let me know when I should swing by and pick you up for the long walk across campus."

"Do you want cute or football leftovers?"

"You're always cute."

"You're a smart man, Henry Tilney," Catie laughed. "Give me 30 minutes, and we shall attempt to outwit calamity and chaos."

An hour later, Catie had to admit she was having fun. The night was cool, the food free, and the crowd surprisingly sober. She and Henry met up with a handful of English majors and the group amused themselves by wandering the quad and people-watching. Catie expected Bella to appear, or at least text wanting Catie to meet her somewhere, but she was strangely silent.

"Hey, it's almost time for the General's performance," Henry said, checking his watch. "Let's head over now, get a good spot."

"Oh, is this the secret project you've been working on all semester, Catie?" asked one of her classmates.

"Yeah, the Northanger Ghost," Catie nodded. "The plan is to present our findings at the big historical conference in Atlanta next month. It will be interesting to hear him tonight, within the context of all the research I've been doing."

"You've totally gotta do that presentation here! It's our ghost, we should get to learn the truth too," another classmate laughed.

"We'll see," Catie laughed. "I think Eleanor was planning to set up something as a tie-in with the Historical Society's new exhibit. Oh, this spot is perfect," she smiled up at Henry as he stopped by the low wall bordering the gardens.

"Great view of the stage, close enough to hear without being too close, and suitably spooky – you never know what might be lurking behind those bushes," he winked. "And apparently the General is starting early, look," Henry gestured toward the temporary stage where his father stood, wearing full battle regalia, in a single spotlight.

As the crowd began to gather and settle, Catie leaned against Henry and sighed. *This is what life is all about*, she thought happily. *Football, nights under the stars with friends and a cute boy, and getting to see research at work in the real world. This might be better than a romance novel.*

"Dad said he was trying something new this year," Henry murmured, wrapping an arm around her and pulling Catie closer. "Apparently you and Eleanor rubbed off on him, and he's entered the twenty-first century." As he spoke, an image of the local battlefield appeared on the wall behind the stage, and the General began his tale. "Are you going to hyper-analyze the story tonight?" Henry teased.

"Nope," Catie whispered back, "tonight I'm just going to listen to a spooky story under the stars, knowing there's a ridiculously nice, very cute guy here if it gets too scary." Henry smiled at her in the dark, and Catie sighed contentedly. *Yep, definitely better than a romance novel.*

The images on the wall behind the stage changed as the General's story progressed, alternating between video clips from reenactments and artsy pictures of the surrounding woods. "Someone did an amazing job editing this," Catie murmured, just as the image changed to familiar slide. "What the," she gasped, sitting up and leaning a little forward.

"Catie, what's wrong?" Henry asked, resting a hand on her back.

Catie shook her head, unable to believe her eyes as the screen now showed another slide from her presentation. "No, no, no," she whispered. The General continued his performance, not realizing anything had changed, until Jack Thorpe walked onto the stage.

"I'm sure you were expecting a treat tonight," Jack interrupted. "But, in keeping with the Halloween theme, you've been given a trick. You've *all* been tricked," he turned to General Tilney, "including you, sir. If you'll take a look at the presentation behind you, you'll notice that these slides are carefully deconstructing your tale. They make the case, sir, that you are," he paused dramatically, as the General turned and glanced over the slides that used to be Catie's presentation, "a fraud."

Henry growled beside her, but Catie could only look on in horror. Her carefully crafted presentation had been tampered with, altered into something sensational. "No, no, no" she continued to whisper. "That's not how it should be at all," she groaned, then gasped as several pictures of herself with the Tilneys appeared.

"You see, sir," Jack continued, "our sweet, innocent Catie has spent the last six months working her way into your family unit in order to disprove the very foundation of who you are. She went undercover, if you will, determined to track down a grisly truth few dared to speculate."

Catie covered her face, daring to peek through her fingers as the General turned several shades of crimson. To her dismay, Jack kept talking. "Not only has Catie been working with your daughter and her research materials, but she has been 'dating' your son – all as means to get closer to your family, and spin a more sensational story. Her end goal? To make a name for herself, and earn the independence, the name-recognition and place in society her status as a local scholarship student will never produce. She wanted so badly to be one of us," Jack shrugged his shoulders nonchalantly, "coming to my sister and I regularly, updating us on her progress and asking for assistance in making this work. Happy Halloween, General," Jack saluted with an overconfident grin.

Unable to take anymore, Catie stood and fled, barely noticing Henry storming toward the stage. Her friends tried to stop her, but she lost herself in the crowd of students trying to figure out what happened, her heart breaking over how completely wrong everything turned out. *That explains Bella's weird mood*, she realized with a bitter laugh. *Worst Fall-o-Ween ever*, she sighed, finally able to lock her door and fall on the bed in tears.

Sunday, November 1, 2015

"Oh my dear girl," Cassie murmured. Jane sat quietly, a thoughtful expression on her face, as her sister leaned across the table to squeeze Catie's hand.

"I told you," Catie sighed. "Henry is never going to want to see me again. Ever."

"I wouldn't be so sure of that," the voice, and the hand that rested on her shoulder, made Catie jump in surprise. "I've been trying to call all morning, why won't you answer?"

"My phone is in my dorm," Catie admitted, blushing. "How, why –" she fumbled for words, as Henry pulled out the chair next to her and sat down.

"You must be Henry," Jane remarked with a knowing smile.

"Yes ma'am," he said, extending his hand. "Henry Tilney. And you are?"

"I'm Jane and this is my sister Cassie," she replied, shaking his hand. "Like your sister and our enchanting friend here, I'm also a member of the literati, and was rather intrigued by the article in the paper. We ran into Catie by chance this morning, and she's been telling us the whole story. It's truly fascinating."

"I feel as if I know you already, Henry," Cassie smiled. "Your Catie is quite the storyteller, and we've been positively engrossed for – gracious, look at the time." Cassie showed Jane her watch. "I'm terribly sorry, but we must leave you now. We have another appointment."

"Oh my, is that really the time? I am sorry, but I think," Jane added, "that you would likely prefer to be alone just now. Please take care to set Catie's concern at ease, young man," she said with a stern glance. "If I find out you've fallen short of your reputation as a hero and gentleman, I will find a way to make your life miserable."

"You have my word," Henry said solemnly. "I've been looking for her all morning, to make sure she's okay."

"Are you sure you can't stay?" Catie asked.

"I wish we could, dear," Jane replied. "But we are leaving you in good hands, and I have a feeling we shall meet again. And Catie," she added, rising to come around and give Catie a hug, "your story is far from over. I promise."

With a flurry of goodbyes, the sisters left, and Catie found herself alone with Henry, a million questions in her eyes. Before she could give voice to one, he leaned close and lightly kissed her. "Does that answer your question?" he asked softly.

"Yes," she whispered with a smile. "Though I may need you to explain why you're so amazing one of these days."

Henry laughed, "that's a secret I will carry to the grave."

"Oh good, you found her!" Catie looked past Henry to see Eleanor hurrying toward them. "Catie, do you realize how many calls the Historical Society has been getting? The answering machine is maxed out, on a Sunday! There are so many people wanting to know more about our research! Oh, what's this?" Eleanor half-rose from the chair she had just taken and pulled a book from the seat. "*Northanger Abbey* – oh, I love this one! Is this yours, Catie?"

"No, I've never read it," Catie answered, confused. "That's where Jane was sitting, I wonder if it fell out of her bag."

"Jane? Wait," Eleanor paused, a strange look on her face. "The two women I passed on my way here, they were just leaving, was one of them Jane?"

"Yes, that was them – Jane and Cassie. They're from England, here on vacation – Jane was in Atlanta for a literature conference and they decided to tour Georgia," Catie replied. "I was telling them the story of everything that happened. They're wonderful listeners, I feel as if I've known them forever."

"Catie," Eleanor turned the book so its back cover faced her. "Is this the woman you've been talking to?"

"Yes it is," Catie said. "She was dressed differently, but that is definitely –" Catie stopped, her eyes wide. "You have got to be kidding me."

Henry laughed, taking the book to get a better look. "Catie," he managed to say, "you've just spent the morning with Jane Austen."

Acknowledgements

This story would not exist without Harris and Jess. No, really. Talking one day about how the writing was going (or not), Harris told me how I should write it instead. I laughed it off – until I realized he was onto something. Something that worked. Something that fixed the problem. Jess, of course, created the amazing Mansfield Perk (why isn't this a real place?), and was the first to bring Jane Austen "to life." As soon as I admitted that Harris's idea was so much better than mine, I realized I needed to borrow Jess's concept and give Jane another adventure. Of course, following his suggestion meant rewriting the entire thing, but I think it's a better story – so I both blame you and owe you, dude.

Thanks as ever to the lovely ladies of *Holidays with Jane* for giving me the chance to write with y'all. We have crazy conversations – about writing and life – but we are creating something amazing and I love it! I am incredibly blessed to call you my friends.

And, of course, my biggest thanks to Jane for writing it first – I learn something new every time I lose myself in her words, and this foray into *Northanger Abbey* was no different.

Of Rivers, Rocks, and Rich Men

A *Pride and Prejudice* Story

For every Darcy trying to get it right,
and every Elizabeth who takes a second look.

Chapter 1

"It is a truth universally acknowledged that a single man in possession of good fortune, must be an arrogant, entitled playboy," Liz grumbled, collapsing on her sister's couch with an exaggerated flop.

"That's only true of the uncivilized north – Southern boys are raised to be gentlemen," Jane laughed, tossing a pillow at her sister. "With or without deep bank accounts," she added arching an eyebrow.

Liz snorted. "Hate to break it to ya, babe, but the only difference between Southern men of fortune and Yankees is the accent." She tilted her head thoughtfully. "Though I must admit, the soft drawl of the Southern playboy does *sound* better. Oomph!" she grunted, another pillow hitting her head.

"You've been away from home too long, Elizabeth Bennet," Jane laughed, batting down the pillow Liz threw in return.

"You take being big sister seriously, and I love you for it. Going to New York or staying here – the end result would be the same." She paused, thinking. "Well, there's one difference."

"Oh?"

"Now I know beyond shadow of a doubt that rich men – particularly good-looking rich men – are the bane of my existence."

"Elizabeth," Jane groaned with a reluctant laugh. "One day, you'll meet someone who doesn't fit your neat little categories, and then you're gonna be in a pickle trying to change your own mind." She smirked. "You may fall head over heels for a handsome man, bearing the weight of both family name *and* fortune." Liz snorted.

"And I still don't understand why you insisted on getting your own place, you could have stayed here," Jane continued. "Or I'm sure Momma and Colin would have been delighted to have you move back and rejoin the family business," she winked.

"Right. That's exactly why I had to get my own place," Liz's voice was firm. "I could handle living with you, and I may – after my summer lease is up – but under no circumstance will I live with the circus. Ever. Never. No way."

"It's not that bad, Liz," Jane sighed.

Liz stared at her sister. "Oh yes," she said emphatically. "It is that bad. If it wasn't, then why don't you live at home?"

"I, ah, well," Jane stammered, "I need to be close to town, so I can be at Bella Gelato at a moment's notice. It didn't make sense to stay so far out, when my life is centered here in Meryton," she finished.

"Mmm, keep telling yourself that, sister," Liz laughed. "We both know you couldn't handle the crazy either, you just have a better excuse." She sighed, "Momma is driving me nuts – and I haven't even seen her yet. I cannot thank you enough, Janie, for keeping my secret. She calls at least three times a day, wanting travel details and making plans for my arrival." Liz pulled a face.

"She's missed you," Jane smiled. "We all have."

"I was only gone 3 years!" Liz yelped. "And I came home for holidays! Y'all make it seem like I spent twelve years exiled in space or something."

Jane laughed. "Think about it Liz, you left mountain haven Meryton for 'The Big City,'" she crooked her fingers in air quotes. "You might as well have gone to space. I understood your need to escape," she continued, "I'm just sayin'."

"Mmm," Liz murmured.

"And that's why I agreed to keep your secret when you told me you were coming home sooner than anticipated and wanted to keep it quiet. Although visiting me in town may not have been your best move – I could have come to you. Are the cabins really as cute as they look?"

"I'm pretending I'm invisible," Liz winked. "Yes, the cabin is ridiculously cute. I haven't had time to really investigate, but Pemberley Acres is beautiful," Liz sighed. "It's everything Daddy dreamed of, and then some."

"I'll come out some evening, let you show me around," Jane said. "I love driving by the place, but never have the nerve to turn down the drive."

Liz laughed. "It's not a private community, silly. In fact, they've even got a park area where people who aren't staying can soak up wholesome natural goodness, or whatever it is people do there."

"You laugh, Elizabeth, but if you didn't agree you wouldn't have rented a cabin for three months," Jane said archly. "In your heart of hearts, you're a hippie chick, a slightly crunchy granola girl, happiest when you've got your hands in the dirt and your feet bare. You *like* what they're doing at Pemberley, and deep down inside you want to be a part of it," she smiled.

Liz raised her eyebrows in mock surprise. "A slightly crunchy granola girl? Why Jane, I can't believe you know that phrase," she laughed. "Okay fine, maybe I do like it. Maybe I could spend my days coaxing nature to thrive like a woodland elf. And maybe," she paused, an impish grin stealing across her face, "I'm only staying there because I want to uncover the deep dark secrets lurking in the shadows. After I discover why the owner is so mysteriously reclusive – and ornery as a wet hen when seen – I shall write a stunning exposé that will win a Pulitzer and set me on my way to owning those lovely green hills."

Jane rolled her eyes. "You're ridiculous. Since when did you become an investigative journalist? What happen to your novel aspirations?"

"New York," Liz sighed. "But let's not talk about that tonight, please. I'm here for the summer at least, which is plenty of time to discuss every possible career alternative – and there are many, including converting to full-time hippie chick," she laughed. "For now, I really want to dig into the gelato I know you have stashed in the freezer, and have a quiet night."

"Mmkay," Jane agreed. "I've got a new dark chocolate mocha you might like, and there's a *Batman* marathon on channel 15."

"That sounds perfect. I'll get the gelato, you make your fancy tv work," she called over her shoulder, rummaging in the freezer before Jane found the remote.

Settling deep into pillows on Jane's oversized couch, with pints of creamy gelato and the cheesy antics of Batman and Robin filling the screen in all their 60s technicolor glory, Liz sighed in contentment. *This is home*, she thought.

Chapter 2

Stretching, Liz closed her notebook, sliding her pen between the pages to mark her place. *This tree must be a hundred years old,* she thought, settling against the broad trunk. *I'm glad they left so many trees, didn't feel the need to clearcut the place. Of course, that would nullify sustainable farming and all that agritourism jazz,* she smiled to herself. From where she sat on the hillside, Liz could see a good deal of the farm sprawling across the slope and wandering down to where the Netherfield River crossed. The other side of the river was more woods than fields, and she knew that's where the owner built his private residence. *I wonder what the house and grounds look like on the other side,* she mused. *With even more of the old trees left standing, I bet it's gorgeous. The guy has taste, if the cabins on this side are any indication.*

According to local gossip, the owner – Dierks or Garfield or Darcy or somesuch, Liz could never remember – wanted to keep his personal life separate from the professional aspect of running a vacation destination. She also knew that not a few of the good people of Meryton found him cranky and even rude – apparently he was not one to entertain meddling or personal questions. Though she had yet to meet the man, Liz could almost understand. *It can't be easy getting a venture like this up and running,* she thought, remembering summers working alongside Jane and their parents. *Pemberley Acres is as far removed from Longbourne Mines as New York is from Meryton,* she crinkled her nose, *and that distance is only going to increase. This is what Daddy dreamed Longbourne would become someday, and instead it becomes more like Mountain Vegas every day.*

Longbourne Mines had been in the Bennet family for three generations, Liz and Jane would have been the fourth generation to run things if not for an unfortunate quirk of estates and her father's kindness in offering an extended cousin a helping hand. When Liz was 3, her fourth cousin William Kent had appeared in the front office, needing to get back on his feet after a tumultuous divorce left him penniless and floundering. George Bennet was fiercely clan-loyal – after some discussion, he agreed to give William a position. Over the years a close friendship developed, and as Longbourne flourished, George offered William a chance to buy into the business, establishing a partnership that proved mutually beneficial. When William's son, Colin, graduated from high school, he reached out to his father, and they restored their relationship. *He was skeevy even then,* she remembered, *with his skinny jeans and aviators.* Liz was 19 when Colin finished college and moved to Meryton. Decidedly out of place in the mountain town, with its bustling summers and quiet off-season, Colin found it difficult to adjust to his new role, though proved himself a diligent worker. He seemed such a positive addition that when William died unexpectedly the next year, George made Colin the offer of his father's stake in Longbourne Mines.

Liz never worked out the particulars of the arrangement, despite handling most of the office affairs during her breaks from college, but things seemed to continue as before so she didn't investigate. She came to regret that decision when things changed again 5 years ago. Upon their father's death, it was revealed that instead of the Bennet daughters, Colin stood to inherit the majority share of Longbourne. Though Momma maintained a portion of the enterprise, the whole kit and caboodle was essentially Colin's. The other surprise was learning that somewhere along the line, Daddy created a savings account for each of the girls. By the time of his death, the amount was substantial, with careful safeguards limiting the dispersion of funds in a way that Liz and Jane were all but guaranteed a comfortable living. Liz often wondered if their father had known all along that Longbourne would change hands, or if the secret accounts were merely a fortunate coincidence.

Under the direction of Colin, Longbourne Mines evolved from a quiet mountain experience into an attention-grabbing tourist trap. *Not that I'm bitter or anything,* Liz thought with a laugh, looking over Pemberley's grounds. *We were never going to have anything like this, but at least when Daddy and Uncle Will were at the helm, there was an air of respectability.* Drawing from his degree in Consumer Entertainment and a bizarre obsession with all-inclusive cruises, Colin set about revamping Longbourne with gusto. Liz often wondered whether his frequent "research trips" were really to inspire his renovations or merely an excuse to spend a week at sea wooing women and pretending to be important. On one such cruise he finagled an introduction to his idol, Catherine D, consultant to the rich and gaudy. In Colin, Catherine D found a starstruck disciple who worshipfully applied her every suggestion, and it was largely at her direction that Longbourne Mines developed into a "family adventure destination!" To Liz's perturbation, but not her surprise, Momma jumped onto Colin's bandwagon and never looked back.

In stark contrast to the hayrides and carnival amusements of Longbourne, Pemberley Acres was a different world, embracing the natural heritage of the area, while gently moving into the future of tourism. Before returning to Meryton, Liz scoured every available piece of literature concerning Pemberley. The more Liz learned, the more she wanted the Pemberley experience. From her research, Liz knew the owner of Pemberley, What's-His-Face, inherited a sizable family fortune, several generations strong. Liz had not determined the source of that fortune, but did discover the Whatsit family had roots in the Charleston area. For reasons unexplained, the reigning heir decided to move inland, west to the gentle Georgian mountains, and proceeded to buy extensive quantities of land, creating the oasis of Pemberley Acres.

According to the promo materials, Pemberley was an homage to bygone days, when people lived in harmony with the land. With the twofold hope of preserving the land and giving city-dwellers a chance to get their hands dirty and engage with the natural world, Pemberley offered vacationers the opportunity to rent cabins and work alongside on-site gardeners and animal caretakers. In spite of the agritourism focus, Pemberley Acres was a working farm – starting small, with plans to expand and provide farm fresh, locally sourced ingredients to local eateries. In truth, Jane was right – Pemberley Acres was Liz's secret dream, everything she would never admit to wishing for. It was also too good to be true: there was no way everything could possibly be as it seemed.

"Two weeks, and this place still seems perfect," she muttered, picking up her notebook and riffling through her notes. *Maybe appearances aren't deceiving.* The thought crept up on her, both annoying and enticing. *If Pemberley Acres really is all it appears, then there's hope for the world.* Laughing to herself, Liz picked up her camera, training the lens on the river and following its lazy trail across the property.

"Hey! Put that camera down!"

The sharp voice startled her; sending notebook and pen flying as she scrambled to her feet, Liz whirled to face the intruder. *Oh my.* Striding in her direction, with the focus of a hunting tiger, was the best looking man Liz had seen in a long time.

"I don't know how you got on the property, but you will leave. Now," he growled. As he closed the gap between them, Liz saw fury blazing in his glacial blue eyes.

"I'm sorry, what?"

"You. Will. Leave. Now," the man barked each word, sparking an answering fury in Liz.

"I don't think so," she retorted. "I paid for the entire summer, upfront. I have every right to be here. Who do you think you are anyway?"

"William Darcy, and this is my property," he snarled. "I don't know what underhanded means you used to procure a place, but I am hereby revoking the lease. Your kind are not welcome here."

"Excuse me? My *kind*?" Liz felt her cheeks flaming.

"Paparazzi," he spat, gesturing at the camera she held, lip curled in disgust.

Liz stared in disbelief. "You have got to be kidding me."

"Dead serious, I assure you. You will be allowed to retrieve your belongings, and you will leave." He suddenly noticed the notebook at her feet. "The notebook stays."

"I am not the bloody paparazzi!" Liz's voice rose. "I paid good money to spend the summer here, hoping for a little peace and quiet. Why in the name of heaven would the paparazzi even care about this place?" He startled, giving her a searching look that left her feeling rattled. "If my camera bothers you, too bad. There was nothing in the paperwork that said I couldn't use one. And if you think I'm handing over my notebook, you're certifiably insane. I'm not sure what your problem is, but you seriously need to get over yourself, buddy."

For several minutes they simply stared at each other. Liz fought the urge to fidget; the way he looked at her, taking her measure, made her want to pick a fight. *Or throw something at his pretty face.* At last, he took a step back.

"You're not a paparazzo, nor are you working for any slimy, intrusive publications?"

"No," Liz snapped. "I wouldn't stoop to such levels. And if I did," she raised an eyebrow, "I wouldn't get caught."

Darcy coughed suddenly, as if masking an impulse to laugh. "Then you may stay."

"You're all kindness," Liz rolled her eyes.

"Just watch where you aim your camera," he muttered, before turning and stalking away.

"So that's the man behind Pemberley," Liz growled. "His reputation in town is deserved. Wait'll

Jane hears about this. Oh!" The *Star Wars* theme blasted from her cell, at full volume. "Crap, crap, crap, where is that phone?" Scrambling, Liz found it a few feet away just as it beeped alerting her to a missed call. *Figures*, she sighed, thumbing her passcode as she flopped back on the grass, returning Jane's call.

"How did you know I was thinking about you?"

"Because I have news to share," Jane laughed in reply. "Where are you anyway, sounds like you're in a hurricane."

"Sorry, I'm trying to do some work outside, and just had the most outrageous encounter with Grumpus. Which is what I was needing to tell you about."

"Who on earth is Grumpus?"

"None other than the lord and master of Pemberley. Lovely man, simply oozing good manners and charm. Get this Janie, he thought I was paparazzi, and tried to kick me off his land!"

"What? How did you – nevermind, I have a feeling I don't want to know."

"Hey now, I can handle myself around rich and snotty. I lived in New York, remember? He's just another obnoxious man with too much money. And he's pretty," Liz laughed. "But oh, that paparazzi bit ticked me off. Seriously? Just because I was sitting here with a notebook and camera? Dude needs to get over himself – and I told him as much."

"Hmm," Jane murmured.

"What?"

"What what?"

"I know you. That's a very significant hmm, Jane Bennet."

Jane laughed. "Sounds like he got under your skin is all."

"Mmm," Liz rolled her eyes. "Anyway, you have news?"

"Well," Jane drawled, "what would you say if I told you I went on a date last night?"

Sitting bolt upright, Liz sputtered. "What!" She coughed, while Jane laughed on the other end of the line. "Okay, I'm breathing again. A date? Like, a real date? With a man?"

"No, a pretend date with a unicorn," Jane quipped. "Of course it was a date with a man, goofball."

"Just to clarify: you went on a real date with a real man."

"Yes, I did. Last night. His name is Charlie," Jane added. "And he's adorable," she giggled.

"Does Charlie have a last name?"

"Bingley," Jane chirped. "He's a history professor at Abbey College in Northanger, but he's rented the Phillips House for the summer."

"Hmm," Liz murmured. "And how did you meet this history professor?"

"He walked into Bella Gelato one day, and we smiled at each other," Jane sighed.

"Hey, wait a second," Liz interrupted. "Is this the guy who walked in when I was there? The one you made sappy goo-goo eyes at, smiling like a Hollywood cliché? Average height, dark goatee, very hometown charming – except his jeans obviously cost more than my electric bill?"

"Yes, that's him," Jane agreed. "He's been coming in every day, and we've progressed from smiling to talking. And he asked me to dinner."

"And you said yes. Because it was a date," Liz prodded.

"Yes!" Jane's smile could be heard over the line.

"And you didn't tell me about this because..."

"I didn't want to jinx it," Jane admitted. "I wanted to make sure it wasn't just dinner, but like, an actual first date."

"And?"

"Oh Lizzie," Jane sighed, "he's wonderful. I mean, I was pretty sure he was, but dinner last night – he took me to Gardiner's, you know, down by the river? And he's so *nice*, Liz."

Liz smiled. "Someone's got a crush," she cooed in a sing-song voice.

"I can't wait for you to meet him, but Lizzie," Jane paused.

"Don't tell me, lemme guess – filthy rich?"

"How'd you know?"

"You don't rent the Phillips House for the summer without having more money than sense. Don't fuss – I'll give him the benefit of the doubt, since he's a professor," she laughed.

"Good. Liz, he's not like the hypothetical rich men who've soured you on the species."

"Not hypothetical, very real. However, I'm giving your Charlie a chance. He had the sense to pick you – that counts for something. And won't Momma be thrilled! Now, tell me everything."

Chapter 3

Engrossed in her thoughts, Liz didn't see the young woman kneeling in the path until she literally tripped over her. With a yelp, Liz fell in a tangle of arms and legs.

"I am so, so sorry," she gasped, catching her breath and trying to extricate herself from the other woman. "I wasn't watching where I was going – I'm usually the only person in these woods, and –" she stopped, realizing the woman was laughing so hard tears streamed down her face. "Are you okay?" Liz asked with concern.

With visible effort, the other woman managed to almost stop laughing. "I thought *I* was the only one who came this far into the woods," she said with a giggle. "Totally my fault, I should know better than to stop in the trail like that – at least you weren't running. I'm Ginny, by the way," she added.

"I'm Liz," she answered. "If you're sure you're okay, let's agree to share the blame."

"Deal. And this will be our little secret. I've been lectured many times about 'not being aware of my surroundings', and 'taking foolish chances,'" she crooked her fingers in air quotes. "I *wasn't* aware of my surroundings this time, so the less my big brother knows the better," she smiled impishly.

"I have an older sister," Liz smiled in return, "I can totally relate. What were you doing?"

Ginny blushed. "I was running and thought I saw something in the trail. So I was backtracking, see if I could figure out what I'd seen."

Liz stiffened. "It wasn't a snake was it? They definitely make you think your eyes are playing tricks, and there are some truly nasty ones around here."

"Oh no," Ginny shook her head. "It wasn't anything alive. I don't think. It was something shiny." She tilted her head thoughtfully. "Probably just mica, huh?"

"Probably," Liz nodded. "Or it could have been a drink tab or some other small piece of metal."

Ginny laughed, leaning close to whisper conspiratorially. "Ever since I learned this area is known for its gems, I've been hoping to find one. I chase sparkles and glints in the dirt far more than I should admit."

Liz smiled. "You can chase the sparkles all day, but the most precious stone you'll find that way is a quartz with heavy mica veins. The real gems keep their colors hidden, and fade into the background."

Ginny's face fell. "Oh. Then I *have* been chasing figments." She sighed, "I know it's silly, but when I learned about the gems..." her voice trailed off.

"If you know how to look, you can find rubies, sapphires, garnets – among others." Liz nudged the girl's shoulder. "I could help you; I have an inside connection."

"Really? You don't even know me, why would you help me? Especially since it's so silly." Ginny tilted her head. With her long hair sliding out of a messy side ponytail, still sitting in the path, the girl looked very young. *There's something about her I like. She's young and naive, but adorably so. I wonder what her story is,* Liz mused.

"My family has made a living helping make silly wishes come true," she offered. Seeing Ginny's confusion, she explained, "my great-granddaddy started Longbourne Mines."

"Oh!" Ginny's eyes widened. "You mean that place on the other side of Meryton with the hayrides?"

Liz scrunched her nose. "That's the one. A cousin is running the place now; he's a little obsessed with 'entertainment culture,'" she rolled her eyes, "thus the shades of Vegas. But I promise, you can still find gems. In fact," Liz continued, standing and offering a hand down to the other girl, "I'll do you one better."

"How's that?"

"I'll spare you the agony of navigating your way through the maze and midway," Liz laughed. "I know where the dirt is stored, and it's been a hot minute since I've panned myself. I've got to put in an appearance at a family meeting tomorrow anyway; while I'm there, I'll grab us a couple buckets and screens, and we can have a rock party."

"Buckets of dirt? Screens?" Ginny blinked. "I know I'm a city girl, but huh?"

Liz laughed. "You don't actually mine in a gem mine, at least not one like ours. We handle the preliminary work, selling buckets of dirt that you pan in water, with a screen, washing the dirt away and see what's left. Some operations sell stocked buckets with pre-cut stones, guaranteeing customers leave with something 'valuable' – hoping to also sell their lapidary services. Longbourne buckets aren't stocked like that, though Daddy did always make sure there was a chance for *something*. We have more uncut native rocks, and my sister and I used to spend a great deal of time poking around the washout, seeing what tourists let slip by just because it wasn't obviously precious."

"Ooooh," Ginny grinned. "I like the sound of this. We can do that here?"

"Sure," Liz agreed. "We just need a water hose or something – I'm not sure Grumpus would appreciate us muddying up the river."

"Who?"

"Oh, sorry. I meant Darcy," Liz shrugged. "I try to avoid him, but when I'm not so lucky, we butt heads. I call him Grumpus Maximus when I complain to my sister Jane."

"Ooooh, I see." Ginny's eyes twinkled. "No, he probably wouldn't like the river getting muddy. Luckily, I know the perfect place, river access and absolute privacy, and Darcy never has to know."

Liz looked at the girl, noting the mischief in her eyes. "Okay, deal. Sounds as if you've had a run-in or two with our charming host," she smirked. "Glad I'm not the only one."

"Darcy's mostly harmless," she shrugged dismissively. "But any chance to ruffle his feathers is a chance I'm going to take."

"You're not a total newbie, huh?"

Ginny laughed, "oh no, definitely not. Darcy and I go way back, if you can believe it," she winked.

"Alright then, we shall ruffle his feathers and see what treasures the earth has to offer. Assuming I survive a blind date tonight," she made a face, "and manage to procure our gem buckets tomorrow – the rest of my week is free. When would you like to have your first panning experience?"

"How about Friday? Day after tomorrow I have to run errands with my aunt," Ginny scrunched her nose, "so knowing I have an adventure planned will help me survive."

"Lord, I know that feeling!" Liz exclaimed. "Bribes are the only way I survive family gatherings."

Laughing, they began to walk toward the main gardens, talking and laughing easily. Liz was impressed to learn Ginny had just graduated *summa cum laude* from Abbey College in three years' time. When Ginny discovered Liz was a writer, she got a scheming look in her eyes, though a strange expression crossed her face when Liz begrudgingly admitted her most recent job was with Dot-Com Weddings. Liz wondered about it, but decided not to pursue her curiosity. Before parting company they agreed to meet at the picnic tables Friday morning; as Liz walked on toward her cabin, she realized meeting Ginny had quite literally knocked her worrisome thoughts out of mind. *And I'm not going to revisit them,* she decided. *There's no telling what harebrained scheme Colin has cooked up, and tomorrow will come sooner than wanted anyway. Besides, if I don't survive the blind date tonight, I won't have to worry about it,* she chuckled, before glancing at the clock. *Shoot, I've got to hurry or Charlie will be here and I'll still be in muddy jeans.*

Chapter 4

Every small town had its hotspot, the local watering hole where everyone seemed to gather. Lucas Lodge was that place for Meryton, and Liz had missed the familiarly shabby ambiance during her stint in New York. *If I have to go on a blind date with Jane, at least I get a good meal*, she sighed. *I wonder what Charlie's friend is like, and why Jane refused to get any details*, she mused, glancing at her sister riding shotgun in Charlie's extended cab pickup. *He's got to be as rich as Charlie, from what little has been said, so he'll definitely be a playboy*, she decided, *there's no way two rich guys as nice as Charlie exist in the same circles.* She sighed quietly, and reminded herself of the breadsticks in her future.

In the month and a half she'd been home, Liz had watched her older sister bloom. Despite her career, or perhaps because of it, Liz never believed in "love at first sight" until she witnessed it firsthand. There could be no other explanation for the sudden and inexplicable bond between Jane and Charlie. Liz was used to seeing men make fools of themselves over her quiet sister, but until Charlie came along, Jane never noticed her would-be lovers. Jane would only laugh when Liz teased her about making half the county and all the tourists fall madly in love with her. Even now, Liz often found herself wondering if Charlie realized Jane was far more smitten than she appeared – her natural modest reserve masking the giddiness brimming behind her smile. *Here's hoping Charlie is smitten enough to see Jane through the shy stage*, Liz smiled to herself, watching Charlie fight to keep her eyes off her sister and on the road before them.

Pulling into the Lucas Lodge lot, Liz was surprised to see a familiar figure pacing back and forth on the sidewalk, engrossed in yet another intense phone call. *Every time I see him, he seems to be in the middle of an angsty crisis. Does he ever not move in stalk-mode, or growl into the phone*, she wondered. *And what on earth is so complicated about his life that he's a perpetual tornado?* She shook her head, Grumpus's frustrated energy apparent even at this distance. *At least I don't have to eat dinner with him.*

"This can't be good," Charlie muttered under his breath. Before Liz could ask what he meant, he was out of the truck and assisting Jane – and herself – out.

"What is it about guys and big trucks?" Liz teased, accepting his hand as she jumped down. "I'm not exactly a hobbit, but climbing up here is like climbing into a treehouse."

"There's your answer," Charlie winked. "Boys never grow up, but we do learn how to take our hideouts with us."

Laughing, the three moved toward the building, just as Grumpus's call ended. Liz nodded, preparing to walk past him into the Lodge, but Charlie stopped her with a "sorry we're late, Will," as he clapped the other man's shoulder.

Liz stopped and stared. *Oh no, no, no, no,* she thought uneasily. *This cannot be happening.* "Jane," she whispered, leaning close. "Jane," she said again, pinching her sister when she refused to meet her gaze. "Please tell me that is not my date. Please, I'm begging you."

Jane turned toward Liz with too-innocent eyes. "I know you hate blind dates," Jane smiled, "but he is Charlie's best friend. How bad can it be?"

"Janie," Liz sighed, but before she could explain her horror at the scene unfolding, the men turned toward them.

"Liz," Charlie smiled, "I'd like you to meet my buddy, Will Darcy. Will," he winked at his friend, "your gorgeous date for the evening is Jane's sister Liz."

Liz smiled politely, wondering how this would play out. To her surprise, Grumpus – *Will Darcy,* she reminded herself – extended his hand and flashed a dazzling smile. *Of course he has perfect teeth. And dimples.*

"Nice to meet you," he said, all charm and civility.

"Likewise," she murmured, with a half-arched eyebrow.

"Liz is staying at Pemberley for the summer, Will," Charlie offered. "I'm surprised you've not run into each other."

"Ah," Will had the grace to look flummoxed.

"You know I keep weird hours and avoid people, Charlie," Liz laughed.

Charlie nodded, "I forget. Will's not one for being social either. Now it makes sense," he smiled. "Shall we go in? I hear the breadsticks are to die for," he winked at Liz.

"That's the only reason I'm here, darlin'! No offense," she added, glancing at Will, holding the door for everyone to file in.

"None taken," he smiled. "I've a similar motivation myself."

As Charlie finally decided on a song, slipping his quarters into the old fashioned jukebox, Liz wondered whether she'd spend the entire number in silence. Will, though painfully polite, had yet to voluntarily contribute to the conversation. *He does make for nice eye candy*, she mused, sipping her tea and glancing across the table. When Charlie and Jane left the booth in favor of the dance floor, Will turned sideways, stretching his long legs under the table along the bench seat and leaning against the wall, watching the crowd. The pose was exceptionally flattering, *the man must know he has a glorious profile* she thought, but did not encourage conversation. The familiar strains of Frank Churchill's ballad "Love Me Tomorrow" drifted from the speakers, and Liz smiled.

"Oh I love this song," she sighed. "I always feel bad admitting that – as a general rule I detest love songs – but it's the perfect love song, don't you think?" Will seemed not to hear. "Earth to William," she teased. "Did you know Frank Churchill wrote this last year for his secret love, Jane Fairfax – I knew her in

New York actually, very nice girl, but rather aloof. You'd like her, she doesn't talk to people either. What're the odds Charlie knows that story and picked this song on purpose? Of course, after the hullabaloo last year when Frank went rogue, I think everyone knows the story of the song. Maybe that's why I like it," she tapped her chin thoughtfully, "because of the story. Whatcha think?" When Will steadfastly refused to acknowledge her chatter, Liz picked up a discarded straw wrapper and tossed it in his direction.

"If you must know," Will began, turning toward her at the exact moment the balled up wrapper reached his side of the table – and landed in his mouth. As he sputtered and spat the paper on the table, Liz fought a rising tide of laughter.

"What in the name of good sense were you thinking?" Will growled, surprise and irritation mingled in his eyes. That was all it took to push Liz over the edge; as she laughed, Will glowered. Unfortunately, the more annoyed he looked, the harder Liz laughed.

Returning to the booth as the song ended, Jane looked back and forth between Liz's tear-streaked smile and Will's thunderous glare. "What on earth happened?"

Liz hiccupped a laugh, but before she could explain, Will answered, "it's my fault, I was ignoring her."

As Liz stared at him in surprise, Charlie chuckled. "You still haven't learned not to ignore the ladies, have you? Whatever she did, I'm sure you deserved more. You must forgive my friend, Liz," he continued, "he never learned how to talk to pretty girls. Perhaps you can teach him this summer."

Will and Liz both blushed deeply in response. "I am perfectly capable of talking to girls, pretty or otherwise, *Charles*," Will growled. "I have a lot on my mind," he added with a significant look, "and warned you I might not make the best company tonight."

"So you did," Charlie agreed. "Well, no harm, no foul. I'm sure Liz won't hold it against you, and you'll both agree to join us again," he smiled.

"If I can, I will, but I make no promises," Will muttered. "We don't all have a professor's schedule, you know."

Charlie laughed. "Jane told me the same thing!"

"Apparently our professor here has grand plans for the summer, during prime working hours," she said, elbowing him playfully in the ribs. "I told him the only person with a schedule that flexible was Liz, but even she works some days."

Will cocked an eyebrow Liz's way. "I thought Charlie told me you work with Jane," he asked.

"I do sometimes," Liz replied. "But that's usually when she's in a fix, or I'm bored to tears. The rest of the time I do my own work," she finished, vaguely waving a hand.

Jane slid into the booth, gesturing for Charlie to sit. He pouted adorably, but climbed over Will's still-sprawled feet and waved the waitress over for another pitcher of tea.

"When I first opened the store," Jane began, "Liz was the best help I could ask for, always ready to pitch in and get her hands dirty – or answer my endless questions," she laughed. "I guess she learned by osmosis, spending all that time in Daddy's office, because when it came to setting up business, she was a pro."

"I wouldn't go that far," Liz murmured, blushing.

"I would," Jane countered, "and since I'm telling the story, what I say goes."

"Fine, fine," Liz conceded. "Try to stay close to the truth," she added with a smile.

"Why didn't your father help you?" Will asked. "If Liz learned enough by observation to offer as much assistance as you say, wouldn't he have been the logical choice to help you?"

Liz and Jane exchanged a quick, silent glance before Liz answered. "Daddy died 5 years ago. He left each of us a generous inheritance, completely unexpected, and Jane used hers to open Bella Gelato."

Will flinched, "I'm sorry. I had no idea, and shouldn't have asked such a question."

"It's okay," Jane smiled reassuringly. "You had no way of knowing. It's a fair question, and I have no doubt Daddy would have happily offered assistance. In his place, Liz was my hero. Without her, Bella Gelato wouldn't be the same. I keep asking her to come on as a partner, but she insists one sister in gelato is plenty," she laughed.

"I'm ever so glad she did help you," Charlie said. "Without Bella Gelato, I wouldn't have met you!"

"This is a very small town, Charlie," Will drawled. "I'm sure you'd have run into her sometime or other."

"It's true," Liz nodded. "If you spend the summer here, you'd definitely run into Janie. Just maybe not in such a storybook way."

"Maybe, but I'm glad all the same," Charlie grinned. "If Jane is the uncontested Gelato Queen of Meryton, what's your claim to fame, Liz?" Charlie cocked his head in a distinctly puppy manner. "I think Jane mentioned you're a writer, when you're not being her personal business fairy?"

"I am a writer," she acknowledged. "I've just completed a 3 year gig in New York," she added, crinkling her nose slightly. "My original intention was to live off my inheritance while I wrote the next great American novel. After helping Jane get things up and running, I realized I'd rather do something. I like earning my money, and I didn't want to become just another trust fund baby. Oomph," she grunted, as Jane's elbow made abrupt contact with her ribcage. Charlie snorted, choking back a laugh. "Sorry," Liz muttered.

"No worries," Charlie grinned. "Trust fund babies are horrible creatures, eh, Will?" Will grunted, preoccupied straightening the sugar packets.

"Anyway. Everybody says New York is the place to be if you want to be somebody in publishing, so I decided to take a wild chance. A fraternity brother of Daddy's had just retired from *The Post*, and we emailed. He found a position for me at a startup, nothing glamorous but the pay would let me live somewhere safe. I enjoyed helping Jane with Bella Gelato, and the idea of working on a writing project from the ground up was too tempting to pass up" Liz pulled a face. "He neglected to mention the startup was focused on everything weddings, with a particular emphasis on the successes of online dating."

"Dot-Com Weddings? My sister is obsessed with that site!" Charlie interjected. "And I do mean that literally," he added with a shudder.

Will stiffened almost imperceptibly as Liz nodded, his whole being shifting slightly, as if trying to express less interest than he actually felt. *That's weird, and very similar to the response Ginny had*, Liz noted, before turning her attention to Charlie.

"I don't doubt that," Liz nodded. "Obsession is eerily accurate for describing nearly everyone associated with the project, readers and employees."

"But not you?" Charlie asked, raising an eyebrow.

Liz shook her head, "definitely not me. I did learn a lot, but never did I fall under the spell. Jane will tell you the experience made me even more pragmatic, that I've not a romantic bone in my body," she added wryly.

"It's true," Jane exclaimed. "I don't know how she's going to write a convincing novel, let alone fall in love herself. She was already a skeptic, and I told her not to move to New York. When I found out her new job was all weddings and romance all the time?" She sighed.

"Hey," Liz protested with a laugh. "I can write the stuff just fine!"

"Liz Bennet isn't a romantic, eh?" Charlie asked. "May curious minds inquire why not?"

"She has too many rules," Jane rolled her eyes.

"Not true!" Liz laughed. "Okay, maybe I do," she conceded, as Jane gave her a sideways glance.

"Good grief," Charlie laughed. "Will has rules too – y'all really are perfect for each other."

"Oh, I don't know about that," Liz replied, as Will shot Charlie an annoyed glance. "My number one rule is 'Just say no to rich men,' and I'm afraid that puts Will outta the running." She smiled innocently, as Jane groaned.

"I'm glad Jane doesn't follow your rules," Charlie exclaimed. "I'd love to know more, but just realized what time it is – we should probably be heading home, eh?"

"Hey Will, since you're both headed to Pemberley, you mind taking Liz home?" Charlie asked.

Liz began to protest, but Will waved aside her concerns with an "of course, it only makes sense." Waving goodnight, Charlie and Jane drove off in the direction of Bella Gelato, leaving Liz and Will staring at each other.

"I'm parked over here," Will said, turning and walking toward the far end of the lot. Walking beside him, Liz took a long look at the Jeep parked in the last space.

"*This* is your car?"

Will raised an eyebrow. "Watch your tone, she's sensitive," he said, patting the hood with affection. "We've been through a lot together, this old girl and me," he smiled sheepishly. "She's old, yes, but reliable. And clean," he added.

"Don't get me wrong, I'm all about good old fashioned American engineering," Liz replied, "but this is *so* not the car I'd expect Will Darcy, lord and master of Pemberley Acres, to drive."

Will winced. "Do you have to put it that way? Thanks," he added with a sideways, almost sheepish, glance, "for not mentioning our previous – ah, encounters."

"You mean the day you accused me of being paparazzi and writing for a tabloid?" Liz spun to face him, hands on her hips. "Or maybe you're referring to the day you called me *a gold-digging spy* because I was wearing a Longbourne Mines shirt on the grounds of Pemberley? Newsflash, buddy: I didn't not tell them out of courtesy to you. Jane knows anyway – she just doesn't realize you were you. I only went along with your charade tonight because I didn't want to embarrass Charlie."

Will looked nonplussed for about thirty-five seconds, before his jaw tightened. "I'm sorry," he ground out, "but if you saw things from my perspective, you would be suspicious too."

"And what perspective is that exactly?" Liz snapped. "The perspective of generations of wealth and a family name that makes the earth bow at your feet? The perspective of a lord among men, old money blue-blood aristocracy come to improve our humble lives with your benevolent condescension? You refuse to remotely consider being part of the community. Every time I see you, you're snapping and snarling. You have insulted and derided myself and my chosen occupation on numerous occasions. You may be playing Lord of the Manor at Pemberley, living in the big house and helping people commune with nature by working the land, but you clearly have no understanding of the Southern graces that should accompany such a position. You, sir," she spat the word, "are no different from any other spoiled brat playboy living off his daddy's money. So no, I'd rather not see things your way if it's all the same to you."

"That's enough, *Elizabeth*," he snarled, enough bite in the growl to make Liz take a step back. "Of all people – is it possible for you to *not* see the money? To maybe see me as a person with struggles of my own, who might be having a bad day? No, of course not. Because you've got some ridiculous notion in your head." He stopped, taking a deep breath and dragging his hand across his face.

"What in thunder are you talking about?" Liz's eyes blazed.

"Nothing I'm going to talk about tonight," Will said, his voice chillingly polite. Reaching behind her to open the passenger door, he gestured, "let's just go home. There's been quite enough said for one night."

"I'd rather walk," Liz muttered under her breath. "Hey!" She squeaked in surprise as Will all but lifted her into the Jeep.

"Whatever else you may think of me," he sighed, "I'm not a monster. No lady walks home on my watch, even in Meryton. Charles was right – we're going to the same place anyway." The set of his jaw made Liz wonder if he'd rather slam the door he closed gently, before walking around to the driver's seat. "If it makes you feel better, while the engine is running we don't have to say a word to each other," he said, flexing his grip on the steering wheel.

"Fine by me," Liz said, looking out the passenger window. "We can't stand each other, why make this situation worse than it has to be?"

Will growled something under his breath she couldn't quite catch, as he turned the key and pulled out of the lot. The ride to Pemberley was fiercely silent, tension crackling in the air. Liz stared steadfastly out the window, watching the lights of town fade into the blackness, listening to Will's steady breathing. *It sounds like he's counting, trying to breathe himself down,* she thought. *Good, I'm glad he's mad. Someone needs to give him a taste of his own medicine – you can't boss people around and make crazy statements just because you have money.*

Finally reaching her cabin, Liz was halfway up the path before Will had the Jeep in park, tossing a "thanks," over her shoulder.

"Elizabeth, wait," Will called, slamming his door.

"What?" Liz asked flatly, turning to face him.

"I told you, no lady walks home on my watch – I'm going to make sure you get inside alright."

"You could do that from the Jeep," she arched an eyebrow.

"I believe in walking a lady to her door," he sighed. "About earlier –"

"I don't want to hear it," she interrupted. "We can play nice around Charlie and Jane, but let's face it: that's as far as this is gonna go."

"Because you don't want it to go farther." A statement, not a question. Will's face was impassive, blue eyes darkly unreadable in the glow of the porchlight.

"Why would I?" Liz asked, hands on her hips. "With the exception of dinner tonight, you've been insulting and rude. Sorry honey, but your money and swagger means nothing to me – totally not impressed."

Will raised an eyebrow. "Have you ever considered how hypocritical your argument is?"

"Excuse me?"

"You hold a grudge against anyone with money, yet you inherited a sizeable sum. *You* are one of the wealthy you profess to abhor. What makes you different from other trust fund babies? What makes you above the degradation of money? It certainly isn't your willingness to accept others – you've made it perfectly clear you won't acknowledge me as a person, as your equal, because of the so-called 'rank' associated with my fortune." As he spoke, Will stepped closer until a hand's breadth separated them.

Liz opened and closed her mouth; she had the uncomfortable feeling there was some truth to Will's assertion, but no words came. His eyes seared into hers, scorching like blue flame. Under the weight of his gaze, Liz felt a queer hitch in her chest. *Oh no you don't,* she thought. *This is definitely not the time for hormones to offer an opinion.*

At length, Will took a step back. "Think about it, Elizabeth," he said, voice low. "I know I'm not perfect, but neither are you."

Before she could respond, he turned and walked back to the Jeep. He waited until she finally stopped staring after him and let herself in the door. Once inside, she peeked out the window, watching him take a last look at the cabin before driving into the night.

"What just happened?" she asked softly, feeling as if she'd lost something.

Chapter 5

When Liz parked under the old oak the next afternoon, Jane was still in her car, talking animatedly on her cell. *Must be Charlie*, Liz thought, laughing as her sister gestured expressively.

"You know they can't see you when you do that," Liz teased, as Jane's call concluded and she joined her sister.

"Oh hush," she laughed, walking toward the house. "Oh, Lizzie," she paused, giving Liz a guilty look. "I am *so sorry* about last night. I had no idea Charlie's friend was Grumpus! I swear I don't remember him saying a thing about Pemberley."

"It's okay, really." Liz shrugged. "We managed to mind our manners during dinner, it's fine."

Jane stared at her sister. "What happened?"

"Um, we may have 'exchanged words' after y'all left."

"What happened?"

"Okay fine. We had a smashing argument, of sorts, which I feel a little ridiculous about today. And I think he considered kissing me, but that's probably because I've watched too many rom-coms with you," she laughed. "I found this when I got back from a run this afternoon," Liz drew an envelope from her bag.

"What is it? Where did you find it?" Jane tilted her head in confusion.

"A letter, I s'pose. It was tucked in the screen door of my cabin."

"Hmm," Jane mused, as they resumed walking toward the house. "From Will?"

"Mmhmm. I haven't read it yet. I didn't want to have – whatever this is – floating around in my head while dealing with Colin and the trick up his sleeve."

"Smart, though I don't know how you can resist opening it," Jane laughed.

"Whose car is that?" Liz wondered, noticing for the first time a very shiny, very red convertible parked near the porch.

"Your guess is as good as mine," Jane shrugged. "Maybe it's Colin's?"

"As much as I hate to admit it, that car is too tacky for Colin," Liz laughed. "Maybe it's part of the surprise."

Taking a last curious look, they let themselves in the house and were instantly assaulted by their mother's flock of toy poodles.

"Janie? Liz, is that you?" Momma's voice carried from the kitchen.

"No, it's Jack the Ripper," Liz muttered under her breath. "Oomph," she grunted, as Jane's elbow made contact with her ribs. "You and that elbow need to chill. I'm going to end up with a permanent bruise, and not be able to wear a bikini!"

Jane laughed, and rolled her eyes. "Because you wear a bikini *so often*," she teased. "Come on, we better get in there before she comes looking."

"Do I have to? We could still sneak out, grab something to-go and hide out at my cabin," Liz offered hopefully, allowing Jane to drag her down the hall.

"Come in, come in, and let me tell you – you'll never guess, Janie, never guess. Would you believe it? I hardly knew what to think when Colin told me, but it's true – I've seen it with my own eyes!" As her words tumbled over each other, excitement raising her voice an octave, Momma gave Liz and Jane hurried hugs and pushed them toward the table where a massive mountain of papers warred for space with a half dozen pink boxes from Hill's Bakery.

"Hill's, huh? What's the occasion?" Liz asked, lifting one of the lids to peek inside. "Ohmigosh, turtle cheesecake. Can I skip dinner and just eat this? What's in the rest?"

"Stop that," Momma said, swatting Liz's hand away. "I didn't raise you in a barn, Elizabeth, show some manners."

As Liz laughed, Colin strolled through the back door looking smugger than ever. *Isn't he the cat who ate the canary,* Liz thought. *Wonder what he's done this time?*

"Liz, Jane," he smiled broadly. "You made it! Since Liz came back, we've barely seen either of you. Though I have it on good authority that you, Jane," he added with a significant waggle of his eyebrows, "have made quite the conquest."

Even as Jane flushed, Colin puffed his chest out. "You're not the only one lucky in love, Jane," he smiled. "I've had similarly good fortune."

Liz raised her eyebrows. "Oh yes, Lizzie," he nodded. "After years of unwelcome, despairing solitude, I have found love, and am the happiest of men."

Jane coughed discreetly, managing an "I'm happy for you, Colin," that sounded sincere.

"Thank you, Janie," he preened. "You'll get to meet her tonight – ah, here she is now."

Coming in from the dining room were Catherine D and a younger woman. *So we finally meet the infamous Catherine D,* Liz mused. *She looks so much like her publicity stills it's creepy.* The thought made her choke back a giggle, earning a raised eyebrow from Jane.

"Catherine," Colin purred, "I'd like you to meet my cousins, Jane and Liz." Catherine gave them an appraising glance. "And this," Colin continued, wrapping an arm around the waist of the second woman, "is Catherine's daughter – and my fiancée – CherryAnn."

Silence met this announcement, as CherryAnn offered a nervous smile.

Jane was the first to recover. "Congratulations! How did you meet?"

"As you know, Catherine has been an invaluable resource as I've taken over the day-to-day running of Longbourne Mines," Colin began. "She often mentioned her daughter, but I've never had the privilege of meeting her – until my last Berkshire Cruise. CherryAnn was vacationing with friends, we met on deck by chance, and it was love at first sight. Imagine my surprise and delight to discover the woman of my dreams was the daughter of my esteemed mentor!"

"Oh, well that worked out perfectly didn't it?" Liz asked, earning another elbow to the ribs from Jane.

"Indeed. Things worked out so much better than I anticipated," Colin sighed happily. "In fact –"

"Liz, was it?" Catherine interrupted abruptly.

"Yes ma'am," Liz arched a curious eyebrow.

"I believe Colin mentioned you were staying at Pemberley this summer."

"Uh, yes, I am."

"And you are acquainted with the owner of Pemberley, William Darcy." Catherine's tone was almost accusatory, and Liz felt her temper flare.

"I am," she replied frostily.

"Oh how wonderful," Colin interjected. "You must introduce us, Liz. I want to discuss some partnership ideas with him."

Catherine shot him a withering look before turning her attention back to Liz. "You are aware of his standing in society."

"Umm –"

"And you have placed yourself in a position to seduce your way into his life in a manner directly beneficial to your ambitions as a writer, and social climbing heiress."

"What the hell?"

"Elizabeth!" Momma gasped.

Catherine didn't bat an eye. "You know perfectly well what I'm talking about. You inherited some money, Elizabeth," she sneered, "but you lack the pedigree my nephew would give you. By inserting yourself into his life, you gain a social standing unattainable on your own, as well as increased financial backing for your scribbling."

"I assure you, nothing could be further from the truth," Liz snapped. "My decision to stay at Pemberley for the summer had nothing to do with your nephew, and everything to do with wanting peace and quiet. Yes, I am acquainted with Will, but I never sought his company and the relationship is quite accidental."

"You admit there is a relationship?" Catherine looked startled.

"Of a sort," Liz retorted. "I assure you it was born of no plan on my part."

"If you have any desire to find success in your career, you will cease all contact with William."

"Are you threatening me?"

"Of course not," Colin found his voice again. "Catherine would never –"

"It's not a threat. It's a promise. You will keep your distance from William."

"I will not," Liz snapped. "I will talk to him as often as *we* decide. I will not be bullied by you and your pretentious assumptions. Nor will I stay here to be insulted. Congratulations, Colin," she said, turning and nodding to the bewildered couple. "I sincerely wish you every happiness, but I hope you understand why I cannot stay."

To her surprise, CherryAnn mouthed "take me with you" and winked, while Colin stammered and Catherine gaped, as Liz walked out – back straight and head high – the poodles yapping in her wake.

Chapter 6

The steady gurgle of the river was soothing. Liz settled herself more comfortably on one of the broad flat stones in its stream. From childhood, she sought the solace of the river when her mind was racing. Often, like today, she preferred to find a seat in the water rather than on the banks. *This one is perfect,* she sighed. *Close enough I didn't get wet, but far enough out I'll know someone is coming.* She'd brought a quilt, but left it beside her, notebook and pen tucked in its folds. The corner of an envelope caught her attention, as she reached for her bottle of tea. Crinkling her nose, she pulled it free of the book, turning it over in her hands. The way "Elizabeth" was scrawled in a bold, hurried hand would have given her a hint at the sender, even without the embossed Pemberley Acres logo on the flap. *What can he possibly have to say that warrants a letter?* Liz wondered, running her thumb over the logo.

Thinking about Will Darcy triggered a whole new wave of thoughts, and Liz shook her head. *Why does that man annoy me so much? I can't even open this envelope, because I feel certain he's going to say something that will set me off. After last night, I don't know that I –* "Eeek!" Lip yelped, almost falling off the rock. A very large dog appeared out of nowhere, tail wagging in delight as he splashed his way onto Liz's rock.

"Beren! Heel!" Will's voice sliced through Liz's shock, even as she scrambled to keep herself and her various belongings on the rock. "Heel," he issued the command again, as he picked his way across the river.

"Easy fella," Liz murmured, catching the dog's collar, "there's a good boy. Sit?" The dog sat promptly, then flopped on his side, head in her lap and a contented grin on his whiskery face. "Well hello," she laughed, scratching his ears. "You're not shy, are ya, pretty boy?"

"I apologize for my dog's abysmal manners," Will apologized, stepping onto the rock. "I hope he hasn't ruined anything," he asked, glancing at Liz's scattered belongings.

"No, he's just a friendly giant," Liz laughed, bending to speak conspiratorially in the dog's ear. "You should give your master some pointers." To her surprise, Will lowered himself to sit next to her, laughing.

"My sister has often said I should let Beren be my ambassador," he admitted. "He's better at first impressions. Although I'm not sure about this river monster impersonation. Are you sure he hasn't destroyed anything?"

"My notebook was in the blanket – nothing fell into the water. Oh, where's –" she stopped, glancing around self-consciously. "Crap, crap, crap," she muttered under her breath.

"Here," Will's voice was low as he picked up the envelope. "You haven't read it?"

"It is from you," she said softly, not meeting his gaze.

"Please," he paused, as if searching for words. "I know I've given you little reason to believe me, but I – I have never intended to offend. I can't make you believe me, nor can I make you read this, but please," his voice dropped still lower, and he offered her the envelope. "Give me a chance to explain."

Giving him a hard stare, Liz reached to take the envelope, jumping slightly when their fingers brushed. "On one condition," she said, to cover her response.

"Oh?" Will raised an eyebrow, clenching his hand at his side.

So he felt it too, she noted silently, raising an eyebrow of her own. "Beren stays, and you go get lost in the woods."

"Fair enough," Will agreed with a laugh. "I'm not sure Beren would leave anyway," he shook his head. "You've made quite the conquest."

"Does he not like people?" Liz asked, running her hand down the dog's back.

"He's friendly, but not typically *that* friendly. But he is a good judge of character."

Liz looked up in surprise, but before she could comment, Will stood. "I'll leave you to your reading. When you finish," he hesitated. "When you've finished reading, if you decide in my favor, come up to the main house – Beren can show you the way if you tell him 'home'. And if you don't, just let him follow you back to your cabin and I'll collect him later." As he spoke, Will jumped lightly to the bank and strode into the woods.

"Your master is a strange, strange man, Beren," Liz said, shaking her head. "He almost seems human sometimes, like someone I could talk to, and we both know that's crazy." Beren's only response was to lick her chin. She looked at the envelope again. "What'd he say, fella? I guess it's now or never," she sighed.

Running her finger under the seal, she pulled out several sheets of cotton-soft paper, folded in half. *Oh sweet delight*, she sighed, *this is paper to make a girl swoon*. Laughing at herself, she unfolded the pages to see the Pemberley logo embossed across the top, Will's bold writing filling the pages. Leaning on Beren, she began to read.

Dear Elizabeth,

I deserved the scathing comments you made last night, and I must apologize, find some way to smooth things over - particularly since we will be in each other's presence frequently. I would also like to explain my perspective in all of this. I ask only that you read with an open mind.

First, let me address our first encounter, which - I admit - was uncalled for, if not bizarre. I have a younger sister, of whom I am very protective. She has a sizable trust fund of her own - and as I'm sure you know, a young woman of large fortune attracts attention and speculation. A few months ago, someone created an online dating profile in my sister's name, soliciting liaisons of a highly suspect nature. At the time, my sister had just begun a romantic relationship with an old family friend, and soon paparazzi were hawking pictures of their budding relationship alongside screenshots of the pseudo dating profile. I was able to silence the issue, but not before it was featured by several online gossip rags. Including, I'm sorry to say, Dot-Com Weddings. Thankfully, someone on staff there managed to present a more compelling story - using the fiasco as a teaching moment for others to be aware of their personal identity and safety in virtual relationships. In the aftermath of this nightmare, I have become even more vigilant about protecting our privacy - even now, fending off daily requests for information. When I saw you that day, with camera and notebook, I assumed you were here for a story. I didn't ask questions, and I did not behave as a Southern gentleman ought. I am sorry, and assure you I do possess better manners.

As for more complicated matters, I'm sure you are aware the anti-wealth sentiments you profess are not universally shared. Unfortunately, my experiences have taught me to be cautious, suspicious, always looking for underlying motives. When Charlie quickly became involved with a local girl, wanting me to meet her sister, and you seemed to materialize everywhere, warning bells started ringing. It appeared the single women of Meryton were on the prowl. As the recipient of decidedly unwelcome feminine attention in the past, I was instantly on guard, sure the quiet friendliness of Meryton had lulled me into a false sense of security. I apologize for things said to you, and - though you may not be aware of them - things said about you and your sister before the particulars were made clear.

Charlie assured me you and your sister are not in need of a rich husband, and would sympathize with our struggle. A refreshing discovery, though one I would have seen myself if I did not assume the worst. You are inclined to distrust and dislike rich men - I confess to distrusting single women, particularly those without fortune. It is a rational distrust, not unfounded, but my failing is in applying it too universally. I think we are alike in this regard. Perhaps we can work together to overcome these prejudices; learn to trust each other, if not the world at large.

Several of the accusations you hurled struck home, and in spite of my desire to keep private things private, I will share with you a little of the Darcy history. To gloss over much American history (ask Charlie, I'm sure he'd be happy to provide a more detailed explanation), after the Civil War, very few in the rice industry were able to bounce back. My family managed to hang on to the family land, slowly regaining fortune and standing. In addition to rice, my family expanded their holdings to include everything from tea to berries to prize sheep, resulting in very substantial economic gain. Following my father's death, and my subsequent inheritance, I began considering alternatives to our lifestyle. I freely admit I enjoy the comfort and ease afforded me by my family's money, but I want to be more than a rich man. I want to make a difference - in college I majored in both business and nonprofit studies, looking for the magic formula to make money work for better.

One day I saw an article on agritourism, and an idea took root. Combining the things I love about my family's heritage - working the land, protecting and nurturing a piece of property - with an educational focus that makes it all mean something. I started researching, learning everything I could, and making plans. I briefly considered using the Darcy plantation, but the Charleston area is awash with similar venues. After much deliberation, I sold the family property to someone looking to keep it running, and visited Meryton. I fell in love with the area, and began buying as much land as possible. I feel certain you're familiar with the Pemberley philosophy, what this place is all about. In a way, it feels as if I'm redeeming my family's fortune - we prospered where so many did not, and now I can give back in a meaningful way. I have no wish to be 'Lord and Master of Pemberley,' or throw my name and wealth around, and if I have given that impression I am deeply and sincerely apologetic.

Thank you for the favor of reading this; it is lengthy, but I feel an intense need to make myself clear to you - to gain your good opinion. I would like a chance to start over, to show you my true self.

With warmest regards,
William Darcy

"Well," she said aloud when she'd read the letter over twice. "I wish Jane were here," she told Beren. "I feel like someone took my brain, put it in a bucket, tossed it in the river and then fished it out again after a stretch of Class 4 rapids." Beren gave her a soulful stare, before sneaking a quick lick on her chin. "You get away with that because you're cute and I've got a weakness for whiskered muzzles, but watch yourself, fella. Not everyone kisses on the first date," she laughed. "Come on, let's go find the big house. I have the uncomfortable feeling I owe your master an apology." Standing, Liz gathered her belongings and carefully picked her way across the stones to the opposite bank. "I feel like an outlaw, slipping into enemy territory," she whispered to the dog splashing happily in the shallows. "Okay, Beren. Home." With an energetic shake, the dog began loping down the trail, stopping at the edge of the woods to look over his shoulder at Liz with a "ya coming?"-glance that made her laugh.

Together, they followed a surprisingly direct path through the woods and came to the edge of a clearing. "Whoa," Liz breathed, standing under the pines, looking with wide eyes. "No wonder he keeps this place off-limits to the public," she whispered. "I would never leave – here's the true heart of Pemberley."

The careful attention to maintaining the natural landscape was even more obvious here; terraced gardens leading to the house and a scattering of old trees spreading protective branches over all. *You'd never guess that house was new*, Liz thought, *it looks as if it's been here from the beginning.* A sprawling house, it reminded her of the Victorians on Northanger's Bath Street, with endless porches and carved woodwork. *It's a welcoming house,* she decided, *opening its arms to wanderers and loved ones.* The thought startled her, and the nudging of Beren's head against her hip prompted her to walk on. The closer she got to the house, the more uncertain Liz felt. How was she supposed to find Will? What should she say if anyone asked her why she was in the family area? Pausing at the fence-lined drive, Liz looked at the house and wondered whether she could dash back to the woods before anyone saw her.

"Elizabeth."

Liz spun to face him, strange relief flooding her at hearing his voice, though softer – kinder – than she was accustomed to hearing.

"You weren't barking, I didn't know you were there," she teased halfheartedly, wondering why she felt so unsettled and flustered.

"You read the letter," he said, taking a step closer.

"I did," she answered, looking down at Beren leaning protectively against her leg.

"And you came to the house," he took another step.

"I did," she shifted her bag on her shoulder.

"You came here to tell me off, didn't you?" Will asked, cocking his head to one side.

"What?" Liz looked up in surprise, eyes widening at the devilish grin on his face. *Be still my heart, those dimples.*

"I thought that'd get a response," he chuckled. "Shake on it and call a truce?" Will took another step closer, extending his hand.

"Truce," Liz agreed. As they shook, Beren suddenly took off down the drive, knocking Liz off balance. "Oh," she gasped, stumbling into Will's chest. His arm went around her reflexively, and she relaxed against him for a half beat. Will's arm tightened briefly before loosening. When she glanced up, the look in his eyes reflected every tangled thought and sensation in her own, making her breath catch. Feeling herself being drawn into the glacial blue of his eyes, Liz heard a voice saying "danger, Will Robinson: step away from the pretty rich man." Somewhere in the back of her mind she knew she should listen, but at the moment the question in his eyes made Liz think staying might be the better alternative. As his gaze flickered to her mouth, Beren's deep bark and the sudden braking of a car made them startle. Liz jumped backwards, a deep blush staining her cheeks. Will gave her an apologetic smile before turning to face the drive, muttering under his breath.

Liz groaned as she recognized the too-red convertible.

"You've met?" Will glanced at her in surprise.

"Unfortunately," Liz sighed. "Last night. I didn't realize I would have a repeat performance so soon," she pulled a face before remembering their connection. "Oh, I'm sorry – I didn't mean, and we just called truce–"

To her surprise, Will laughed. "Don't worry, I didn't expect a repeat performance just now either," he said. Turning he greeted the overdressed woman stepping out of the car. "Aunt Catherine," he said stiffly. "To what do I owe this unexpected surprise?"

"Fiddlesticks, William," Catherine sniffed. "You knew perfectly well I was in town."

"And you are supposed to be having lunch with Georgianna," he said evenly, though Liz could see his jaw clenching. At that moment, Ginny popped out of the passenger door, an apologetic look in her eyes.

"Oh!" Liz said softly, the pieces clicking into place.

"I was having lunch with Georgianna, until she mentioned having met one of the daughters of that Bennet woman. I questioned her, and discovered they have plans for tomorrow – William, you must not allow her to fraternize with this, this," Catherine paused, searching for a suitable epithet, while Liz edged slowly behind Will's tall frame. "That woman is not proper company for Georgianna," she continued. "I met the family last night, at Colin's bidding. The eldest is acceptable I suppose, but this 'Liz' your sister befriended – is the most obstinate, headstrong woman I've ever encountered."

Will choked back something suspiciously resembling a laugh, before Catherine continued severely, "William, she is a writer at that devilish internet wedding rag."

"I don't know what that has to do with anything," Ginny interjected.

"You don't know what you're saying, Georgianna. People of her ilk, parading around as 'writers,' only want one thing – the scoop. She's pretending to be nice to get the story. If I've seen it once, I've seen it a dozen times. No, Georgianna, you will not see that woman again."

"That's enough," Will growled.

Catherine bridled at his tone, but before she could respond Liz stepped into view, eyes blazing.

"If you have a problem with my association with your niece, I wonder that you would allow your daughter to marry into my family. I had no inkling of Ginny's background or family affiliation when we met, and knowing she's a Darcy changes nothing. As I told you last night, I have no ulterior motive – not where William is concerned, and definitely not about Ginny. She's a charming, articulate young lady whom I look forward to calling my friend." A charged silence followed. Ginny looked like she wanted to cheer but didn't dare.

"Where I'm concerned?" Will finally ventured.

"Don't ask," Liz said, continuing to stare down the fuming Catherine D. When the older woman didn't say anything, Liz gave Ginny a quick smile before turning to Will. "I –" she paused, not knowing what to say.

Will smiled, understanding in his eyes. "Make your escape while the getting's good," he said softly. "We'll talk later."

Liz smiled her thanks, and walked into the woods. "I've really got to talk to Jane," she muttered, pausing at the river and looking back towards the Darcy home.

Chapter 7

"So," Ginny smirked. "You and my brother, huh?"

Liz buried her face in her hands. "Here I was thinking you didn't notice," she groaned. "You let me get all the way here, and *then* pounce?"

Ginny laughed. "Hey, I learned the hard way if I want a real answer, the trick is to catch someone off guard. And," she waggled her eyebrows impishly, "since your face tells all, I'm not gonna apologize."

Liz swiped her hand through the water, sending water drops flying. "I should have known," she sighed, rolling her eyes. "However, I could get my revenge by not telling you which stones are which."

"What if I told you that Will and Aunt C got into a huge argument yesterday, after you bolted? Or," she continued with a grin, "what if I told you that Will has never looked at anyone the way he looks at you."

Liz cast a sideways glance at Ginny, making a noncommittal sound.

"Oh it's true," Ginny teased. "I had a hunch my bear of a brother's growling was because of a woman – I just didn't know who. When I tripped you the other day, and you called him Grumpus, I started wondering; my suspicions were proved yesterday."

"You mean he doesn't normally growl?" Liz looked up incredulously. "Since I met the man, he growls and barks more than speaking."

Ginny cocked her head slightly. "Okay, I'll admit he's particularly ferocious this summer, but I think he told you some of what's been going on?" Liz nodded, thinking of the letter she'd memorized rereading the night before. "*But,*" Ginny let the word linger, "he has never been so riled up about anyone. You, dear Elizabeth, got around his armor and under his skin, and it annoys the heck out of him. Mega kudos to you!"

Liz distractedly raised her hand to meet Ginny's high-five, confusion still evident in her eyes. "I thought you said he was – the fact that I annoy him is a good thing?" Liz finally asked.

"Oh yeah," Ginny nodded. "Haven't you heard that phrase about strong emotions? Like, the ability to provoke heated anger can also provoke heated passion?"

Liz felt her face flame. "Ah," she stammered.

"I know it's not easy to let go of thinking he's a Class A jerk, but give him a chance. Get to know the real William Darcy, instead of Grumpus Maximus," Ginny smiled. "And *please*, don't hold the illustrious Catherine D against us!"

Liz laughed. "Of course not. Speaking of bears – is Beren named after Beren and Luthien, or ...?"

Ginny smiled. "Yup. Will is a Tolkien geek, if you can believe it, and wanted to name him Huan – since, you know, that's the dog. But he looked so much like a bear when he was a puppy, that's what I insisted on calling him. Will finally relented, and Beren he is – as faithful and true as Luthien's." She leaned forward conspiratorially. "Don't think I didn't notice you changing the subject either, but I'll let it slide. This time," she added with a wink.

"Thanks," Liz rolled her eyes. "I wondered about that yesterday. The name fits him, of course, I was just curious."

"You'll find my brother is full of surprises," Ginny teased. "Now, let's put your family legacy to work, and dig into these buckets. I want to find something pretty!"

With a laugh, Liz handed Ginny a wooden framed screen and showed her how to wash the dirt away. The morning was warm, the water cold, and the company pleasant. In spite of the difference in their ages Ginny was an engaging companion; their conversation ranged from the task at hand to the best flavors at Bella Gelato, from guilty pleasure reading to favorite haunts in New York. As they worked through two buckets, talking and laughing their way into what promised to be a solid friendship, the river worked its magic and Liz was able to forget the whirling questions as the morning passed. The reprieve lasted until the moment the women walked out of the woods and stood beside the long, winding driveway of the Darcy home. Beren came bounding to meet them, tail wagging enthusiastically.

"You seem to have bewitched my dog, Elizabeth," Will said as he approached. "Ginny, you've got company," he added with a wink.

"Oh! I completely forgot!" With a laugh, Will waved her toward the house. "Hey Will, you should walk Liz home," she called over her shoulder. "I'll tell Charlie you'll get here when you get here, so take your time!"

Will shook his head, but Liz felt a telltale flush creeping up her cheeks. Kneeling to adjust her shoelaces, she hoped Beren hid her pink cheeks from Will. *Dangit,* she thought, *I've blushed more this week than my whole life put together. Of all the times to learn a new trick.*

"Beren and I would be happy to walk you home," Will smiled.

"If you don't mind the walk, I don't mind the company," she said, standing. "Oh, you don't have to take those, I can carry them."

Shaking his head, Will gently took the empty buckets from her hand. "No ma'am," he said, "a gentleman never lets a lady carry heavy, bulky, or dirty items. Besides," he smirked, "I can't have people think you're stronger than me, what would that to do my masculine pride?"

As they walked, they fell into a comfortable silence, occasionally broken by Will pointing out an area he hoped to improve in the future. When they reached the river, Beren splashed his way across, but Will stopped Liz with a light hand on her shoulder. He gestured to the rock she'd been sitting on the day before. "Do you mind if we sit here a moment?"

"Okay," Liz nodded.

"We haven't been able to talk," Will continued, fending off a dripping Beren as Liz settled herself on the sun-warmed stone. "Thanks to Catherine," he grimaced. "I wanted to make sure – to see – to ask," his voice trailed off.

Liz smiled, turning so she faced him. "I've read your letter so many times I have it memorized," she blushed. "I owe you a rather large apology, and planned to do so yesterday before Hurricane Catherine arrived."

"Hurricane indeed," Will laughed. "She managed to disrupt the entire afternoon, and evening, and frankly I'm happy you're still speaking to me. Please believe me, Elizabeth," his tone deepened, eyes serious. "Nothing she said represents what I – nor Ginny – think of you. She was out of line with her accusations, and I set her straight after you left."

Liz looked down, toying with a hair elastic on her wrist, unable to hold his gaze. "Some of what she said – you have said though," she said softly.

With a gentle touch, Will raised her face to look her in the eyes. "I owe you the apology," he said softly. "I should never have spoken to you the way I did – even before I realized you were the sister of Charlie's beloved, you were my guest. A paying guest. I was a wretched host." He paused, as if making sure every word was heard. "You were right. I have taken advantage of my position, using it as an excuse for abysmally bad manners. If Ginny knew how abominably I acted toward you, she'd make me pay – and be completely justified. I am deeply sorry, Elizabeth. I'd much rather make you laugh than furious, but you'd never know from the way I've behaved. I don't know why I lashed out at you so – obviously Charlie was right: I don't know how to talk to pretty girls. But I'd like to learn, because you are beautiful and intelligent and I think," he paused, "there's a very real chance I've mistaken annoyance for attraction." He fell silent.

"So," Liz breathed softly, raising an eyebrow, "my Janie is Charlie's beloved?"

"Everyone knows their story is going to end in happily ever after. But don't change the subject," Will smiled, holding her gaze. Liz's breath caught. She had the queerest feeling that time stopped while the world kept spinning, and she was terrified of the answer that crept, unbidden, into her mind.

At that moment, Beren leaped off the rock in pursuit of a fish. The sudden spray of cold water made Liz and Will jump, breaking the spell. Liz took a deep breath, and felt time and space aligning again. The moment passed and with a wry grin, Will stood – offering his hand to Liz with a gallant bow. "Shall we continue, m'lady?" His voice teased, but she knew they were both keenly aware of the unspoken, unanswered question.

"Why thank you, kind sir," she smiled, accepting his assistance, surprised when he tightened his grip as she moved to withdraw her hand. Glancing sideways as he whistled to Beren, she felt something coiled tight inside beginning to relax. With fingers interlaced, they walked in silence, each lost in their own thoughts.

"In light of our truce and – starting over – can I ask a question?" Liz said abruptly, knowing the secluded part of their path was drawing to an end.

"Of course," Will agreed, squeezing her fingers lightly.

"How, exactly, are you related to Catherine D? You call her 'Aunt', but I haven't been able to put all the pieces together in a way that makes sense."

To her immense surprise, Will laughed so hard he dropped her hand and had to brace his hands against his knees, gasping for breath. "I'm sorry," he finally managed, "but of all the things I thought you'd say, that was not one of them. Elizabeth Bennet, what goes on in that beautiful head of yours?"

"I asked first," Liz teased. "And I'm not sure how to explain it anyway, it's a strange, strange place up there."

"Mmm," Will murmured. "Well, to answer your question – distantly. Very distantly. Actually, she's not really our aunt, but we've always called her 'Aunt Catherine' out of respect. Her mother and my great-grandmother were first cousins, and after my grandmother died, Catherine essentially raised my mother – but she refused to be viewed as our grandmother, so Ginny and I have always simply called her Aunt Catherine."

"Hmm," Liz murmured. "Interesting. Where'd the 'D' come from?"

"When she was creating her public persona, Catherine didn't think Rosings, her married name, was mysterious or distinguished enough to suit her purposes. The D is a nod to Darcy, although she will never admit to the connection. For which I am incredibly grateful," he laughed.

"She'll use the letter, but not the name? That's weird."

"She won't acknowledge the Darcy name because she didn't like my father. She wanted my mother to marry," he paused dramatically, "the blueblooded heir to a Yankee fortune," he waggled his eyebrows at Liz. As Liz laughed, Will shrugged. "Ironically, the Darcy family fortune – and name – were greater than the New Yorker Aunt Catherine picked."

"Why the preference then?" Liz asked, eyebrows raised.

"Does Hurricane Catherine need a reason?" Will rolled his eyes. "Come on," taking her hand again, "I do actually need to be there when Charlie arrives. When he called this morning, he sounded positively frantic."

"Poor Charlie, he does work himself into a frenzy," Liz laughed.

They talked easily the rest of the way, soon standing on the porch steps of Liz's cabin once more. "Thank you for walking me home," she said softly.

"Beren has great ideas," Will smiled. "I think we'll be repeating this one."

"Yeah?" Liz asked.

"Oh yes," Will whispered, drawing her close. Liz's heart raced as his gaze drifted to her mouth, but before he could kiss her, the *Star Wars* theme broke the silence.

"You've got to be kidding," Liz muttered, reaching for her pocket at the same time as Will growled and grabbed his own phone. "Wait, that wasn't me – it was yours?"

"Appears we have the same ringtone," Will laughed, silencing the call. "That's Charlie, I should head back, but I'll see you soon," he said, kissing her forehead. "Promise."

Liz leaned against the porch rail, watching Will and Beren leave. *Well then*, she sighed. *This summer just got a lot more interesting, even if he is rich.*

Chapter 8

June passed quickly, and before Liz was ready, the Fourth of July arrived, in all its humid glory. Between helping prepare for the festivities and her growing relationship – such as it was – with Will, the preceding weeks were a whirlwind. Even though the day could end in chaos, Liz looked forward to the revelry. When she heard the community celebration would be held on the grounds of Pemberley, Liz assumed the City Council approached Will; to her immense surprise, Will contacted them – several months in advance – to make the offer. Over the last few weeks, Liz discovered Will was deeply involved with community affairs, behind the scenes. Rather than be perceived as a deep-pocketed savior, he preferred to offer insight and assistance in ways that could not be seen. For the first time in memory, Liz was delighted to be proved wrong – and about so many things.

The day passed in a flurry of festive activities ranging from the traditional to novel. Will approached Colin about operating a small-scale gem mining booth – it took little convincing for Colin to agree to the idea. The booth was a rousing success, and when Will suggested increasing mining operations at Longbourne, Colin enthusiastically agreed to look into the matter. To Liz's great amusement, Colin transferred his idol worship from his future mother-in-law to her nephew. Will was less amused, but hoped to use his newfound influence to restore balance to Longbourne Mines. Ginny teased Liz that it was proof of her brother's feelings for her, something Liz wanted to believe. After their almost-kiss the day they agreed to start over, there had been hugs and hands held, but no more.

As afternoon turned to evening, an expectant calm fell over the crowd. The Bennets and Darcys, with various friends and bystanders, gathered under an expansive tent, eating and visiting quietly until the fireworks began. Will had just made his way to where

Liz was camped out, people-watching and sipping tea, when Charlie stood and tapped his glass with a knife.

"Friends," he began with a grin. "When I decided to rent the Phillips House for the summer, I never imagined meeting so many interesting people, or making such wonderful friends. I certainly never thought I'd fall in love." The look of adoration he gave Jane elicited soft awws from his audience. "This summer has been so much more than I expected, and it's not over yet!" At his pause, Jane stood and laced her arm through his with a smile.

Liz squinted, as something caught the light. "If that's what I think it is," she said softly. Will chuckled, wrapping his arm around her shoulders and brushing a light kiss against her temple. "Oh," she gasped, turning to look at him.

"Shh," he whispered. "Charlie's up to something."

"After many walks by the river and countless conversations, I realized I don't want things to end when I go back to teaching in August. So," he drawled, "I asked Jane to marry me."

"And I said yes!" Jane exclaimed.

With whoops and whistles, the happy couple were quickly lost in a crowd of hugs and questions. Liz laughed, grabbing Will's hand and dragging him into the fray. Momma's voice could be heard over everyone, repeatedly exclaiming "bless me, a daughter married!"

"You don't mind being surprised, do you?" Jane asked, giving Liz a tight hug.

Liz shook her head. "It was cute. And Charlie obviously enjoyed the joke," she smiled. "Now if you elope without telling me, it'll be a different story."

"Promise that won't happen," Jane laughed, before someone else swooped in to gush over the ring.

Liz found herself passed from friend to friend, quickly losing sight of Will, everyone wanting to know if she'd been in on the secret, and would she be next? When Ginny climbed on a chair and announced the fireworks were minutes from beginning, Liz heaved a sigh of relief and ducked into a corner, waiting for the tide to ebb before making her way outside.

With a quiet "Elizabeth," Will drew Liz to the side, out of the flow of revelers migrating to better fireworks viewing. She stepped into his embrace, sighing happily. "Were you surprised?"

"Mmhmm," she murmured, tucking her head against his shoulder. "Well, yes and no," she amended. "I had a feeling something was cooking, but wasn't sure what exactly. Did you know?"

"Yeah," she could feel him nod. "That's what he wanted to talk to me about that day. He's lucky," Will laughed. "If it'd been anything else, I might have tossed him in the river for cutting our moment short." His arms tightened, and Liz felt her cheeks flame. "Maybe we can try again," he whispered, breath warm against her ear.

Leaning back to meet his gaze, Liz smiled. The lights along the paths, and spilling from the tent, cast shadows dancing over them both. "What have we been doing then? Moment is a very open-ended word, William," she teased.

"So it is," he smiled. "But I was thinking about one particular kind of moment." His gaze drifted to her mouth and back with purpose.

"Oh," she breathed, nodding slowly. "I see."

"Yes?" Will quirked an eyebrow, raising a hand to cradle her jaw.

"Yes," she murmured, closing her eyes as he leaned in. Just before their lips met, the first firework exploded. Liz startled, bumping into Will's nose before losing her balance. With a muffled shriek, they fell in a tangle of arms and legs. Shifting to cushion Liz's fall, Will "oomph"ed on impact.

"Talk about making an impression," Liz groaned, attempting to disentangle herself.

"Where are you going?" Will asked, tightening his arms around her waist.

"Um," she paused. "Off the ground?"

"Why? It's actually not bad. It's dark, nobody bothering us, and fireworks behind you –" A loud cheer cut him off. Liz turned to glance over her shoulder, before rolling to sit next to him, laughing. "What?" Will asked, sitting up.

Unable to respond, Liz pointed in the direction of the hill where the fireworks were launching.

"I don't see –" he stopped. "Is that what I think it is?"

"Uh-huh," she gasped. "I wondered if he'd make an appearance, with the show moved to Pemberley," she giggled.

"You know that … that person?" Will stared at her.

"Everyone knows him," Liz smirked. "That's No-Clothes McGee."

"No-Clothes McGee."

"Yup. Every year when the fireworks start, he takes off streaking. He's a Meryton tradition!" At the bewilderment on Will's face, Liz began laughing again.

"You're telling me every year, this McGee fella strips down and takes off running, with bombs bursting in air?" Will's lips twitched, the beginnings of a smile.

"Yup," Liz nodded.

"And the rest of the year?"

"He's just your normal, keeps-to-himself hermit."

"And nobody finds this strange?" Will arched an eyebrow.

"Nope. He's just one of those characters that makes small-town living colorful."

"Ah. I suppose I should get used to it, huh?"

"Yup. One of many things to get used to. If you're serious about staying," Liz teased, though there was a seriousness in her eyes the darkness couldn't hide.

"I'm very serious, about all the things," Will said softly, resting a hand on her shoulder.

"Good," she smiled, leaning closer. "Because Meryton is serious about you," she whispered, right before she kissed him. She felt his smile under her lips for a half-beat, before he pulled her closer and deepened the kiss.

Liz lost herself in the moment, in the feel of his mouth on hers and the security of his embrace, as the crowds oohed and aahed over the fireworks display. When they parted, a moment or a lifetime later, Will smiled.

"Meryton *is* serious about me. Good to know we're on the same page. I think I'll stay awhile," he winked.

"Welcome home," she laughed, as he drew her close and rendered words unnecessary.

Epilogue

The days flew by, details lost in the blur of things happening. In keeping with their whirlwind summer romance, Jane and Charlie wanted to be married before he returned to Northanger for the start of classes. Since they wanted a small, informal wedding, Jane told Momma she was planning a simple engagement party, and the wedding would be the following summer, with the intent of springing a surprise wedding on everyone. It was a brilliant idea, though Liz wondered how long the ruse would last. As the big day approached, everything seemed to be falling in place, and the happily ever after Will foretold seemed possible.

At the suggestion of Liz, Ginny would become manager of Bella Gelato in Jane's absence, as well as housesitting. Ginny was giddy about the prospect, and spent nearly every free moment with Jane, learning the secret ins and outs of Bella Gelato. Liz suspected some of Ginny's excitement stemmed from getting to "play house" on her own, and proving to her brother she wasn't a little girl anymore. When the Bingleys returned the next summer, they'd evaluate the success of the venture, and Liz felt certain Ginny would be offered a partnership in the enterprise.

For her own part, Liz's cabin rental expired the day of the wedding, but Will asked her to consider staying on through the fall. Ginny convinced her brother to expand his reach, by way of social media and blogs, or at the very least a quarterly newsletter. To accomplish this, Liz was asked to join the team behind the scenes of Pemberley Acres, beginning a formal partnership she knew would only strengthen and deepen with time. In addition to becoming better acquainted with the vision Will had for Pemberley – and it was grand – working alongside him provided the perfect excuse to steal a kiss or few during the day. As their personal relationship thrived, Liz found herself thinking a Bennet daughter might get married next summer after all.

When she fell into bed every night, Liz was the tiredest she'd ever been – but also the happiest. Perhaps, sometimes, rules were made to be broken.

Acknowledgements

The phrase "it takes a village" is so true of this story, but more than that – it takes friendship. From the first inkling of the idea to the naming of characters, and the addition of one scene in particular, this story is the result of numerous conversations over dinners and frozen yogurt, the Scrabble board and driving through town. It's the result of bets, inside jokes, mischievous plotting, summers in the mountains, and a long-standing love affair with Fitzwilliam Darcy. To everyone who has played a part – even unknowingly – I offer my deepest thanks, and many hugs.

Thank you also to my fellow *Holidays with Jane* writers – this is our fourth volume, and we're still coming up with crazy awesome ideas! I'm so privileged to be along for the ride.

And, as ever, my unending gratitude to Jane for writing it first.

Melanie Perceived

A *Mansfield Park* Story

*For every girl who has loved the wrong guy,
and had the courage to start her story over
again.*

*In loving memory of Dr. James W. Stitt,
my own "Grampa Jamie," who believed I could.
Thank you.*

Chapter 1

The late afternoon sun fell slanting across the cemetery, casting a long shadow behind a squirrel investigating something in the leaves. Melanie quietly snapped a series of shots, suppressing a giggle as another squirrel approached from behind. *This could get interesting,* she held her breath. As the second squirrel pounced the first, Melanie's fingers flew; she didn't have to think, making adjustments to the camera came as natural as breathing. After the squirrels raced off, Melanie leaned against a nearby tree and thumbed through the photos. The images made her laugh, and she couldn't wait to get back to her room and open them in her editing program. *These would be so fun in a grouping,* she thought, already visualizing them matted and framed.

The familiar strains of the *Superman* theme pulled her back to reality. With a sigh, Melanie fished her phone out of her messenger bag. "Hiya," she chirped.

"Frankie! Where are you?"

"Umm," she hesitated, glancing at her watch and realizing she was running very late.

"Don't tell me, lemme guess – you found the perfect photo op, and completely lost track of time. Am'right?"

She smiled at the teasing note in Eddie's voice. "Guilty as charged," she laughed. "But Eddie, wait'll you see!"

"Can't wait," Eddie laughed, "but first, think you'll make it back to campus before the meeting's over? Mr. Gee has an announcement to make, and he refuses to budge until you show."

"I'm coming, I'm coming," she groaned. "I'm actually not that far away, Smartypants; I'll see you in less time than it takes MaryJo to order a latte at Mansfield Perk." Gathering her things, she kept her camera strap looped around her neck, *just in case,* and walked the two blocks back to campus. Abbey College was an old campus, and Melanie loved it best in the fall, when the leaves finally started to change and lazily drift down on sidewalks and stairs. *The bricks glow in this light,* she sighed dreamily, stopping to snap a few pictures before hurrying down the quad. *Superman* blared again just as she walked into newspaper office.

"Perfect timing, Price," Mr. Gee, the faculty advisor, grinned. "Bertram is having kittens over there, but I told him you were working on a Campus Charm piece. Please tell him I was right," he winked.

"Of course!" Melanie grinned, setting her camera on her desk. "I got an excellent picture to start with, just need a quick trip to the archives, and the piece will be perfect."

"See, Bertram? Everything's under control. And now that everyone is here, I've got some news – pun intended," Mr. Gee chuckled. "As you know, *The Lion's Den* has been a monthly publication since the first issue was printed back in the thirties. We have recently received a generous donation from an anonymous donor," he paused with a smile, letting the playful whoops die down. "We now have more than enough to cover the cost of updating the equipment here in the office, and giving it a general makeover, as well as extending our printing contract. This is particularly important since there was one requirement for receiving the money."

"Whatcha mean?" Eddie asked, glancing around the room. Everyone wore confused and puzzled expressions, and looked expectantly at Mr. Gee.

"Our generous and mysterious benefactor requests that we begin biweekly publication. Beginning in January." As the paper staff sat in surprised silence, their fearless leader leaned back in his chair and smiled. "Okay, newsies, I know you have questions or you wouldn't be on my staff. Let's hear them."

"With all due respect, sir," Eddie began, "are we going to be able to produce enough quality material on a biweekly basis?"

"Perfect opening question, Mr. Editor-in-Chief," Mr. Gee nodded. "You raise a valid point of concern, and one I've mulled over considerably. We'll discuss things, of course, but I think our best course of action is to make slight adjustments in terms of scope and range. We now have room to cover more, and I think we should."

"We'll have to get more people involved," Melanie mused. "There's no way we could keep the same standard without expanding."

"Right on the money, Price. Thankfully we have a healthy pool of potentials to draw from, and as we make adjustments to our regular features, we can actively recruit for additional positions."

"When are we going to start implementing changes?" Laura, the assistant editor, asked. "If possible, we should start adding new writers sooner than later, so we can get a feel for their style and whether they're keepers or not."

"What kind of changes to coverage are we making?" Eddie asked, and Melanie could see the wheels in his head turning. "Obviously we can feature more on-campus events, and we should probably offer more reviews in A&E with the increased space – they always generate a lot of buzz."

"Yes and yes," Mr. Gee nodded. "Additionally, we will run more feature stories, and I'm adding a new editorial position." He paused, as Hank Crawford strolled into the office and sat on Melanie's desk.

"You always have to make an entrance," she muttered, rolling her eyes.

"You know it, babe," he winked. "How's my timing, Gee?"

"Crawford, how long have you been standing in the hall, waiting to make that entrance?"

Hank laughed, "touché, Gee, touché. I was running late anyway, so I decided to play it up a bit. I was trailing Melanie into the building, so I've heard pretty much everything."

"Yes well," Mr. Gee chuckled. "Do try to be on time from now on. Especially since you're our newest editor." He held up a hand to silence the questions buzzing. "As you know, Crawford has been writing Greek features since January. They've received a lot of positive feedback, and with increased publication, I think it will work in our favor to establish a permanent Greek section. To that end, Crawford is officially Greek Life editor – that goes into effect immediately."

Laura cocked her head. "Okay, I can see this working. What kind of material are we talking about though? Hank's features have been a good addition, true, but if we're going to make this a permanent section, we need more."

"I plan to continue my features," Hank drawled, "as well as highlight events and whatnot taking place in the Greek community at Abbey. Additionally, I think it'd be a nice touch to feature a different Greek house each issue – share the history, interview a few members, talk about the sponsored charity. You know," he shrugged, "sharing the other side of Greek life."

"Will you be writing all the pieces, or will new staff writers be handling Greek pieces as well?" Eddie asked, making notes.

"Actually, Bertram, we're making some changes to staff writing," Mr. Gee answered. "We have an exceedingly talented team on staff, both as editors and writers, and many of you have potential beyond the pages of *The Lion's Den*. I want to help you grow, to be the best writers you can be – even if it means writing something outside your comfort zone."

"Okay, you look like you're up to something. What are you planning?" Laura asked.

Mr. Gee smiled. "Instead of designating staff writers for particular areas, we are going to have a pool of writers. All writers will be assigned stories on a quasi-lottery basis, giving everyone a chance to write something different. This will also help prevent stagnation, repetition and burnout – of particular concern with our increased publication."

Eddie whistled. "That's going to be quite a change for some of our writers."

"It will," Mr. Gee nodded. "I think they'll find it has merit however, especially once they realize even you, editorial darlings, will be flexing your writing muscles."

"Uhoh," Melanie laughed. "I knew it sounded too good to be true. What's the catch?"

Mr. Gee leaned back in his chair with a devious smile. "You will each maintain the monthly features you've been writing, in your department. With the addition of at least one other issue a month, you will be assigned a story from the pool – not necessarily in your department. And of course," he added with a laugh, "there will always be the odds and ends you pick up along the way."

"Hmm," Eddie murmured. "I like it," he decided. "We keep the regular columns that people expect, and then we mix things up a bit. It's different, but you're right – it will only help us in the long run."

"What about photography?" Laura asked, tilting her head in Melanie's direction. "As amazing as she is, Melanie won't be able to get all the shots we'll need and keep up with her writing."

"Not without going crazy in the process," Melanie laughed, eyes wide. "I hadn't even thought about that!"

"I've thought about that too, and I propose Price and I meet with the chair of the art department, and see how the photo students can help. I know they already shoot sporting events for class, and that will be the hardest new demand to fill."

"Maybe we could accept photographic submissions from students – sort of like a 'photo to the editor,'" Melanie mused. "Things that could be used as Campus Charm pieces, or even make it a standing feature. It would get students involved, as well as give us a more varied photographic representation. Everyone has a different eye, and I can only be in so many places," she laughed.

"Hey, you might be onto something," Hank exclaimed. "My sister is actually pretty good with a camera, and I know she's chomping at the bit to join *The Lion's Den* team," he added with a sly glance in Eddie's direction. "I'm certain she'd be willing to step in and help in any way."

Melanie sighed. *MaryJo strikes again,* she thought, biting her tongue to keep from grimacing.

Mr. Gee arched an eyebrow. "Have her submit some sample photos, Crawford. I make no promises, but we'll look at her stuff same as anybody. Did she work on the paper at State before transferring to Abbey?"

Hank shrugged. "I mean, she takes pictures all the time – drives me nuts, actually," he rolled his eyes with a laugh. "And no, she didn't work for the paper at State, she was a bit preoccupied with social engagements," he waggled his eyebrows at Melanie. "When our old man made her transfer here, she decided to start over entirely – and that includes getting more involved with campus activities. Plus she knows how much fun I've had working with y'all, and she's rather fond of our editor."

Melanie cringed, as everyone chuckled and Eddie blushed. *So much for imagining things.*

Mr. Gee, realizing the meeting was too far gone, released everyone with reminders about the next deadline. While the others chatted and laughed, Melanie dug around in her bag. *If I look busy enough, maybe Hank will just go ahead and leave,* she thought. *Or not.*

"Hey man, no hard feelings, eh?" Hank greeted Eddie with one of the brotastic handshake-shoulder slap routines Melanie found so peculiar.

"Nah," Eddie shook his head. "It's all good. Not like it's a secret," he laughed.

Melanie glanced up in surprise as Hank whooped, quickly dropping her eyes back to the tangled chaos in her bag.

"Dude, she didn't make you have 'The Talk' did she?" Hank cackled. "The DTR talk, man," he continued, seeing the confusion on Eddie's face. "Dude, how do you not know this? You and Melanie are inseparable, you should at least have heard about this stuff!"

"What's Frankie got to do with it?" Eddie asked, brow furrowed in ever-deepening confusion.

"Um, hello? She's a girl."

"Your point?"

Hank paused long enough for Melanie to hazard another glance. He was staring at Eddie with an expression equal parts surprise and sympathy. "Dude," he finally sighed. "You – she – how – I just don't even know what to say right now. But I think," he added with a smirk, "I owe my sister a very large margarita for apparently achieving the impossible."

"I have absolutely no idea what you're talking about. Do you?" Eddie asked, turning to Melanie.

"Ah," she stammered, feeling her cheeks flush. "I uh, have some work to do and I'll see y'all later," she muttered, hastily zipping her bag and grabbing her camera. To her dismay, Hank hopped off her desk, pulling back her chair as she stood.

With a lazy grin, he looped an arm around Melanie and Eddie's shoulders. "Hey, whaddaya say we blow this popsicle stand, get something to eat or catch a movie?"

Eddie laughed, shrugging off the invitation and the arm. "Hank, you heard the announcements – I'm gonna pick Mr. Gee's brain about how this is going to work, so I can start planning."

"Whatever, dude," Hank laughed. "Melanie?"

"Hank, I have work to do," she reminded him, trying to casually step away.

He slipped his arm around her waist, pulling her in for a half-hug. "Girl, you're always three weeks ahead of everything. Can't you make time for a friendly cup of coffee? Aren't you girls s'posed to be, like, addicted to pumpkin spice lattes? I'll buy you the biggest one they've got – and a cookie – if you'll keep me company."

Melanie sighed. Hank's wheedling face was one-part boyish charm and two-parts puppy eyes. "Why?" she asked, stalling for time.

Hank cocked his head. *He's totally got the puppy thing figured out,* Melanie thought. *He's such a hound dog. I'm going to end up regretting this, just watch.*

"Why not?" Hank sounded genuinely confused.

Melanie smiled in spite of herself. "That's not an answer, Hank. *Why?*"

"Because I need caffeine and sugar and you work too much. And," he lowered his voice and leaned closer. "Unlike our fearless leader over there, I happen to know you're a girl. A very fascinating, not to mention cute, girl. I happen to have a thing for cute, fascinating girls." His breath tickled her neck, and Melanie felt her cheeks flaming in a blush.

"Lay off, man," Eddie laughed, before Melanie could respond. "Frankie isn't another one of your conquests, she's not gonna fall for that schmoozy charm."

"Schmoozy charm? Conquest?" Hank raised his eyebrows. "Nah, man. I'm just telling the truth. 'Sides, what girl doesn't like to be told she's cute? Whaddaya say, Melanie?"

"Ya know what? Caffeine and sugar sound really good right now, so I'm gonna say yes," she shrugged. "I'll do better work riding a sugar high anyway, so be prepared: I *am* going to be taking you up on the biggest drink they sell."

"Hey baby, I don't make the offer if I don't intend to follow through," Hank winked, releasing Melanie to open the door with a flourish. "After you, m'lady."

As they left the office, laughing, Melanie couldn't resist looking over her shoulder to see if Eddie was watching. *Of course not,* she chastised herself. *Because I'm just Frankie, and apparently MaryJo is – well, I'm not sure what. He hasn't told me, which is weird. He tells me everything.* Catching herself before she got sucked into a vortex without answers, she shook her head slightly. *Stop it, Melanie. Right now, it doesn't matter. Just be a normal girl for once, and enjoy the fact that one of the Pretty People wants to buy you coffee.* The thought made her smile; Hank, watching her as they walked, saw it and his own smile broadened.

Chapter 2

Later that evening, Melanie was thankful, yet again, to have a private room. There were too many new developments to process, and after the steady chatter of what turned into a two and a half hour excursion with Hank, she needed the calm, restful sanctuary of her dorm. Curling up with her laptop and a mug of steaming peppermint tea, she settled in for a quiet evening of work. The upcoming change from monthly to bi-weekly editions of *The Lion's Den* was exciting, and she looked forward to seeing how things would play out. She opened a document on her laptop and started jotting down ideas and questions to bounce off Eddie and Mr. Gee. *I know we're going to need another photographer,* she sighed, *we've needed one, truthfully. But I really don't want to have to work with MaryJo. And I don't want to think about her tonight either.*

Wrinkling her nose, she saved the file and grabbed her camera to transfer her shots from the day. As the squirrel pictures loaded, she smiled. "Yes," she whispered. The series of pictures had turned out even better than she hoped; her favorite captured the moment before the surprise attack – the first squirrel happily rummaging through the leaves, unaware of the second squirrel in midair, about to land on his back. Realizing the images would need very little editing, she quickly selected the six best, copying them to a folder on the desktop labeled "Someday."

On a whim, she opened the folder, sighing happily as the thumbnails loaded. Taken over the last decade, these were the pictures she felt had the most promise. It was a truth universally acknowledged that Melanie was a shutterbug, but few people realized just how deep the passion ran. *Even Eddie doesn't really understand,* she mused, stopping at a series of photos from a high school game. On the surface, or to the casual observer, these images resembled countless others – they could be of any football team, at any high school. Melanie clicked on the first, opening the viewer and letting the image fill the screen. Her eyes roved, taking in the little details that made it one of her favorites. Far from being any other game, this was the game when everything changed – when Eddie became a star.

The pictures told the story; Melanie had filled her memory card that night, taking picture after picture as Eddie got his first start and showed everyone that bookish boys can catch. Turning her lens to the crowd and sidelines as often as it was directed toward the field, Melanie had recorded the reactions as well as the game. Coach Norris's proud appraisal; the surprised expressions of teammates turning to respect as Eddie caught pass after pass; the enthusiastic delight of Momma B in the stands – Melanie managed to capture them all. Looking at the pictures now, Melanie could still feel the excitement and energy of that night; the feeling that a new world was opening welcoming arms – not just for Eddie, but for her too. Over the years, she had taken so many pictures of Eddie in action – on and off the field – he had his own folder. Every now and then however, she managed to capture particularly special moments, like these, that told a bigger story.

Once Eddie established himself on the gridiron, things started shifting and changing. Looking back, Melanie couldn't say exactly how they ended up where they did, but she knew it'd been a wild ride. *If Coach hadn't given Eddie a chance that night, how different would things be?* Melanie wondered, grimacing as she sipped her now-cold tea. "Ugh," she said aloud, "that's gross. If you're going to wax nostalgic, girl, at least get a real drink," she laughed at herself. "Oh crud," she groaned, seeing the time. "And that's the end of this trip down Memory Lane," she sighed, closing out the open windows and shutting down her computer for the night. *Probably just as well*, she thought, getting ready for bed. *The Eddie and Frankie story is really just one big game of "what if" and that's never a good idea before bed.*

Chapter 3

The rest of the week flew by, and Saturday – game day – arrived before Melanie was ready. Between homework and stuff for *The Lion's Den*, she'd been almost too busy to miss Eddie. *Almost being the operative word*, she thought, gathering her things for the game. *If I didn't know any better, I'd think Eddie is avoiding me. But that's ridiculous – isn't it?* Once she would have known the answer, but things felt strange between them this semester. *Ever since MaryJo waltzed in with her blonde highlights, pink cowboy boots and cheerleader perkiness.* Melanie sighed. If she was the literal "girl next door," MaryJo was the girl next door fantasy. Pretty, but not "too pretty," she was comfortable in her own skin and not afraid to live a little. Even though she transferred in August, MaryJo was already the darling of her sorority and a favorite among the frat boys. *All boys*, Melanie corrected herself. *She's fluent in flirting, like it's her native language or something. The boys have got to know she's playing all of them, but she's so gosh darn sweet about it they don't even care.*

When Hank had his sister meet them at Mansfield Perk for a post-meeting coffee one afternoon, Eddie was positively starstruck. In the weeks following, MaryJo looked for reasons to bump into Eddie and Melanie, randomly appearing in unexpected places. Melanie, used to girls fawning over Eddie, was less accustomed to those girls sticking around once they realized he wasn't one to frequent parties or cash in on his star receiver status. She assumed MaryJo would be no different, and as more time passed without her disappearing, Melanie worried Eddie's schoolboy infatuation might develop into something more. *And then he'll get his heart broken*, Melanie thought. *Girls like MaryJo never really like guys like Eddie, even though guys like Eddie always like girls like MaryJo.* She sighed, double-checking her bag. *And I get to spend the entire game with her. Lucky me.* "Let's get this show on the road," she muttered, slinging her bag over her shoulder and beginning the trek across campus.

After much discussion, it was decided the most tactful way to appraise MaryJo's photography would be having her shadow Melanie during a home game. While she would cover predominately non-sporting events if she joined *The Lion's Den* team, seeing how MaryJo handled the fast-paced action and demands of a football game would tell as much about her skill as the images she produced. Melanie was curious how things would turn out, but dreaded spending the afternoon in the other girl's company. *Although,* she mused, *maybe I can figure out what's going on, feel things out and find out what her intentions are – since Eddie is being weird and sharing nothing, and MaryJo loves to talk.*

"There's my football girl! I was beginning to think you weren't coming."

The friendly greeting startled Melanie out of her thoughts, and she smiled at the familiar face. In every small town, there are local legends – retired professor James Stitt was Northanger's resident football guru: never missing a home game and even attending many away games, for both the college *and* high school. Over the years, his faithful support of all things football, and willingness to teach new fans the secrets of the game, had earned the respect of the entire community. He was also an adopted grandfather to many, including Melanie. Grampa Jamie, as he was affectionately known, was always available to provide a listening ear and sage advice – or motivating nudge – whenever such was needed.

"Am I that late?" Melanie laughed, breathing deeply as she stopped by the impressive tailgating setup. "Mmm, I'm don't know what you're grilling, but it smells like heaven."

"Late for you is still early for everyone else," he smiled. "Did you eat before you came over? You look –" he paused, taking a long look. "You look distracted. Bad week?"

"Eventful week," Melanie sighed. "And not over yet."

"It's still too early for them to let you in the stadium; have a seat and tell me what's going on. Want some coffee?"

Melanie smiled as she sat in a folding chair, "Gramps, you've known me how long and you still have to ask? Especially if it's game day coffee."

"It is polite to ask, even when one knows the answer. In fact, I've already prepared it the way you like: with extra cream." As he spoke, he handed her a tall purple thermos.

"You're the best," Melanie sighed, taking a sip of the hot drink. "Perfect. Seriously, if you ever decide you need something to break the monotony of retirement, you should work at Mansfield Perk. And yes," she said, raising a hand, "I'm stalling. I don't know where to begin," she shrugged. "A lot of it doesn't even make sense in my own head."

"Hmm. Start with what you do know," the older man suggested.

"I took some great pictures this week," she smiled. "And *The Lion's Den* will be moving to biweekly publication starting in January. Which is totally awesome and exciting, but also part of what has me feeling so – so –" she paused, searching for the best word. "Disgruntled, I guess," she sighed.

"I would have expected you to say excited or maybe nervous, rather than disgruntled," Jamie arched an eyebrow.

"Increased publication means expanding the staff, which is generally a good thing." Melanie shrugged. "One of the positions we are discussing is another photographer, and," she crinkled her nose, "the leading candidate is MaryJo."

"Ah, I begin to see the problem."

Melanie gave a wry grin. "Yeah. It gets better. She apparently doesn't have 'professional' experience, so we can't ask her to submit a portfolio. So she's going to shadow me during the game, and we'll see what kind of photos she gets and how she handles herself. I have a feeling this will be an experience."

"But that's not what's bothering you is it?"

"It's Eddie," Melanie sighed.

"Mmhmm," Jamie nodded knowingly.

"He's been weird all week, not quite ignoring me but –" she hesitated, "no, actually, he *has* been ignoring me. Unless it's something directly related to the paper or class, he has been MIA this week. He even stood me up Wednesday for pizza night, and it's been a tradition since we were in the third grade! Nobody bails on Wednesday night pizza unless you're dying." She felt her temper sparking, and took a couple deep, calming breaths.

"What happened to bring about radio silence?"

Melanie shrugged. "I don't know. It was an away game, you know, but we hung out like normal Saturday night once we got back to campus. Everything seemed fine. Sunday I had a paper to finish writing, and he was s'posed to be working on a project for his marketing class. We talked about getting dinner Sunday night, depending on how much work got done, but nothing concrete. That's nothing unusual though, and when I didn't hear from him I figured he was lost in his project and just grabbed a sandwich with a girl from the dorm. Wait a second," she cocked her head thoughtfully. "Sunday. That's gotta be when it happened."

Jamie raised an eyebrow. "When what happened?"

"I don't know, but something!" Melanie laughed. "I told you: I don't make sense in my own head." She sipped her coffee, gathering her thoughts and letting the sounds of the growing crowd wash over her. "Something happened," she began slowly, "between Saturday night when Eddie walked me home and Monday afternoon. By the time I saw him again at the emergency paper meeting, it had already taken place. Something with MaryJo." She paused again, idly running her thumb along the ring on her finger. "I don't know if they went out, or what, but something shifted the Eddie-MaryJo dynamic. And I don't know *what*," she continued, "because Eddie won't talk to me!"

"You and Eddie have been friends a long time. Has he ever stopped talking to you before?" Jamie asked.

"Yeah," Melanie rolled her eyes. "Whenever he got a new crush in high school, he'd clam up and moon over the girl. But the silence never lasted long, a couple days," she laughed wryly. "He always needed my advice on how to talk to her."

"Hmm, interesting," Jamie murmured.

She shrugged. "It hasn't happened since then, though. Once we started at Abbey, things settled down and it's been just us. He's been more focused on football this year, but it's his senior year – of course he wants to savor every minute."

"Maybe it's just the college version of the high school crush thing," Jamie offered.

"Maybe. And here I was hoping he grew out of that," she sighed dramatically. "Okay, duty calls. Wish me luck, I have a feeling I'm going to need it today." Melanie stood, looping her bag over her shoulder again.

"You'll be fine; you've got more gumption than you give yourself credit for."

"Ha, thanks, but I'm not so sure about that."

"Trust Grampa Jamie, he knows these things," he laughed. "Now get in there and make everyone look good. Maybe after the game, everything will get back to normal."

"One can hope," Melanie smiled. "Thanks for the coffee, and letting me vent. Time to get this show on the road! Or, well, home stadium. Okay, I'm leaving now," she laughed. "Go Lions!"

Chapter 4

Ten hours later, Melanie kicked her shoes into the corner, set her bags on her desk, and threw herself onto the bed. "What a day," she groaned, wishing she had a close girlfriend. *Or even a roommate.* For the first time in a long time, she wondered whether she should have tried to make more friends along the way. *It's always been Eddie. Only Eddie,* she thought. *But who do you talk to when the person you talk to is who you need to talk about?*

MaryJo had arrived at the stadium as perky and cheerful as ever, eager to please and listening to every suggestion or comment Melanie made. As she'd watched the other girl, Melanie had to admit MaryJo was confident in her handling of the equipment, and she suspected the photographs would be more than acceptable. Working alongside each other, Melanie also noticed there was far more to MaryJo Crawford than met the eye – and she found herself wondering whether MaryJo cultivated the effervescent, cheerleader-sorority queen persona with a purpose. As anticipated, MaryJo spent most of the afternoon talking – in the space of a few hours, she more than covered topics ranging from the game to photography, from her favorite drink + snack combinations at Mansfield Perk to comparing Greek life at Abbey to that of State. Used to being in her own bubble on the sidelines, Melanie found the constant stream of chatter distracting at first, before realizing that MaryJo didn't seem to need responsive feedback. Surprisingly, it was late in the third quarter before MaryJo mentioned Eddie.

❧❧❧

On third and long, quarterback Tom Rushwood took a wild chance, lobbing a ball that – somehow – landed perfectly in Eddie's outstretched hands. After a thrilling forty-three yard run downfield Eddie was tackled, setting the Lions up with first and goal from the seven. While the officials moved the chains, and everyone in the stands went wild, MaryJo turned to Melanie and squealed.

"Ohmigosh, did you see that?! I can't believe he did that! Eddie did that!!"

"I know!" Melanie smiled back. "I've been watching him play for years, but it's always amazing to see something like that from the sidelines. Especially when you can see just how big the defenders are," she winked, glancing up as one of the Lions players walked by on his way to the water cooler.

"Aww, Mel, we're not so big, you're just teeny tiny," he laughed, reaching out and giving her ponytail a tug.

"Funny, Ralph, real funny," Melanie rolled her eyes at him. "Don't you have a game to play?"

"Yeah, and you're gonna make me look like a star in all the pics, right baby?"

"Only if you play like a star. I don't waste my time on benchwarmers."

As Ralph walked, laughing, back to the group huddled around one of the assistant coaches, MaryJo stared at Melanie.

"What?" Melanie asked self-consciously, running a hand down her ponytail. "Did he stick something on my back?" She turned, trying to see over her shoulder.

"No, you're good," MaryJo shook her head. "I just didn't realize –" she paused, thinking.

Melanie arched an eyebrow. "MaryJo," she began, "I've known Ralph almost as long as I've known Eddie."

"Oh," MaryJo said. "So, um, do you know the whole team?"

"Mmhmm, pretty much. I've been covering the games since freshman year; we've spent almost every Saturday together for years now. People are used to seeing me with Eddie too," she added with a shrug. "Sometimes it feels like I've got way too many protective 'big brothers,' but it's not all bad, being the only girl in a boy's world."

"I can imagine. Would that we could all be so fortunate," MaryJo smirked.

"Right, like you need to be 'one of the guys,'" Melanie snorted. "You're gorgeous. They love you, whether you speak football and sweat or not."

"Mmm, maybe" MaryJo murmured, her gaze strangely appraising. "Though I think, with things working out the way they are, I should learn to speak football. Not fluently, but enough to impress Eddie," she added, turning back to the field as the referee blew his whistle. "They're finally ready!"

The first play from scrimmage was a quarterback sneak, that didn't sneak past anyone. On second down, Tom dropped back and lobbed an easy pass to Eddie for the go-ahead score. Melanie whistled, keeping her camera pointed at the action, while MaryJo let her camera hang from the strap, clapping and shouting along with the rest of the Abbey fans – and bench. After Neil Turner made the point-after kick, a media timeout was called, and MaryJo turned to Melanie.

"So you'll help me right?"

"Umm," Melanie blinked. "Help, huh?"

"Learn to speak football, without, like, having to spend every waking moment memorizing this stuff." MaryJo arched an eyebrow. "I need to know enough to keep up with what is going on, and impress Eddie, but still be just dumb enough to be cute. Can you make it happen?"

"Why?" The question surprised them both, and Melanie smiled a little to see the perplexed look on MaryJo's face.

"Because you know football, like one of the boys. And if I take lessons from you, it won't be as weird or obvious as if I asked Eddie or one of the others."

"But that still isn't *why*," Melanie responded, holding her smile even as her heart started to realize what was happening. "*Why* do you feel a sudden need to speak some football to impress Eddie? Especially since, again, you clearly don't need to do anything other than smile at a guy to have him worship you." The bite to her tone surprised her, and she hoped MaryJo didn't notice.

"Because," MaryJo drawled, arching one eyebrow with a satisfied smile, "if I'm dating the star receiver, I should know what he does. Other than look incredibly hot in his uniform, of course," she added with a laugh. "I don't know how you manage, being here every week, surrounded by football boys – has it really never occurred to you, the gold mine you're sitting on? Even if you didn't want to date them yourself, like, you could offer matchmaking services or something."

Melanie barked a laugh, feeling a blush flood her cheeks with color. "What are you talking about? Football and matchmaking don't even come close to belonging in the same sentence, MaryJo. Are you sure you're from the South?"

"Nice deflection," the other girl smirked. "I'll let you off the hook this time, but your face tells more than you think, Melanie. Now are you gonna help me or not?" She poked her bottom lip out in a pout that was equal parts annoying and adorable.

This is the moment of truth, Melanie thought, taking a deep breath. "Are you asking me to teach you so you can catch Eddie's attention, or –" she left the question unspoken, lingering.

"Oh!" MaryJo exclaimed. "I thought you were playing coy, but it makes sense now. He hasn't told you, has he?"

"Since I'm getting more confused by the minute, I'm gonna go out on a limb and say no," Melanie answered wryly.

"Girl, we had the world's most perfect first date Sunday afternoon," MaryJo gushed.

"Sunday afternoon," Melanie repeated, mentally putting the pieces together.

"Mmhmm," MaryJo purred. "Oh, they're starting again. I'll tell you later."

With a sigh, Melanie let herself get lost in the zone, allowing the energy of the game and the familiar routine of photographing it distract her from MaryJo's announcement. The final quarter was intense, as the teams traded scores. Before they realized, the clock was down to 1:47 of game time, and the Lions were driving downfield, intent on extending their three-point lead and securing the win. The frenzied pace of the game kept MaryJo distracted, and Melanie hoped she'd be able to slip away from the other girl during the post-game chaos. *I know it's childish,* she thought, *but I need some alone time before I find out any more details.*

After several missed plays, Rushwood finally connected with Eddie on a long ball and he scored the winning goal with mere seconds left in the game. The crowd went wild, and the coaches and officials barely managed to get things wrapped up before the celebration took over. Melanie stood on a bench, trying to get higher and capture the happy scene. With another win on the books, a perfect season was that much closer. Scanning the crowd through her camera, she paused, her heart sinking beyond her stomach. Unable to look away, she watched MaryJo fling herself into Eddie's arms, lacing her own around his neck, and plant an enthusiastic kiss on his lips. For his part, Eddie's initial surprise at the onslaught quickly vanished, as he wrapped his arms around her waist and – from what Melanie could tell at a distance – returned the kiss with equal enthusiasm. The boys around them whooped, and MaryJo broke the kiss, casting a surprised look over her shoulder before hiding her face against Eddie's shoulder. With the benefit of her lens, Melanie was able to see the smug smile the laughing crowd could not.

Seeing the smile broke the spell, and Melanie hopped off the bench and headed toward the stadium gate. *If I can slip away without anyone noticing, everything will be fine,* she thought, ducking and dodging her way along the sideline. She was almost home free when she heard someone call her name.

"Melanie! I've been looking for you everywhere!" Hank cried, catching up with her. "You're headed the wrong way, girl." He cocked his head, in perfect imitation of a puzzled puppy, and Melanie smiled in spite of herself.

"I've been here all day, Hank. I'm tired, thirsty, and ready for some quiet," she said with a shrug, hoping he'd let her slip away.

Before Hank could reply, MaryJo appeared out of nowhere, looping her arm through Melanie's. "Eddie said I should find you and wait for him," she cooed. "We're all going out to celebrate! You're coming too, Hank." Melanie sighed, knowing there was no escape.

"Let's find a shady spot then," Hank said, placing a hand on each girl's back. "It may be late October, but the sun can still get to ya, and y'all have been on the sidelines the whole game."

Melanie blinked in surprise, letting him gently propel her toward a bench off to the side. "I'm not all bad," he leaned close to whisper. "I can try and get you an early out, if you want?" His eyes were kind, and she smiled. She was tired, but the energy from the victory was contagious.

"Thanks," she whispered back. "Maybe it won't be so bad. I've got to eat anyway, might as well have company, yeah?" She shrugged, "I just hope it's not too much company," she added, as MaryJo began calling out to people she knew as they filed out of the stadium.

I should have taken him up on that offer, Melanie thought now, hugging a pillow to her chest. Watching MaryJo and Eddie together had been torture. It'd been so long since Eddie had a crush, let alone a girlfriend, Melanie had forgotten the unique agony of watching her best friend flirt with another girl. *Not that he's ever flirted with me,* she reminded herself. *I just hope MaryJo is serious about him, because he has fallen hook, line and sinker. At least Hank was there, that helped.* The upside of the evening, other than riding the football high, was the company and conversation of Hank. Prior to their Mansfield Perk jaunt earlier in the week, Melanie's interactions with Hank had been limited to paper meetings and the odd post-meeting coffee stop – he tended to tag along, but she attributed that to his outgoing personality. Hank and MaryJo were the kind of people who never met a stranger, and were "friends" with everyone. Hank had proved himself surprisingly observant during the course of the evening, keeping an eye on Melanie and running interference when his sister got too excited. *Maybe there's more to Hank than meets the eye,* she thought. *I could use a friend right now, although it'd be really weird to talk to him about Eddie + MaryJo.*

Chapter 5

Eddie apologized for flaking out and going MIA, saying that MaryJo caught him so by surprise he wasn't sure what to do. He'd had a crush from day one, but never thought she'd be interested – so when she asked him out, and then kissed him, he was over the moon. "It was just so unexpected, Frankie," he'd explained. "I thought I was dreaming, and was afraid telling you would break the spell. Now it's real, and talking won't change anything, so we can go back to the way things were."

Or not, Melanie thought, as she arched an eyebrow. "MaryJo may take offense at that," she pointed out. "We spent a lot of time together. Most girls don't want their boyfriends hanging out with other girls."

"Oh, that's not a problem," Eddie assured her. "She knows you're not some other girl, you're Frankie."

Ouch. Melanie winced. "Umm. I honestly have no idea how to take that, Eddie," she said softly.

Eddie cocked his head. "It's a good thing! It means we can still hang out, and nothing has to change. Because you're Frankie – you're like my twin or something." He paused, his gaze softening in the way that never failed to win her over in any argument. "You know I wouldn't be here without you, Frankie," he said quietly. "And I can't imagine my life without you beside me."

"I know," Melanie sighed. *That's the problem. I can't imagine my life without you either.*

In the days that followed, Melanie found herself spending more and more time with her camera; the quiet routine a welcome escape. Wednesday night pizza remained strictly Eddie and Melanie, but MaryJo tagged along for trips to Mansfield Perk, lunches on campus, and even study sessions. After submitting her trial photos, which were more than adequate, MaryJo was a regular fixture at *Lion's Den* meetings too, as the team worked out the particulars for increasing publication. Everywhere she turned, there was another reminder that Eddie was now MaryJo's, that the "Eddie and Frankie Show" had a new leading lady, and the adjustment was proving painful.

It was a particularly glorious fall in Northanger, and Melanie spent hours roaming the quaint town, camera in hand. Photography was second nature, as easy as breathing, leaving her mind free to wander and process all the changing relationships. She felt most at ease with things when looking through the viewfinder, seeing the world in scenes. The number of files in her "Someday" folder was growing steadily, and Melanie began to toy with the possibility of submitting one or two for publication. She was surprised to discover she did not always miss Eddie. *No, that's not it,* she thought one night, waiting for her afternoon's work to transfer to her laptop. *I miss Eddie, painfully. But I don't miss having to explain my need to photograph things.* It was a startling revelation, but one that felt familiar – as if she'd been burying it deep, in case acknowledging it meant things would have to change. *He's never fully understood that it's so much more than a hobby, the picture taking. It's a need. I have to take pictures – to look through a lens and see things from a new perspective. To take in the light and shadows, to do everything I can to capture the little details. The ones you miss in the moment, but when you look at a photo later, you see them.*

Melanie discovered photography in middle school, one rainy afternoon when she and Eddie were prowling around the Bertram's expansive attic. They stumbled upon a box of old camera parts, and another full of old photographs and negatives. Together they pulled the boxes into the light and spent hours going through the albums and bundles of photos. As she laughed with Eddie over the wild clothes and made up far-fetched stories about what was going on when the pictures were taken, Melanie found she wanted to try it herself. When Momma B called them downstairs for dinner, Melanie had taken the most functional of the cameras and asked if she could use it. Momma B shrugged a "sure, good luck – it's old as the hills," and Melanie officially began her photographic journey.

From that first point-and-shoot, and learning the hard way that film is expensive and you should make every shot count, Melanie progressed to a secondhand SLR and fell in love with the ability to fine-tune an image. When she received her first digital camera, and subsequent freedom to take as many pictures as her heart desired, Melanie knew she had discovered a whole new world. Over the years, she tried to share her world with Eddie – while he was indulgently supportive, even surprising her with a top of the line digital SLR for graduation, he was never able to see beyond the surface. *I think he views it as something I'll outgrow, a phase,* she thought, *when I would dearly love to make it my life. And he hasn't the foggiest idea.* Her file transfer completed, and she hesitated a moment before opening a folder marked "Yesterday."

These pictures were the record of her entire relationship with Eddie: digital scans of her favorite snapshots from childhood mingled with images she'd captured on her own; formal portraits and pictures purloined from friends' facebook pages added to the mix. Growing up next door to the Bertrams had been an interesting experience for Melanie; it was years before she realized her family's cozy bungalow was owned by Eddie's parents. She still wasn't sure of the particulars, but she and Eddie decided ages ago it didn't matter. They were inseparable, and might as well have been twins – when they were younger, you never saw one without the other. As they got older, with diverging interests and occupations, they were still the closest and best of friends.

Melanie set the contents of the folder to play in a slideshow, leaning back to watch with a sigh. *Nothing like a trip down Memory Lane to make you realize just how much you miss your best friend,* she thought. *At least one of us remembers the story.* She smiled, watching the images play across the screen, reliving their childhood escapades. Seeing their young faces, dirt-smudged and smiling, she remembered the first time she met Eddie. Melanie and her parents had been in their new house for a few weeks, and the family was coming back to "the big house" next door after a lengthy summer holiday. An only child, Melanie was giddy: there was a little boy, just her age, and she *knew* they were going to be best friends. With that expectation, as soon as she saw him in the backyard, she ran over and climbed on the fence.

"Hi! I'm your neighbor," she called, waving enthusiastically.

The boy stared at her, before slowly walking over to the fence. "How old are you?"

"Five, but almost six," Melanie answered. "How old are you?"

"Just turned six." He smiled. "I'm Edmund Thomas Bertram. The Third. But everyone calls me Eddie."

Melanie was impressed. "I'm just Melanie Frances Price," she sighed.

"Hmm," Eddie thought. "Now you're Frankie."

Melanie crinkled her nose. "That's a boy name."

"But I'm Eddie, and Frankie sounds better. 'Sides," he added with a cheeky grin that sealed the deal and ruined Melanie forever, "Mum says I'm too little for a girlfriend."

"Okay," Melanie shrugged. "So are we friends now?"

"Yup!"

And it was as simple as that, Melanie remembered. *If I could go back in time, would I do anything differently? Eddie has always called the shots, with a charming grin and a way about him that makes ya think he set the whole world spinning – he changed my name, he changed my world. And he has no idea.* She paused the slideshow, a picture from last Thanksgiving filling the screen. Standing in front of a bonfire, arms around each other, laughing – they looked like they belonged together. *That was a perfect moment,* she smiled.

Thanksgiving was A Big Deal in the Bertram family, which meant it was A Big Deal for Melanie too. The festivities started early, with everyone gathering in the media room to watch the Macy's parade on the big screen, nibbling muffins and sipping cocoa or cider. Afterwards, everyone helped get the meal on the table, even Eddie, Frankie, and miscellaneous cousins in town for the holiday were expected to help out. It was messy, chaotic, and loud – everyone talking over everyone else, and laughing when nobody could hear. It was Melanie's favorite day. Before they were allowed to eat, everyone had to share their "thankful thoughts," big or small, and more than one big family announcement had been made over the years. The afternoon was devoted to board games and football, and Melanie treasured every minute. *It's almost Thanksgiving. Wonder if MaryJo's gonna crash that too. Or if I'm even still invited,* she mused.

Chapter 6

It'd been three weeks since she witnessed The Kiss, and Melanie was looking forward to seeing Grampa Jamie before the game. After a bye-week and an away game, she was in dire need of unburdening herself, and maybe getting some insight into the inner workings of the boy brain.

"You're here early," Jamie remarked, looking up from arranging charcoal briquettes.

"I know," Melanie smiled sheepishly. "I need to vent. But I come bearing gifts!" She raised her hand to show the Mansfield Perk bag containing still-warm muffins.

"I've got a thermos of coffee on the tailgate," Jamie nodded, "pour yourself a mug and you can start talking while I finish getting this grill ready."

Melanie opted to sit on the tailgate rather than one of the chairs, and sniffed the coffee appreciatively. "Mmm, feeling better already," she laughed. "So. A lot has happened since last we chatted," she began, quickly giving him the rundown of MaryJo and Eddie becoming an official couple, and MaryJo's subsequent infiltration of daily life. She told him about the extra time she'd been spending with her camera, and the revelations she'd been resisting. "Eddie is my absolute best friend in the universe," she sighed, "and it kinda feels like a betrayal to say this, but he really and truly has no clue what photography means to me. And I think I maybe always knew that, and while I hoped he'd 'get it' one day – I also just sorta, filtered myself." She groaned. "Oh man, does that sound as pathetic out loud as it did in my head?"

"It sounds like you've been doing a lot of soul searching," Jamie countered. "You're looking at the relationship from a new perspective – and being open to the truth."

"Yeah, well. There have been a lot of new perspectives going on," she wrinkled her nose. "We had a fight Monday. A real one. I haven't spoken to him since, and we even canceled pizza night."

Jamie raised an eyebrow. "This sounds serious. What was the fight about?"

"It started with Hank," Melanie began, rolling her eyes. "Or rather," she continued, "the fact that Eddie doesn't want to date me – but he doesn't want anyone else to either." She felt her temper flaring again, remembering the encounter. "He came over to pick up something for class, and happened to arrive the same time Hank was leaving. We had dinner, because Eddie and MaryJo were on a date, and he walked me back to my dorm. When he said goodnight, Hank leaned in and kissed me on the cheek. *That's* when Eddie walked up, and completely lost his cool. I've never been so embarrassed in my life! He all but drug Hank out of the building, before coming back and lecturing me on how Hank isn't right for me, and I should know better than to get involved with someone like that, and all sorts of crazy talk. I finally asked him if he was jealous – he didn't answer, but he blushed like fire. Like, what the heck? *He has a girlfriend.* He can't all of a sudden decide that I can't date someone, if he's not going to do anything about it!" Melanie growled. "Sorry, I know I'm ranting. It ticks me off. At least he finally realized I'm a girl? Too little, too late. But there is some victory in the knowing, I s'pose?"

Jamie gave her an appraising look. "You said it started with Hank. There was more?"

"Mmm, you could say that." She reached for the thermos to top off her coffee, buying time. "You know Eddie is a religion major, right? And football has always been this kind of hobby, one he's very good at it, but it was never the focus. The plan has always been graduate and go on to seminary, start a sports-based student ministry. We've talked about it for years, had everything worked out. And now –" she paused. "Eddie is rethinking things," she said simply. "No doubt encouraged by MaryJo, he has decided to explore the possibility of playing football professionally. He hasn't even mailed his applications for any of the graduate ministry programs! After his rampage against Hank and laying the groundwork for his new 'Put Frankie in a convent so the only guy she needs is me'-plan, I was so mad. I told him I didn't know him anymore, and I felt like I lost my best friend when he started dating MaryJo – that maybe he should rethink *his* relationship, because it seemed to be ruining everything."

"Somehow, I don't think that went over well," Jamie said with a small smile.

"Oh no," she shook her head. "I knew better, but I couldn't help myself. I *don't* know him right now – she's had such a strange, and strong, influence on him, in such a short amount of time. He's a completely different person right now, and –" she trailed off, lost in thought.

Jamie sat quietly, eyes thoughtful, letting her sort through the thoughts and emotions. For all that she'd just said, there was more bottled up inside; she had to work her way through it and find the answer in her own time, or she'd never be able to fully embrace it.

Melanie laughed softly. "I think," she began, hesitantly. "What really bothers me about everything – changing his mind, and pursuing football – is that I was as much a part of The Plan as any of it. I honestly thought we were going to end up together – he was just waiting for the right time to make the transition from friends to more-than-friends." She studied her coffee before whispering, "I was wrong."

The silence lingered, broken only by the sounds of tailgaters calling greetings to friends. Melanie concentrated on taking deep breaths, gently probing the truth of what she'd just said. *I was wrong.* It was terrifying, and hurt like hell, but it was also – strangely – liberating. *I was wrong; wrong about everything. Wrong about him ever seeing me as anything more than Frankie, wrong about things working out the way we planned, wrong about shaping and changing myself to fit better alongside him. I was wrong.* She looked up, smiling slightly when she met Jamie's gaze.

"How does that feel?"

"Actually, it feels kinda good. Weird, I know. I'm *so* not normal," Melanie rolled her eyes. "But it's almost like – finally admitting it? I don't have to let it make me feel like crap anymore. Ya know?"

Jamie smiled, "I know. And I'm proud of you. What are you going to do now?"

Melanie cocked her head, thinking. "I have no idea. Absolutely, positively no idea. There's this big empty space now where The Plan was, and I don't know what's going to happen with me and Eddie." She sighed. "He's been part of my life for so long, I don't want to lose him entirely."

"But –" Jamie prodded.

"But things can't go on the same, either. It may take a little time to convince my heart he's got to go in a different place now. Okay, that sounded weird," she laughed softly. "He can be my friend, but I can't keep waiting for him to decide he's ready or wants to be my lover."

"If he hasn't figured that out by now, he probably won't. He has a few years before his personality is wholly set, but generally speaking the way a boy behaves now, in his twenties, is how he will behave for the rest of his life," Jamie remarked. "My guess is he is either genuinely clueless – about everything – or he doesn't have the guts to take the next step, that he's content to keep coasting in the familiar – safe – way things have always been."

"Hmm," Melanie murmured. "It might be a combination of the two. And I made it so easy for him, because I love him – I always have. Just maybe not the right kind of love." She pulled a face. "Ugh. This is exhausting," she laughed. "And I still have to cover the game!"

"Have some more coffee," Jamie passed her the thermos. "What about Thanksgiving?"

"Umm," she hedged. "That's a really good question. My parents always celebrate with his family, it's a given. This could be awkward. But," she said, standing with a dramatic flourish. "In the words of the great Scarlet O'Hara, I'll think about it tomorrow. Thanks for the coffee, and for listening. I didn't realize the venting would turn into a therapy session. But I think we had quite a breakthrough, Doctor," she smiled. "Truly, thank you."

"What are grampas for?" Jamie asked, standing to give her a hug. "You're stronger than you think, and I really am proud of you. Oh, I almost forgot," he turned and reached into the truck. "I saw this and thought of you. Maybe it can be part of your new Plan."

Melanie glanced at the flyer, and tucked it into her camera bag. "Okay, I'll check it out. Thanks. Into the fray I go, wish me luck! And if I don't see you before Thursday, happy Thanksgiving!"

"Good luck, happy Thanksgiving, and I expect a full report next Saturday."

"Aye aye, Cap'n," Melanie saluted with a laugh. "Go Lions!"

Chapter 7

Thanksgiving morning dawned bright and sunny, with a distinct nip to the air. Melanie lingered, she told her parents she wanted to get some pictures of the Bertrams' house in the morning light, but she was really prolonging the inevitable. Eddie had texted her, saying he hoped she would still come, and she'd replied "of course." *Because really, what other option did I have?* Stooping to take a closer look at some half-hidden acorns, she jumped at Eddie's voice.

"You scared me to death! What are you doing sneaking around the yard like that?" Melanie whirled to face him. "Geez, Eddie."

"Sorry, thought you saw me coming," he said, shuffling his feet in the leaves. "I'm glad you came, Frankie." He glanced at her briefly, before looking back at his feet, hands shoved in his pockets. "I know I was an idiot, and I think I probably deserved more than you told me, so ... I'm sorry. For everything."

Melanie sighed heavily. "You definitely deserved worse than you got." She laughed a little at the look of surprise that crossed his face, as he finally met her gaze. "Thought that'd get your attention. I know you were an idiot, but I also know that things happen sometimes. I accept your apology."

"Thanks, Frankie," Eddie half-smiled. "You really are the best."

"Why do you look like crap?"

Eddie winced. "Um, is it that noticeable?"

"Mmhmm, to me it is. I know you don't look that bad just because I yelled at you."

"Ha. No. Well, not entirely." Eddie fidgeted. "The things you said? About how you didn't recognize me anymore and how in such a short amount of time I'd let MaryJo change everything about me?" At Melanie's nod, he continued. "I started thinking about it, like, really thinking. Because you know me better than anyone, and if you didn't recognize me – that was big. I tried talking to MaryJo about it, and it was the strangest conversation. She thought I'd found out about her and Rushwood – yeah, I was surprised too. Apparently they hooked up at a party, and would see each other on Wednesdays, when I was with you for pizza night."

Melanie choked on a laugh. "How did nobody know this? And oh gross, dude – you were secondhand kissing your quarterback."

Eddie cringed. "Thank you, Frankie, for putting it in such delicate and ladylike terms. I was trying not to think about that. *Anyway,*" he continued, over Melanie's snickers. "Obviously, that relationship is ended."

"I'm sorry, Eddie," Melanie said. "I know you really liked her."

"I did, but I'll be okay," he shrugged. "I think I knew it'd never really last, not with a girl like MaryJo." As he spoke, he took a couple steps closer. "Um. Fran– no, Melanie," he corrected himself, ignoring her raised eyebrow. "Um, so, ah – this is probably the worst timing ever, but the other part of my thinking was, well. It's like this – when you slammed your door in my face, and didn't talk to me, I missed you. I realized that I needed you there. I need *you*. Maybe," he paused, hesitating, as his eyes searched her face. "Maybe we could, you know, give more than friends a try?"

"Oh Eddie," Melanie sighed. "I adore you, I always have – and I waited so, so long for you to say those words. But," she placed a hand gently on his arm. "I can't. Not right now."

Eddie took a step back. "Oh. You're with Hank, aren't you?"

"No, and I never was," Melanie stated. "I tried telling you that, and you wouldn't listen, remember? Hank's a surprisingly decent friend, but that's it."

"Then – why?" Eddie looked genuinely confused.

"Because right now? I'm concentrating on me," she said softly, her eyes pleading for understanding. "I've lived my whole life waiting for you, Eddie –

making plans for an 'us' that was never gonna happen. It's time I find my own place in the story."

Eddie stood there, uncertainly. "What are you going to do?"

"I've got an idea," she smiled. "Grampa Jamie gave me a flyer advertising this new gallery coming to Northanger, and I'm going to see about getting some of my work included. I've been playing with the idea of doing something 'official' with my photography, and this may be my in."

"Hey, that's great! You've got mad skills, and it'd be cool to see your pictures somewhere other than the paper," Eddie smiled. "Need an assistant?"

Melanie laughed. "Nah, I'm good. But I might need a friend – know where I could find one of those?"

"I know a guy – he's kinda dumb sometimes, but teachable. You may know him, fella by the name of Edmund Thomas Bertram. The Third. But his friends call him Eddie."

"Hey, that's an impressive title," she grinned. "I like the sound of this Eddie guy, think he'd wanna be friends with a girl named Melanie Frances Price?"

"Yup," Eddie grinned back. "Friends?"

"Friends," Melanie nodded, stepping into his familiar hug.

❧❀❧

At the table later, surrounded by family and friends as close as family, when it was her time to share her thankful thoughts, Melanie smiled at Eddie sitting across from her as she said simply "Old friends and new vision."

Acknowledgements

To my own, real life "Grampa Jamie" – there aren't enough words to say how deeply I appreciate your investment in my life, and I know that I wouldn't be who I am today without the encouragement and truths you shared over the years. For the hours spent talking life (and football!): thank you, from the bottom of my heart. You will be missed, so very much, but never forgotten.

Another holiday, another story, and I still can't quite believe this is happening. I consider myself so blessed to be a part of the *Holidays with Jane* ladies – Jessica, Cecilia, Jennifer, Melissa and Nancy (Kimberly too!): y'all are awesome, and so much fun to write with. I love the insanity we cook up, and wish there was a real life Mansfield Perk where we could hang out.

And, of course, thanks to Jane for writing it first. Even though *Mansfield Park* is officially my least favorite of all her novels, I have a greater appreciation for the story she was telling now, after spending so much time with the characters. I like to think she'd understand, even approve, the change I had to make.

Design by Chance

A *Persuasion* Story

*To the lovers, the dreamers, and the
fairy tale believers:
May we all get a[nother] chance at our own
Ever After.*

Chapter 1

Gracie stared at the screen, wondering if she was reading the message correctly. *No way,* she thought. *There is absolutely no way. Except, it kinda makes sense–if a nightmare can make sense.*

"Ohmigosh, Gracie, you have got to try the new cookies at Mansfield Perk, they are to die – whoa, you look like you've seen a ghost. Are you okay?" Setting her bag in the chair by the door, Eleanor Tilney-Grey hurried to Gracie's desk. "Seriously, you're scaring me. Here, have a sip of my Marianne Dashwood, it'll help. What's going on?"

Gracie turned her laptop so the screen faced her friend, watching Eleanor as she read aloud.

"'Gracie, my name is Sophie Croft and I've recently moved to the Northanger area. You may be aware that I purchased Kellynch Hall, and am in the process of renovating it into an art gallery. Having seen several examples of your work in the last month, I've decided that you are – without doubt – the person I want handling the interiors. You have a wonderful eye, and your attention to maintaining historical character and integrity are exactly what I am looking for in bringing Croft Galleries to life.'

"I don't know what to say," Eleanor said, looking up. "Does she know Kellynch was like, your family's legacy?"

"Keep reading," Gracie whispered.

"'As much as I would adore working with you on this project, I know it might be a difficult undertaking for you; I understand your family has a long-standing connection to Kellynch. In truth, that family connection strengthens my desire to have you work with me – you have an intimate understanding of the house and, I think, a wish to see it restored. Please allow me the impertinent privilege of inviting you to dinner next week, so I can share my vision, and – I hope – entice you to help me restore the house to its former glory. My number is below, or feel free to stop by anytime I'm at the house – I drive a red Tahoe. I look forward to hearing from you soon, Sophie Croft.'"

After she read it through, Eleanor sat on the edge of Gracie's desk and gave a low whistle. "Wow. So ... whatcha thinking?"

Gracie shrugged. "I have no idea. I knew the house had been sold again, obviously, but I had no idea ..." her voice trailed off, as she turned the laptop and stared at the screen again.

Eleanor cocked her head thoughtfully. "You're reacting to more than just the sale of the house and being asked to come refurbish the place – probably with a limitless budget, by the way. The Crofts? They're Vanderbilt-caliber old money. By logical reasoning, this should be a dream job, even if it would be weird fixing the Elliot place up for, well, non-Elliots. Spill, what's really bothering you?"

"It's a long story," Gracie sighed.

"Then let's move this show down the road," Eleanor said. "You, me, Mansfield Perk, a plate of cookies and two very strong drinks."

"Don't you already have a drink?" Gracie asked, standing and reaching for her coat.

"It'll be gone by the time we get there," Eleanor laughed. "'Sides, I can always get something different. I hear a rumor Parker has created a new off-menu drink, wonder if I could sweet talk him into letting me have one?"

"If you're referring to the Pemberley's Attic, I've had one. Several actually," Gracie grinned. "And it is *so* delicious. He made them as bribe and payment to wrap his Christmas presents."

Eleanor stopped in the middle of the stairwell to stare at her friend, eyebrows raised. "Come again?"

"He needed someone to wrap his Christmas presents," Gracie said simply.

"That's what I thought you said," Eleanor shook her head. "What on earth are you talking about? I thought he was like, this artistic savant or something?"

Gracie laughed, nudging her friend to keep moving. "You would think the art thing would give him an edge, wouldn't you? But there's more to gift wrapping than simple creative genius. I took pity on the guy, he brought his gifts over, and I wrapped them for him."

Eleanor rolled her eyes. "I wonder if he tried to pass off your work as his own?"

"He could try I s'pose, but I used those nifty gold 'Graceful Design' labels on the gift tags," Gracie grinned.

"Free advertising," Eleanor squealed. "Love it! You're an evil genius on top of being the world's most amazing decorator ever. I'm glad you're my friend, I'd hate to be on your bad side."

Walking into the welcoming, coffee-scented warmth of Mansfield Perk, Gracie looked around with a low whistle. "You can tell the semester starts tomorrow," she said. "You find us somewhere to sit, and I'll order. You wanna try a Pemberley's Attic?"

"You got it," Eleanor flashed a thumbs-up. "And don't forget the cookies! Oh, there's a spot opening up, I'm gonna stake a claim."

Gracie joined the line waiting to order and pulled out her phone. Scrolling through her newsfeed, she half-listened to the chatter around her. Just as she found herself getting interested in the story the girl in front of her was telling about introducing her New Yorker boyfriend to a California Christmas, Gracie was startled by a sharp tug on her arm. "Oh," she gasped, turning to see who had approached her. "Russ, I swear," she began.

"Not so fast," he interrupted. "I come bearing good news."

Gracie arched an eyebrow.

"Eleanor told me to take over ordering duties," he explained. "Apparently something has come up and your presence at the table is required *immediately*. Don't ask me," he raised his hands, "I know only what

I'm told. Which reminds me, you're supposed to tell me the name of the drink I'm ordering?"

With a laugh, Gracie leaned close and whispered "Pemberley's Attic," in Russ's ear, smirking at the confused expression on his face. "I promise, it's worth it. You should order one for yourself while you're at it. And don't forget –"

"The cookies," he finished. "I know, Eleanor told me three times. And," he paused, looking at the phone in his hand, "she just texted me a string of cookie emoji. That girl has a problem," he shook his head. "Go, sit, do whatever you need to do while I wait in this incredibly long line."

"You're a doll, Russ," Gracie smiled. "Have I told you lately that I love you?"

"Can't hear that too often," Russ smiled back. "Just save all the juiciest gossip 'til I get there, okay?"

"No promises," Gracie quipped as she began to weave her way to the window table Eleanor had managed to secure.

"I hope you don't mind," her friend said as soon as Gracie was close enough to hear. "But when I saw Russ walking by, I couldn't resist asking him to join us – especially since it got you out of line duty."

"How did you manage that, by the way?" Gracie asked, settling in a seat and looking over at the line. "He hates lines."

"I know," Eleanor grinned. "It took some conniving, but beyond that I won't say."

Gracie rolled her eyes. "Before he gets over here, I'll fill you in on the short version of the story, okay?"

"Won't he be mad? He's got to know we're here for A Reason."

"Nah, he won't be mad. Well, he might be mad, but not for the reasons you think. 'Sides," she shrugged slightly, "he knows the story anyway – he was part of it."

Eleanor raised an eyebrow. "How complex is this story?"

"Not complex so much as ..." Gracie hesitated, searching for the right word. "Okay, so maybe it is complex. Short version? Once upon a time, freshman year, right here at Abbey, I met two guys."

"Is this going to be a dramatic love triangle?" Eleanor leaned forward conspiratorially, an impish glint in her eyes.

"No, not a love triangle. But it did get dramatic," Gracie's laugh was sharp. "One of the guys was Russ, and the other was a guy named Derek."

"I still crack up over how you and Russ met," Eleanor interrupted again. "It's a wonder y'all are still friends after all these years."

"You don't know the half of it. And if you don't stop interrupting me, you won't get the rest of the story."

"Sorry. So, who was Derek? Why have I never heard of him and what is the connection to Croft Galleries?"

"Derek was an art major, we met in Art History I, and I fell head over heels for him at first sight." Gracie smiled at her friend's exaggerated sigh of delight. "It was such a cliché – freshman girl falling for tall, dark and mysterious older student. He started college later than most, he worked several years to pay his way through school, so even though he was five years older, we were both freshmen. Long story even shorter, we dated all four years. He proposed the week before graduation. I said yes, but –" Gracie paused.

"Who called things off?" Eleanor asked softly. "You're not married, and I've never heard his name cross your lips – the engagement either didn't last, or there was a very quick divorce. I'm banking on the former," she continued, as Gracie raised her head in surprise. "Historically-minded literature professor," she smiled. "I excel at reading between the lines."

"Oh right," Gracie nodded, smiling slightly. "That makes sense. I was surprised is all, because you're right. The engagement didn't last. I called it off." The last words were a whisper.

"You didn't want to," Eleanor said simply.

Gracie shook her head. "Derek was my everything – my True Love. I wanted to marry him. And I didn't." She paused, pursing her lips slightly. "The timing was bad, that's what I told myself. And sure, it wasn't great, but that's not why I broke the engagement – the truth of the matter is I allowed myself to be convinced that marrying him would only make things worse. For myself, but more so for my family. I can blame people who gave me advice, like Russ, but at the end of the day *I* made the decision." Gracie sighed. "Needless to say, that conversation did not go over well, and I've not heard hide nor hair from Derek in eight years."

"Hmm," Eleanor murmured. "What's the connection with Sophie Croft's new gallery?"

"Derek had an older sister, married to a Naval officer stationed overseas. I never met her, but he used to tell me about the places they went and the artistic hideaways she'd discover. That sister was Sophie Croft."

"Wait, so –" Eleanor paused. "I'm still confused. If you never met her, does Sophie Croft know you were engaged to her brother?"

"I don't know," Gracie shrugged. "I guess not, or she wouldn't want me to work on her project. I mean, would *you* want the snob who broke your little brother's heart to do your interiors? I don't think she knows. But I do, and it's going to feel strange." She pulled a face, glancing over to see where Russ was in line, before adding, "did I mention that Derek, my one-time fiancé and The Great Love Of My Life, is Derek *Worth*?"

"Derek Worth? Derek Worth?!" Eleanor squeaked. "Even I know who he is, Gracie! How the heck? Man," she shook her head. "And you broke the engagement, so you didn't even get to keep the ring!"

"It ended so fast, I never even *got* the ring," Gracie sighed.

"Derek Worth," Eleanor murmured, "I just can't believe it. The Derek Worth." Tilting her head, she gave Gracie a speculative glance. "What else have you been hiding?"

"Nothing interesting, I promise," Gracie laughed.

"What's not interesting?" Russ asked, approaching with a loaded tray.

"Oh, just that Miss Secretive over here has been hiding some very interesting – and famous – people in her past," Eleanor smirked.

"Her past?" Russ raised an eyebrow. "I would say she has very interesting people in her present. I mean, I'm here – and *nobody* is as interesting as me."

"Nor as humble," Gracie quipped, rolling her eyes.

"Remind me why we put up with him?" Eleanor asked, reaching for a drink.

"I haven't the foggiest," Gracie shrugged. "Especially when you consider that he stole my scholarship."

"Oh brother, don't start that again," Russ groaned, handing Gracie her drink and setting a plate of cookies in the middle of the table. "I never stole anything! See, I'm the soul of generosity, bringing gifts of cookies and sugary drinks to a confab during which, I feel certain, I will be subjected to any number of girlie remarks and/or diatribes against the stupidity of man." He paused, as Gracie and Eleanor exchanged glances and succumbed to a case of the giggles. "Obviously, it's going to be one of those days," Russ sighed good-naturedly. "I have nothing else to do this afternoon, I might as well watch you two act like schoolgirls."

Later that evening, Gracie reread Sophie Croft's email for what felt like the thousandth time. *I would be completely stupid to turn this job down,* she thought.

And if I'm completely honest with myself, I don't want to turn it down. I want to work with Sophie and restore Kellynch to its former glory – with an updated twist. With a determined nod, she typed out a quick reply, telling Sophie she was very interested in the proposition and looked forward to meeting with her soon to further discuss the project.

Chapter 2

"We changed very little of the actual architecture and original design. Thankfully, once we started 'digging in,' there was much less structural damage than we thought. There were a few tweaks I couldn't resist making, but overall we tried to keep it as close to original as possible." As she spoke, Sophie Croft gestured for Gracie to enter Kellynch ahead of her.

"That's good," Gracie murmured, stepping into the familiar foyer and looking around. Signs of the newly finished construction work lingered, from the scent of sawdust heavy in the air to walls and trim begging for a coat of paint.

"The contractor couldn't believe it when I asked him not to repaint anything," Sophie laughed. "I assured him I was working to secure the services of an expert decorator, but he made me promise to call him if you were unable to take the job."

Gracie smiled. "Did you use Brandon Delaford?"

"How'd you know?" Sophie nodded an affirmative.

"I recognize his style – in both the work, and that concern. He's a good guy; we've ended up working the same project before." Gracie moved further into the welcoming space. "I can already tell he's done an amazing job," she remarked, running her hand along the banister. "I'm not sure Kellynch has ever looked this good."

"Wait until you see the rest of the place," Sophie said. "I know it's a gallery and arts center, but I couldn't resist indulging a whim – the kitchen is to-die for!" As she spoke, she flashed an excited grin so like Derek's that Gracie's heart momentarily slammed to a halt. "My husband teases me about the extensive overhaul, especially since this kitchen is nicer than our own, but I told him it was a business investment."

Gracie, heart beating again, raised an eyebrow. "A business investment?"

"But of course," Sophie smirked. "With a professional-grade kitchen in-house, we can cater functions at a lower cost. Simple logic, wouldn't you agree?"

"Totally," Gracie laughed, starting to walk down the hall. "Let's go check out this investment kitchen, I confess to being intrigued. I always wanted *more* for that space, it seemed so lonely somehow." She stopped, realizing Sophie hadn't followed. Turning, she saw the other woman still standing in the foyer, a strange expression on her face. "Is everything okay?" Gracie asked, feeling a jolt of concern.

Sophie shook her head a little, "I just realized how strange this must be for you. Kellynch is my new project – I saw a house with potential, and fell in love along the way. But for you," she paused, waving her hand vaguely, as if reaching for the right words. "I knew the house belonged to your family in the past, but it struck me just now, seeing you here – this was *home*. And I know this must be hard for you, I'm sorry if I've brought up painful memories. You don't have to do this if you don't want to, please know that," Sophie continued.

If you only knew, Gracie thought, feeling a wave of emotion building. She moved back into the foyer, surprising them both when she reached out and gave Sophie a tight hug.

"Thank you," Gracie said softly. "I cannot tell you how deeply I appreciate that you care," she continued. "I'll admit I had my doubts at first, I wasn't sure what it would be like to come in here and see someone making changes to Kellynch. But I was also very curious. And truthfully, I haven't lived here in nearly a decade; I sometimes think my memories are imaginings. I told myself I'd keep an open mind, come see what you were thinking, and then decide." She shrugged slightly. "I made my decision the minute I walked in the door. I want to do this. I think I *need* to do this," she smiled.

Sophie gave her a searching look. "I believe you," she said at last. "But if it gets to be overwhelming at any point, please let me know."

"That I can do," Gracie laughed. "Now, show me the kitchen, please! I won't be able to talk business until I see what you've done. I love a good kitchen."

"I knew I liked you," Sophie grinned, leading the way. "Tell ya what, we can even break in the new coffee bar, if I can figure out how the machine works, while we talk details."

The next few weeks were a blur of activity as Gracie and Sophie fine-tuned the aesthetic for Kellynch's new life as Croft Galleries. While deciding paint colors and debating lighting methods, the women found themselves settling into a friendship as well as a creative partnership. Sophie was an ideal client: communicating her wants for the space without hindering the creative process, and a budget that left Gracie breathless. With her natural cheerfulness and what Gracie dubbed "big sister instincts," Sophie was an even better friend. Her open, relaxed manner set Gracie at ease, and she found herself wondering what could have been, if she hadn't ended things with Derek so many years ago. She often reminded herself not to focus on the what ifs, but to enjoy the chance to get to know Sophie now. Russ, on the other hand, was less than enthusiastic about the development.

Gracie knew he was genuinely concerned, they'd been the best of friends through so much, but as her phone pinged with yet another text, she couldn't help but groan. "I'm working," she muttered, glancing at the screen. "Oh, not Russ. And why am I talking to myself?" Shaking her head, she opened the text from Sophie. "Come by Kellynch when you get a chance," she read aloud. "I've got a surprise."

Chapter 3

As Gracie let herself in the back door of Kellynch, she breathed deeply. *Few things smell as new and promising as fresh paint.* She sighed happily. Brandon's crew had finished painting a few days earlier, and she was ready to start putting the finishing touches on the basic structure of the rooms, before the artwork arrived. At this rate, they would be able to get everything polished and in place well before the deadline. *I wasn't sure about Sophie's opening Gala timetable, but the work has gone much quicker than anticipated, and Valentine's will make for a special celebration. Cheap date too,* she smiled to herself. *Art, heavy hors d'oeuvres, seeing and being seen by the community. Sophie definitely knew what she was doing.*

"Gracie? We're in the dining room," Sophie called, hearing the door.

Shrugging out of her coat, Gracie laughed. "Do you think we should rename the rooms, so we don't confuse people," she asked, "or at least give them code names?" Walking into the room, Gracie saw Sophie was not alone. "Sorry, I didn't realize you had company, or I wouldn't have –" she stopped abruptly, as the man by the window turned her way. His hair was shorter, and the earrings from college were gone, but she'd know him anywhere.

"Oh don't worry about it," Sophie laughed. "Gracie, meet my infamous little brother Derek – he's arrived earlier than expected, and will help us get things ready for the Gala on Valentine's!"

"Hello, Gracie," Derek said, his voice low and rumbling.

"Derek," she said softly, heart racing. *Breathe, Gracie, breathe,* she reminded herself. *You knew it was going to happen eventually. You can do this, you're a professional.*

Sophie looked between them, a searching expression in her eyes. As the charged silence lengthened, she asked "am I missing something?"

"Gracie and I knew each other in college," Derek said, giving a casual shrug. "It's been a long time," he added. "I'm surprised you're still in Northanger, I thought you'd be in Atlanta or somewhere, making a name for yourself."

Gracie felt her temper flare. Before she could respond, Sophie walked over and looped her arm though Gracie's.

"Our girl Gracie has made a name for herself, and I'm glad she's here in Northanger. It'd have been much harder to convince her to take on this project if she were elsewhere," she said. "I didn't realize you knew each other," she continued, giving Gracie a curious look.

"It's been a long time," she said quietly. "When we were art students at Abbey."

"That's the truth," Derek nodded. "So long ago, it's as if we're starting over, eh Gracie?"

Gracie looked at him, trying to read between the lines. His eyes, dark as ever, revealed nothing. *Of course*, she thought. *Why would he want to pick up where we left off?* "Yeah, I guess you could say that," she said at last. "After all, we've been out of school twice as long as we were in school. That's a world of living taking place, neither of us is who we once were."

"You'll have plenty of time to get reacquainted," Sophie interjected. "I've just had the most brilliant idea."

Gracie glanced curiously at her friend, as Derek sighed. "Soph, what are you cooking up now?"

"I'm making some changes to the Valentine's Gala," she said. "With you here to help us, we'll be able to get the Galleries public-ready even more ahead of schedule, which leaves us a good deal of extra time. I think we should add a special, sparkling, element to the Gala."

"I've got a bad feeling about this," Derek muttered.

"You know we've talked about having an exhibition of some of your pieces," Sophie began. "I propose we weave it into the Gala. After all, diamonds and Valentine's go together like milk and cookies."

"What exactly do you have in mind?" Derek asked, raising an eyebrow.

"Okay, hear me out, I'm making it up as I go," Sophie laughed. "But I'm picturing your pieces on special display, maybe mixed in with the other work or maybe a separate room. The first real rotating, traveling collection. I know you're concentrating primarily on custom designs, but don't you have a selection of standard stock? Oh!" Sophie gasped, eyes wide. "I know, I know! We can spin it as a 'returning to the beginning' kind of thing, with examples of your early work, that you did here as a student, and show your progress as an artist."

Gracie smiled as Derek listened to his sister, his inscrutability faltering in the face of her enthusiasm. *Didn't see that one coming, did ya? I think she's been plotting this for months*, she thought.

"Sophie," he sighed.

"I know, it's genius right?"

"I was going to say it's very short notice," he replied. "I admit the idea has a certain marketing appeal – you've already got a great idea going, having an opening Gala on Valentine's. Add jewels to the mix, and it does flirt with genius territory. But to do it right takes time, Sophie."

"It's doable, if you really wanted to," Gracie said quietly. As Derek turned to her in surprise, she squared her shoulders, a determined look in her eyes. "Is it short notice? Yes. But it's not impossible. In fact, you wouldn't even have to have a large inventory on hand to make it work. In this case, less is more. Especially since we really don't want to run the risk of anything going missing," she smiled slightly. "I suggest no more than a half dozen pieces on display. A mix of early work and current designs, maybe even something that isn't complete. Fill the rest of the 'exhibit' with framed images of other pieces and sketches; maybe have an assortment of tools or raw materials. Play up the artistic journey, tease them, and leave them wanting more. Not only will it make for a nice addition to the Gala, but you'll probably generate interest in commissions as well."

Derek was silent, obviously appraising the idea, though Gracie still couldn't read his eyes. At last, he nodded slowly. "Quality, not quantity," he murmured. "Okay, I'm convinced. I have thousands of sketches to choose from, so that's easy – and a nice touch. It'll fill the space, and make it a more complete experience, as opposed to popping a few rings in a case and calling it done."

"So you'll do it?" Sophie asked.

"Sure, let's do it," Derek smiled.

"Great!" Sophie threw her arms around her brother. "This is going to be magnificent, trust me. And Gracie," she added, turning to flash a grin her way. "You're in charge."

"Uh," Gracie stammered. "What?"

"Yeah, what she said," Derek added, with a wary expression.

"With you here to help, I can focus on getting the behind the scenes, paperwork stuff taken care of," Sophie shrugged. "Gracie's official design work is essentially complete, so the two of you can work together to make sure things look beautiful. Especially this new element."

Derek and Gracie exchanged a look. "Here goes nothing," Derek shook his head. "Guess we're back on design duty. It'll be almost like old times, eh, Gracie?"

With a sigh, Gracie accepted the new development with as much grace as she could muster in the moment. "Almost like chicken," she snorted. "Well, this'll be a new line for the resume at least," she quipped. *What on earth have I gotten myself into*, she wondered. *And how will I survive working with Derek again?*

"Are you out of your mind? And I mean that seriously. I go out of town for a week, and everyone loses their mind! Why does nobody else see the problem with this?"

Gracie rolled her eyes before turning from her design board. "Good morning, Russ. Pull up a chair, have a seat. What's on your mind?"

"Is it true?" Russ asked.

"Is what true?"

"Are you working with Derek Worth on a special Valentine's project?"

"Yes."

"Are you out of your mind?" Russ repeated.

Gracie raised an eyebrow. "I don't think so? I've been working with his sister for a couple weeks now. This is an extension of that project; it's just another job, Russ."

"Gracie. It's *not* just another job. This is Derek Worth we are talking about. And it's Valentine's. Valentine's! Gracie, honey, are you sure about this? I know it's been a long time, but this kind of scenario could spell disaster for your heart."

Gracie leaned back in her chair, considering Russ's concern. Taking her silence as an invitation to continue pressing his case, Russ leaned forward. "We've been friends a long time, I know you. I know that when you called things off with Derek, it took a long time for you to get over it. There were times I wasn't sure you would get over it, but that's a discussion for another time. The point is: you're going to be working closely with your ex fiancé, at Valentine's. This can only end in disaster."

If you only knew, she thought. Standing, she leaned over the desk to give him a quick hug. "I know you're only looking out for me, but I'll be okay. As you said, it was a long time ago. I'm not the same girl I was then, and Derek has given no indication that he'd be interested revisiting the past. In fact, Sophie has hinted that she anticipates an engagement in his future – to some girl who is not me. I'm not expecting him to fall in love with me again, Russ."

"But you might fall in love with him. Again," Russ sighed. "That's what worries me."

Gracie smiled. "I'll be careful, I promise. Now I need to fine-tune this sketch, we have to finish placing Derek's pieces today, and I want to make sure we maximize the space. If you can sit quietly, you can stay. Otherwise: vamoose," she laughed.

Russ glanced at his watch. "I've got some time to kill, so I'll just kick back and read a little. I've found the most amazing blog, *The Felicity of Reading*, and it's full of great book recommendations. I know it's early in the year, but if I'm going to read more than you, I can't afford to get behind."

"Make yourself comfortable," she drawled, as Russ pulled out his tablet and propped his heels on the desk.

"I always do," he replied with a grin. "And you have work to do."

Gracie rolled her eyes, turning back to her design board. In truth, there was very little left to do, on paper anyway. Sophie had called that morning, letting her know that Derek had finally decided which sketches and photographs he wanted to use. *He's getting them framed today, simple black frames for minimal intrusion but optimal showcasing*, Gracie thought, mentally running through her checklist. *The jewelry itself won't be placed yet, but we do have the glass cases–those can be put into position, and give us a better sense of how traffic will flow in the room. We also need to make sure we aren't forgetting the obvious in the other rooms*, Gracie scribbled a note in the margin of her sketch.

"Hey Gracie," Russ interrupted her train of thought. "You're an interior designer. I can understand Sophie Croft hiring you to redecorate Kellynch, and even help with the initial layout of the galleries. But how did you end up as, like, party planner-slash-designer?"

"Oh," she blinked. "Umm, it just happened. When I started working on Kellynch, Sophie wanted to make sure it'd be ready by Valentine's, so she could have an opening gala. I assured her it would be ready in plenty of time, after all, the hard part was finished. I was mostly supervising colors and handling miscellaneous furnishing and layout. That didn't take long, since Brandon volunteered his crew to handle the painting. As Sophie and I worked through details, we would talk about the Gala, and somewhere along the way I became part of the planning and execution," she shrugged. "It's been fun though," she smiled. "This is going to be the Valentine's party of all Valentine's parties."

"Hmm," Russ murmured. "I'm still not happy about you spending so much time with Derek. I don't want you getting hurt, and I will get involved if I feel like I need to."

"Please don't," Gracie snapped. "That's what got us in trouble in the first place."

Russ's eyes were wide with surprise. "Wow," he said softly.

"I don't know where that came from," Gracie shook her head. "But please, don't get involved. Whatever happens will be between me and Derek. I love you, and I appreciate you wanting to protect me. But I'm a big girl, and I have to make my own decisions and take my chances."

For a long moment, they sat in silence, taking each other's measure. "Okay," Russ said at last. "Okay, I'll stay out of it. I'm here if you need someone to listen, and I'm willing to get as involved as you need me to be. But you're calling the shots."

"Thank you," Gracie whispered. "Really, I mean that. Now, you're gonna be my date to this thing, right?"

Russ laughed. "As if I'd let you go with anyone else! Just let me know what color tie to wear, and I'm there. Oh," he jumped, as his phone buzzed. "I should take this, but I'll see you for lunch," he added, grabbing his things and walking out of Gracie's attic office.

Chapter 4

Gracie stood in the middle of the room, looking at her surroundings with a practiced eye. The local art collection, in the former living room, was her favorite part of Croft Galleries. *I'm glad Sophie is so willing to support the local community*, she mused, taking in the paintings and photographs on the walls, the blown glass and ceramic sculptures on specially designed stands. *It all came together beautifully, and I can't wait for everyone to see it at the Gala,* she sighed happily.

"It always surprises me, how much talent hides in plain sight," Derek said softly, joining her.

"Oh," Gracie gasped. "You startled me. I didn't realize you were here."

"Just got here; couldn't find Sophie at home," he shrugged.

"She ran to town for something," Gracie replied. "What did you mean?"

"Hmm?"

"When you said the talent in plain sight surprises you – what did you mean?"

"This," Derek gestured to the art surrounding them. "Every piece displayed in this room came from someone who calls Northanger, or the near vicinity, home. These are the people you pass on the street, make your drink at Mansfield Perk, live quiet unassuming lives in a quiet unassuming town. Would you expect them to produce art like this, if you didn't know?"

Gracie raised an eyebrow. "Now who's the snob?" she asked, instantly regretting the quip. "Sorry," she amended. "I get what you're saying, but you forget – I was one of those unassuming people from this unassuming place. I like to think that any of us could be hiding artistic genius, or at least a creative spark."

"I forget nothing."

Gracie shivered, the low rumble of his voice rendering her speechless. She tried, for the thousandth time, to read the expression in his dark eyes. As the silence lengthened, she sought frantically for something to say. *Preferably something that won't lead into the danger zone,* she thought. Before she could come up with anything, Derek stepped away from her, toward a grouping of photographs.

"These are excellent," he murmured.

"Yes," Gracie said softly. "Melanie Price is the student photographer for *The Lion's Den* at Abbey. She's never shown her work before, outside of the paper, and her nervous enthusiasm is adorable. She's spectacular; I'm glad Sophie accepted her pictures."

"She's got a good eye," Derek nodded toward a series of scenes from around town. "Hey, there's Grampa Jamie"

"Mmhmm," Gracie nodded, stepping closer. "I think this is my favorite, especially –" she fell silent.

Derek looked at her, and for the first time Gracie could read his eyes. Seeing the raw emotion in his dark eyes, Gracie felt tears sting her own. To her surprise, Derek reached over and gave her shoulders a quick squeeze. Before she could react, he stepped back quickly, raking a hand through his still just-too-long curls. "Charlie told me. It's hard to believe he's gone; he's the kind of guy who lives forever. I always thought I'd get to come back, tell him thanks. But I waited too long," Derek shook his head. "He used to give me the worst lectures. I hated them at the time – I was convinced I knew best – but I would give anything to be able to talk things over one more time."

"I know what you mean," Gracie smiled slightly. "When I," she paused, rethinking her phrasing. "After graduation, when I was making decisions about what to do next, he definitely gave some tough love advice. I took some of it, and some of it I ignored." She hesitated, hazarding another glance at Derek, but he was focused on the candid portrait of their mentor and friend. "Sometimes I wonder what would've happened if I changed up the advice I took," she whispered.

"'What if' is a dangerous game," Derek said quietly, several minutes later.

"I know," she nodded. "But that never stopped anyone from asking."

Several minutes passed in silence, and Gracie wandered over to take another look at Parker's paintings, debating whether the grouping should be separated or not, when Derek's voice stopped her. "Why are you still here?"

"Excuse me?" Turning, she raised an eyebrow.

"In Northanger," he amended. "Why are you still in Northanger?"

Gracie thought about it for a moment. "Northanger is home," she said at last. "Just because my father squandered the Elliot fortune and had to sell the family estate, that doesn't change. When he moved to Atlanta to live with Elizabeth, I stayed. I couldn't bear the thought of leaving, not when so many memories were here."

"I'd think you would want to escape the memories," Derek said quietly.

"I considered it," she admitted. "I really did. But running away doesn't mean you forget."

"No, no it doesn't."

"I was homeless for a bit, living on couches and spare beds in the homes of various friends," she continued. "It was a dark time, with so many changes and departures. But I worked my way through it, and found a new path."

"That how you ended up selling your soul to interior design?" Derek's lips twitched in a quick smile that made Gracie's heart skip a beat.

"In a roundabout way, yes," Gracie laughed. "It's not altogether a bad way to earn a living. I get to spend other people's money bringing their dreams to life. I've even gotten to work on some big name projects, like that haunted hotel in Savannah."

"Is it enough though? Are you happy?"

Gracie was quiet, weighing her answer. "Yes," she said at last. "I am. I have found my place, and yeah, sometimes I miss creating the way I did in college. But that was a special time," she smiled wryly.

"And I did earn my MFA along the way, and teach a class at Abbey sometimes. It's fun, and gets my hands dirty. Art is still in my life, it's just...different." She shrugged, uncertain how to decipher the intensity of Derek's focus.

Before either could say anything else, they heard the front door open and Sophie calling a greeting. *Saved by the bell*, Gracie thought, as Derek walked out to meet his sister. *That was strangely uncomfortable.*

Chapter 5

Gracie took a moment to breathe in the crisp morning air before heading into Kellynch. She leaned against the porch rail, eyes wandering over the open yard and tracing the gravel drive leading out to the main road. *It's so quiet, peaceful out here*, she mused. *Too bad Dad never understood that, maybe things could have turned out differently.* The thought surprised her; she tried not to think about the decisions her father made, and the impact they had on her life. *That's a path that benefits no one*, she reminded herself.

Over the past weeks, she'd had a lot of time to think about decisions and their repercussions. The decisions of others, as well as her own. She remembered telling Eleanor, when she first explained the Derek/Croft Galleries connection, that at the end of the day she was the one who called off the engagement. Not her family, not Russ. *It was me*, she thought sadly. *I've regretted it every minute since, but never as much as I have since he came back to Northanger. Today is Valentine's, and the Gala; I have no idea if he's staying in town or will be gone tomorrow.*

The thought of Derek walking out of her life, again, made her heart twinge. Working together bringing Sophie's plans to life had given them a common ground, a way to start over, and they developed an easy almost-friendship. There was a tacit understanding that The Past was off limits, but they'd been able to talk about work and mutual friends, even crack jokes over late working suppers of pizza and tea. As Croft Galleries bloomed, Gracie found hope stirring again. *Who am I kidding*, she thought now. *I'm crushing like a schoolgirl. He's still the tall, dark and mysterious older artist, and I'm the local girl in the shadows. With the dubious honor of having once broken his heart. Russ was right to be concerned.* She sighed. *If anything is going to happen, it'll be today. One way or another, I will know by the end of the day.*

The sound of a car coming up the drive made her straighten. Gracie's heart skipped a beat as Derek's old truck pulled to a stop beside her Honda. She waved as he got out of the truck, hiking a duffle bag over his shoulder and balancing a to-go carrier from Mansfield Perk.

"I come bearing gifts," he said. "Parker said you would want some drink called Pemberley's Attic?"

Gracie laughed. "He's right. Smart man, bringing drinks to the work site. Morning meetings always need caffeine; and morning meetings on Valentine's? I hope you have some baked goods hidden somewhere too, this job needs sugary carbs."

Derek smirked. "You and your carbs," he rolled his eyes. "Yes, I've got cookies and muffins to go with the drinks. Sophie threatened my life if I showed up empty handed."

"I knew I liked your sister," Gracie smiled. "Although I hope her drink is decaf, she is beyond antsy about tonight. She was blowing up my phone before 8!" She laughed. "Not that I really blame her, things are falling in place beautifully and I think it's going to be an amazing event. And we finally get to see which pieces you've decided to display," she continued, unlocking the door and gesturing for Derek to go through first.

"Yeah," Derek murmured, ducking inside and making sure Gracie made it in before heading toward the kitchen. "All will be revealed in its own time."

That was weird, Gracie thought, following him down the hall. *Maybe I'm not the only one not sure what's going on here.*

"Derek, these are gorgeous," Sophie breathed, as he opened the jewelry cases one by one.

"Thanks," Derek's casual tone belied the pride in his eyes. "I decided having a few non-rings would be good," he gestured toward the brooch and bracelet.

"Everyone knows my engagement rings, but I can do more. Between the sketches and these, I think it shows a better scope. Plus," he added with a wink, "you can't give your girl an engagement ring but once. There's more holidays and reasons to give someone jewelry than that."

As Sophie and Gracie laughed, he moved to the last case. Gracie gasped when he stepped back, and she got a clear view of the ring within. Derek gave her a loaded look, as Sophie stepped closer.

"This is incredible," she breathed. "How is this available for you to display during my Gala?"

Derek hesitated. "I made it for someone whose engagement didn't happen," he said at last.

"Oh how sad," Sophie frowned.

"Very," Derek murmured. "It was one of my earliest designs. I've kept it all these years," he added. "I've had a couple offers, when clients would notice it in my studio, but I believe this ring could only ever suit one woman."

Gracie choked on her drink, as Sophie cooed. "Aww, Derek, you really are a romantic under all the cynical charm."

"A sentimental fool, perhaps," he shrugged. "But I thought it would be a good ring to have here. Today." His eyes found Gracie's, searing with intensity.

"It's beautiful," she managed at last. "I remember the sketches for that one, I think," she dared to add. "I didn't realize you ever made it."

"Do you? I wasn't sure if you would or not," his voice laden with meaning. Gracie's heart raced, and she felt a dozen questions vying for attention, but couldn't find her voice.

"I know just where that ring should go," Sophie gently broke the spell. "We've got a lot of work to do, before it's time to get gussied up for the party."

Chapter 6

Gracie wove in and out of the crowd, fighting off a sense of impending claustrophobia by staying moving. Sophie's Gala was a marked success, with guests representing towns from Northanger to Atlanta, nearby Barton and even the mountain resort of Meryton. *Makes for great people watching*, she mused, catching bits and pieces of conversation as guests oohed and aahed over the works on display. She was particularly pleased by the enthusiastic reception Melanie's photography received. *Good for her*, she smiled. *I hope this encourages her to keep chasing her dreams. Abbey girls can change the world, if we believe in ourselves.* There was also quite a buzz of chatter about Derek's jewelry, and even more about the sketches themselves.

Gracie was surprised to discover that not a few women in attendance were happily wearing a Derek Worth original. Many of the sketches Derek selected were for pieces being worn tonight, a touch that brought the art to life. *He had to have selected these on purpose*, she mused, wondering how many other connections to the area Derek was hiding. She stopped to greet one of the Abbey professors in attendance; Charlie Bingley was pointing out details to his wife Jane, whose earrings were clearly the subject of the sketch in question.

"Gracie, hi!" Jane's smile was warm. "Isn't this amazing? When Charlie told me the jeweler who made my earrings was going to be here tonight, I could hardly wait! I want to thank him for matching them so perfectly," she laughed. At Gracie's puzzled look, Jane held up her left hand. "Charlie requested earrings to complement my ring, and Derek Worth was able to match them perfectly. You'd never know one was a family heirloom and one was made for Christmas."

"Oh wow," Gracie leaned forward to get a better look. "You aren't kidding; he did a great job mimicking the lines. That's an Art Deco ring, yeah?"

Charlie raised an eyebrow. "How'd you know – oh wait, is it an interior design thing? Knowing the historical styles?"

Gracie laughed. "Sorta. I had two concentrations for my Art History degree: architecture and jewelry, and my studio work was in metals."

"Why didn't you go into design?" Jane asked, a thoughtful look in her eyes.

"That's a long story for another time," Gracie said, stepping back. "If you'll excuse me, I must check in with Eleanor." As she ducked back into the crowd, smiling a response to the Bingleys' friendly farewell, Gracie heaved a sigh. *Okay, that got a little too close to dangerous territory*, she thought.

"Well, what do you think?" Gracie asked, sliding into the space between Eleanor and Russ at one of the ring cases. "Wait a second, that's the wrong ring."

"What do you mean?" Eleanor asked. "That's a gorgeous ring. I've been trying to coax Mark into getting me something similar," she smiled sweetly at her husband.

"It is," Gracie agreed. "But it's not the ring that was in the case when I left earlier today."

"How do you know?" Russ asked. "Never mind, stupid question," he said, raising his hands as if to ward off the glare Gracie directed his way.

"The ring that was there was the one–" she paused, as Russ gave her a strange look. "It was a ring he designed at Abbey; I watched him sketch it over and over before he was satisfied. He didn't make it at the time, but when he unpacked the rings earlier, I recognized it immediately. I've never seen that ring," she pointed at the three-stone band in the case, "before in my life. Or, you know, in the process of setting up for the Gala."

As she spoke, movement by the door to the kitchen caught her eye. Derek was standing just inside the room, looking her way intently. When he caught her eye, he held her gaze before tilting his head slightly and slipping through the door. *That's funny,*

Gracie thought. *Am I supposed to follow him, or...?* As if in answer, Derek stepped into the room again, giving her another significant look before ducking back out. *Okay then, I guess I follow him.*

By the time Gracie was able to extricate herself from the crowd and slip into the kitchen, Derek was gone. "Craptastic," she muttered, turning to venture back into the fray. Something made her pause, and instead of rejoining the party she moved further into the kitchen. On the counter, leaning against the toaster, was a creamy white envelope with her name scrawled across the front in familiar script. Picking it up, she paused to admire the red seal on the closure. "Cupid's Secret," she murmured. "How fitting."

Carefully working the flap free, she withdrew a card, elegant in its simplicity, the muted reds and pinks of a watercolor wash bringing the roses to life in a way that made her heart sing. Opening the card, she saw many words in that same familiar hand, and her heart stuttered to a stop. Breathless, she moved to sit at the small breakfast table and began to read.

I've guarded my heart and kept my silence for so long, I don't know how to break it now. These past weeks I have been relearning a language I once spoke fluently. The language of Gracie. I only hope I'm not too late.

After years of running from the memory of you, the truth has made itself known. Here, where it all began, I have come, hoping to start again. You pierce my soul, and I am half agony, half hope. I have been stubborn and resentful, but never inconstant—there was never anyone for me but you. My heart is even more your own than when you nearly broke it eight years ago. Everything I have done and said and plan to do—it is all for you, surely you know this, my Gracie.

If I have a chance—if we have a chance—surely now is the time to start again. Together.

Forever and always your own, Derek

Chapter 7

Gracie read Derek's card through twice, hardly daring to believe what she read. "It's too wonderful to be true," she whispered. "After so long, could it really be this simple?" Standing, she held the card close against her chest, feeling her own racing heartbeat. *I have to find him,* she thought. *I have to tell him... tell him, what?*

"I'll figure it out when I see him," she said aloud. Taking a deep breath, she left the kitchen and immediately ran into Emma Knightley.

"Oh! I'm sorry, I wasn't watching where I was going. Why didn't you tell me you were coming?" Gracie exclaimed, reaching to give her friend a hug. "I have something for Baby K, and I would have brought it with me."

"Noah's schedule changed at the last minute, so we decided to surprise you," Emma grinned.

"I'm glad you did," Gracie smiled. "And you look amazing! How do you feel? I can't believe we're a month away from meeting Baby K."

"See?" Noah smiled at his wife. "I told you you looked beautiful. Hi Gracie," he added, giving her a quick hug. "Do I detect your hand in the details tonight?"

Gracie nodded, "it's possible. Sophie and Derek did most of it, but I was around for the process."

Emma gave her a speculative glance. "Derek, huh?"

"Yeah," Gracie blushed. "Say, have you seen him? Something has come up and I need to talk to him, like, 12 minutes ago."

Noah looked over the crowd. "He was here a minute ago, walking toward the foyer. Maybe he needed to get some air?"

"Thanks, Noah. I'll come find you guys later, okay? Don't leave without saying goodbye!"

"Not a chance," Emma assured her. "I need this story. The whole story."

With a laugh, Gracie began to navigate her way through the crowd again. *I'm starting to feel like a salmon,* she mused. *Always moving against the current, not knowing what's around the next bend.* Walking into the foyer, she quickly realized the space was empty. Taking a chance, she stepped out onto the front porch. At the sound of the door closing, movement at the far end of the porch caught her eye. There, beyond the party lights spilling from the windows, stood Derek.

For a moment they simply stood there, looking at each other through the shadows.

"Gracie," Derek said softly, hope and wariness in his voice.

Instead of answering, Gracie walked toward him. Slowly at first, before half-running the last few steps and launching herself into his arms. As he wrapped her tight and close, hanging on as if his life depended on her and her alone, Gracie felt all the hurt and regret from the past eight years fall away. Nuzzling in close, she relaxed into his familiar embrace. *It is real,* she thought hazily, feeling his heart pounding against hers. Moving her head, bringing her mouth to rest gently against his ear, she whispered "I'm sorry."

Derek tightened his grip slightly, before releasing her enough to look her in the eye. "I am too," he said quietly. "But no more apologies. No more yesterday. You found the card?"

"I did."

"And you..." Derek paused, his heart in his eyes, waiting for her response.

Gracie looked at him, drinking in his features – so familiar, and yet somehow new – before rising on her toes to press a soft kiss on his lips.

"Words, Gracie," he growled softly.

"I keep trying to find words," she shrugged. "There's too many in my head, in my heart. But they're all saying 'yes' and 'I love you.'"

His grip on her waist tightened. "Do you?"

"I do," she nodded. "I always –" The rest of her sentence was lost as he bent and claimed her mouth with his, a kiss so hungry and desperate it took her breath away. A kiss eight years in the making.

When they separated, breathless, Derek shifted Gracie in his arms and slipped his hand in the pocket of his jacket. She gave him a curious look.

"I have a question," Derek said.

"Another one?" Gracie raised an eyebrow.

"Mmhmm, a very important one," he nodded, sneaking a quick kiss. "Put out your hand," he instructed.

"I thought you had a question. That's a direction," she countered.

"They're connected. Hand first, then question. Put out your hand, palm up," he said again.

With an indulging roll of her eyes, Gracie opened her hand, palm up. When Derek placed a small navy box in her palm, her eyes widened. "Oh," she breathed.

"Open it," he rumbled, low and husky.

Taking a deep breath, she lifted the lid and gasped when she saw the ring inside. It was the ring, their ring.

"I asked you once before, but now that I have the ring, I'm asking again," Derek said quietly. "Will you marry me?"

Gracie looked at him, eyes shining. "Yes," she whispered. "Ring or no ring, yes."

Derek released her long enough to slide the ring on her finger, before drawing her close again. As they stood in each other's arms, Gracie looked at the light playing across the ring. "Why?"

"Because I love you, silly," Derek laughed.

"Not that why. Why did you switch the rings?"

"Ah," Derek rested his chin against her head, holding her ring-clad hand. "I wasn't sure, not until this morning. I hoped, but I wasn't sure if you could still love me or were content with a new friendship. But I saw your face, when you recognized the ring –

then I knew. This afternoon I snuck in and switched the rings, gambling that you weren't hiding some secret romance. Your date to the Gala was Russ, so I knew I was safe."

Gracie laughed. "He'll be so disappointed to hear that."

"We've already had our talk," Derek said in an offhand manner.

"What?" Gracie turned in his arms to stare at him.

Derek shrugged. "This evening, when Sophie was dragging you around and introducing you to her friends? Russ and I talked it over man to man. It's all settled."

Gracie gave him a hard look, before shaking her head. "I think I don't want to know."

"A wise decision, my love," Derek grinned. "Think we should go tell them?"

"Not yet," Gracie shook her head. "We have some unfinished business."

"Oh?" Derek arched an eyebrow. "You've got the ring, I asked my question. What more is there?"

"I can't believe you have to ask," she said with a saucy grin, tugging his face to meet hers. "We didn't finish this," she whispered, kissing him.

"This is something we will never finish," he said, his voice vibrating across her skin, as he trailed kisses along her jaw. "I promise," he breathed, kissing her as if they had all the time in the world.

Acknowledgements

I owe the biggest debt of gratitude to the amazing ladies of *Holidays with Jane* – Jessica, Jennifer, Cecilia, Melissa, Nancy and Kimberly – we made it! I can hardly believe we've written our last stories. This has been an incredible experience, and I am so very, very blessed to have been a part of the adventure. One day, I hope we're all able to spend an afternoon in a Mansfield Perk, talking about life, love and other mysteries as we sip drinks and nibble cookies.

And, of course, a very sincere "thank you" to Jane Austen for writing it first, and best.

Acknowledgements

Every story has its own set of "thank you"s, and this collection echoes those sentiments and more.

I'm forever grateful for the opportunity to write alongside the ladies of *Holidays with Jane*, and especially to Jess for believing I had it in me and answering all the oddball questions along the way.

A special shout out to Jamie for working design magic and bringing my vague ideas to life. Thanks to you, I have an amazing logo and feel official.

And for the readers who want more, keep asking – something new is coming, I promise.

About the Author

Rebecca M. Fleming is a dreamer, writer, quarterback fangirl, lover of all things Austen, and the next Elven Queen of Middle Earth. A fervent believer in fairy tales and the power of Love, she often describes her purpose as "the distributor of tough love and fairy dust," and is determined to tell all the stories.

Connect:

Website: http://fairyjane.blogspot.com
Twitter & Instagram: @FairyJanePress
Email: fairyjanepress@gmail.com